"THE CIA BLAMES ONE OF THE NUCLEAR POWERS."

The President ran his hand through his hair in frustration. "But if another government had such a weapon, they could never use it. And if terrorists had a neutron cannon, the death toll would already be in the millions."

"Unless this was a field test," Hal Brognola stated. Taking out Air Force One in midflight would certainly make a statement. "What can my people do to help?"

"Stopping these people is more important than getting our hands on the cannon. It has to be top priority. Kill them with extreme prejudice. No mercy."

DON PENDLETON'S

STONY

AMERICA'S ULTRA-COVERT INTELLIGENCE AGENCY

MAN®

NEUTRON FORCE

A GOLD EAGLE BOOK FROM

WORLDWIDE®

TORONTO • NEW YORK • LONDON
AMSTERDAM • PARIS • SYDNEY • HAMBURG
STOCKHOLM • ATHENS • TOKYO • MILAN
MADRID • WARSAW • BUDAPEST • AUCKLAND

First edition June 2007

ISBN-13: 978-0-373-61973-3
ISBN-10:   0-373-61973-1

NEUTRON FORCE

Special thanks and acknowledgment to
Nick Pollotta for his contribution to this work.

Printed in U.S.A.

NEUTRON FORCE

PROLOGUE

"What was that?" the pilot of the 747 demanded, leaning forward in his seat.

For a split second the man could have sworn that he saw a flock of birds tumbling out of the night sky alongside the speeding jumbo jet. In an instant they were gone, left far behind. But the image remained in his mind. Hundreds of falling bodies, wings spread wide.

"Trouble?" the copilot asked, looking up from the clipboard in his hands. He had been busy working on the fuel consumption figures.

"Not sure," the pilot replied, looking over to check the radar. They were flying low enough for birds to reach the 747, only ten thousand feet, but the scope was clean, and the flight plan showed that no other planes should be near them for a hundred miles. Aside from the flight of F-18 fighters flying escort, the nighttime sky was clear with only a few sporadic clouds on the horizon and the infinite heavens above. Then what the hell knocked down a flight of birds? he wondered.

There was no moon. Below the speeding plane, the world twinkled with the city lights of the villages and towns of Ohio. The digital clock blinked into midnight, and the pilot saw the map on the plasma screen monitor shift position slightly. Okay, make that Pennsylvania.

Briefly the pilot considered contacting the Secret Service agents in the rear of the plane, but decided against disturbing the men. What could he say? Some dead birds fell out of the sky? How could that possibly be a threat to the armored 747 and its august passengers?

Ever since 1995, there were three Boeing jumbo jets that bore the designation VC-25. The planes only assumed the call sign Air Force One when the President was on board. The three planes were in constant service, sometimes flying empty across the continent, to make it all but impossible for an enemy of America to precisely track the whereabouts of the nation's political leader. Thankfully, the current flight from Los Angeles to Boston was a milk run. The jumbo jet was almost empty, bearing only a couple of Homeland Security agents, a civil servant, an elderly scientist and a dozen Secret Service agents. Nothing to attract a terrorist attack.

Adjusting the trim slightly, the pilot couldn't shake the feeling of dread. Those birds had only been in sight for a moment, yet he felt certain that they had been dead and not merely knocked unconscious from the wash of the turbojets. A former combat pilot in the first Gulf War, the man had learned to trust his instincts. And there was definitely something odd about a hundred birds tumbling from the nighttime sky.

"What's wrong, Chief, see a UFO?" The navigator chuckled as he poured himself a cup of coffee from an insulated carafe.

"Maybe you've finally burned out your brain on caffeine," the pilot suggested with a wane smile.

The navigator laughed. "With Jamaican Blue? Not possible."

"Coffee that sells for more than cocaine." The copilot sadly shook his head, placing aside the clipboard. "Waste of money, if you ask me."

"If I gave you a sip, you'd never say that again," the navigator said, holding the cup in both hands to savor the delicious aroma. Then he took a taste, the thick rich Jamaican coffee filling his mouth with scalding flavor.

"Really? Okay, so pour me a cup."

"Ha! I said a sip, besides…" Pausing in the middle of the sentence, the navigator stopped talking and slumped in his seat. The hot coffee splashed across the console, seeping into the banks of controls.

"Bob, are you okay?" the copilot asked, looking over a shoulder. Then he shuddered and went limp, easing down in his seat as both hands dropped to his sides. The clipboard on his lap slipped away to clatter on the deck.

Instantly alert, the pilot flipped the alarm switch and the autopilot at the same time. One odd thing could be ignored, but two always spelled trouble. First dead birds falling from the sky, now this. Was the plane being attacked?

"Report," said a brusque voice over the intercom.

Reaching for the hand mike, the pilot suddenly felt a tingling warmth engulf his body, then an infinite blackness swelled to fill the universe.

"I smell Jamaican Blue!" a flight attendant called out jokingly, opening the hatch to the flight deck. Just for a split second the man saw the still bodies of the crew before he also crumpled into a heap, dropping a tray of sandwiches.

In the main galley, the other attendants turned at the noise, then reeled and toppled over, one of them splashing hot soup everywhere.

From their seats, the Secret Service agents looked up at the commotion and started to rise when they also paused, then limply collapsed back into their seats.

The door to the private washroom swung open and the director of special projects for the Department of Defense stepped into the aisle. The man gasped at the sight of everybody sprawled in their seats, and felt the hairs at his nape rise in warning. Something was horribly wrong.

"Get Himar off the plane!" the man shouted, lurching toward a rack of emergency parachutes. But that was when a wave of warmth filled his body and the director tumbled onto the carpeting.

At the aft of the 747, Himar glanced up at the sound of his name, then the scientist slumped in his seat, both hands motionless on the keyboard, the plasma screen filling with lines of total gibberish.

Unstoppable death swept through the 747, touching everybody on board. In moments, the jumbo jet was a flying coffin, totally devoid of life. The only sounds were the drip of the spilled coffee, the hushed whisper of the air vents and the muted thunder of the powerful engines.

Staying a loose combat formation, the wing of jet fighters kept a careful watch on VC-25. As per standing regulations, the Air Force pilots stayed in constant communication with SAC headquarters, and through them, the situation room of the White House. But there was nothing to report. The flight was on course, and on schedule. Everything was normal.

Rigidly maintaining the last heading, the 747 continued toward distant Boston, guided solely by the autopilot...

CHAPTER ONE

Washington, D.C.

Impatiently, Hal Brognola honked the horn of his car, and the armored entrance to the underground parking lot for the Old Executive Building rumbled aside.

As big Fed eased the vehicle inside, two Secret Service agents carrying M-16 assault rifles stepped out of a small brick kiosk. Two more stayed inside, one of them touching his throat as he subvocalized into a throat mike.

Flashing his federal identification, Brognola waited while one man checked its authenticity on a handheld device and the other walked around the car, looking underneath with a steel mirror at the end of a pole.

Brognola knew all of the men by name, but this close to the White House, the Secret Service wasn't taking any chance with anybody. He had already passed through a barrage of EM scanners and chemical sniffers checking the driver and vehicle for explosives, biological agents or other illicit materials. This was an understandable precaution.

Maintaining the classic "rock face" of the U.S. Secret Service, the agent looked at Brognola without expression, then waved him by.

Driving past a line of cars, Brognola angled onto a steep ramp and proceed to a sublevel, and then another, until reaching the bottom. He paused to let a security camera get a good view of his face, then went to a far corner and parked near a construction zone, the area marked off with bright yellow cones. Bags of cement were stacked high on wooden pallets and a small portable cement mixer chugged away, blast dust puffing from the rusty exhaust. A canvas tent covered the work area, and several large men stood around adding sand to the mixer or inspecting blueprints spread across a table made of a sheet of plywood placed across two sawhorses. They wore bright orange safety vests marked with the letters DPW: Department of Public Works.

Getting out of the car, the big Fed walked over to the workers, his hands held deliberately away from his sides. Even this far away, he could see the small bulges in the clothing of the workers. They were carrying guns at the waist, small of the back and ankle. The men were heavily armed and seemed even less friendly than the Secret Service agents at the front entrance.

"How is the work coming on the foundation?" Brognola said, stopping a few yards back. "Seems like you've been here for an ice age."

"This is dangerous work," one of the men replied,

looking up from the blueprint. "If we go too fast, people could die."

"Fast as lighting?"

"Slower than a glacier."

Sign and countersign given, Brognola used only fingertips to spread open his jacket and display the holstered weapon at his side, a snub-nosed S&W .38 Police Special.

The workers stayed where they were and did nothing. But their sharp eyes never left him for a second.

"We've been expecting you, Mr. Brognola," a worker said, pushing aside the flap of the canvas tent. "This way, please." The man was wearing a bright yellow hard hat, marking him as the foreman.

Proceeding inside, the big Fed followed the man around a large stack of crates blocking a direct view of the interior. More canvas covered the wall. The foreman agent pushed the material aside to reveal the burnished steel doors of a modern elevator.

Going to the wall plate, Brognola pressed his palm against the warm metal and kept it there until there was an answering beep that his five fingerprints had been accepted. With a soft sigh, the door parted and he stepped inside. There were no buttons.

As the foreman entered, the doors closed, cutting off the thumping of the cement mixer. A moment later the cage began to descend.

Slowly building speed, the elevator moved swiftly along the shaft until finally slowing to a complete stop. The doors opened on a wide brick-lined tunnel. Standing behind a low concrete carrier was a squad of U.S.

Marines in full combat gear, M-16/M-203 assault rifles held ready in their hands. The 40 mm grenade launcher slung under the 5.56 mm assault rifle was a daunting sight to anybody, even if they were wearing body armor.

While the foreman and a Marine exchanged passwords, Brognola looked the tunnel over. Folding steel gates had been pushed back, allowing access, but this tunnel could be closed off at a dozen points. It had to be one of the private government tunnels rumored to honeycomb Washington.

Satisfied, the foreman went back into the elevator and a lieutenant waved at Brognola to follow him down the tunnel.

At an intersection, they took a side tunnel, then zigzagged twice more before reaching a plain steel door with a dozen Secret Service agents standing outside holding Atchisson autoshotguns.

Without a word, the big Fed showed his ID again and submitted to a pat-down. His S&W revolver was taken, then returned. Because of his position as the head of the Sensitive Operations Group, Brognola had the unique distinction of being one of the few people in the world who could be armed in the presence of the President.

"Bird Dog is here, sir," a Secret Service agent said into his throat mike. There was a pause, then the man nodded. "Confirm."

"Go right in, sir," another agent said, tapping a code into a small keypad in the wall. There came the soft hiss of hydraulics and the metal portal ponderously swung aside, revealing that it was two feet thick.

Stepping through alone, Brognola heard the door

close behind him as the lights came on overhead. Not surprisingly, he found himself in a kill box—an enclosed space with both doors closed. Just another layer of protection for the President. Lull the enemy into thinking that they were successfully getting past the security, then let them walk directly into the kill box and start firing through the hidden gunports. Nice and simple. And extremely deadly. A tense moment passed in silence, then Brognola relaxed slightly as the second door opened with a soft hydraulic hiss.

Stepping out of the box, he suffered a moment of disorientation as he appeared to be walking into the Oval Office at the White House: curtain-draped bay windows, massive hardwood desk flanked by American flags, the great seal of the presidency woven into the carpeting, twin couches set parallel to the fireplace filled with a crackling blaze. A Franklin clock ticked away on the mantle, and he could hear typing from a nonexistent secretary. The curtains were open, and he could dimly see the Washington Monument masked by the Potomac River mist. Obviously this was one of the many duplicate offices designed during the cold war so that the President could address the nation on television from a hidden position of safety.

Sitting behind the desk, the President was writing furiously in a black leather journal. Positioned carefully at strategic spots around the office were a dozen more Secret Service agents. These men openly wore body armor and were carrying a wide assortment of deadly weapons.

Off by himself in one corner was an Air Force colonel

carrying a steel briefcase handcuffed to his wrist. In Washington slang that was the Football, the portable computer console used to activate the hellish nuclear arsenal of the United States. The colonel's job was to carry the briefcase for the President, and to guard it with his life. No matter how peaceful the world was, the colonel was never more than fifty feet away from the President, day or night.

"Sir," Brognola said as a greeting.

"Good to see you, Hal." The President rose from behind his desk and offered his hand.

Respectfully, Brognola advanced and they shook. "Always glad to be of service, sir," he stated, releasing the grip.

"Sit down, old friend." The President sighed. "We have a major problem, and time is short. Very short."

"How can my people help?" Brognola asked, leaning back in the chair. The fabric was warm. Somebody else had just been conferring with the President only moments ago.

"Gentlemen, if you would be so kind as to leave us for a few minutes?" the President asked politely, glancing at the armed agents about the office.

The Secret Service agents showed no emotion.

"This is a Code Moonfire situation," the President added.

Inhaling deeply, the chief Secret Service agent nodded. "We'll be right outside, sir," he said, leading the others out through a side door.

As they departed, Brognola caught a glimpse through the next room, a large concrete-lined area filled with crates of MRE food packs, and a small emergency medical station. Many weapons hung on the unpainted walls.

"Are we at war?" Brognola frowned, loosening his necktie.

"If only it was that simple," the President said, sitting again. "What do you know about neutron weapons?"

"Weapons? I thought there was only the neutron bomb," the big Fed stated carefully, rubbing his jaw.

"Originally, yes," the President said.

"But you suspect different?"

"Judge for yourself." The Man slid a sealed envelope across the desk.

The dossier was covered with stamps from DOD, NORAD, SAC, FBI, CIA, NSA and Homeland. Hail, hail, the gang's all here, Brognola thought. Breaking the seal with his thumb, he lifted out the red-striped papers inside, the edges immediately turning brown from contact with his fingers. A Level 10 document. For the President's eyes only.

Reviewing the reports, Brognola skimmed the photos of the crashed 747 on a rocky beach, and concentrated on the autopsy reports. There was one for every passenger and crew member, including a couple for the bomb-sniffing German shepherd dogs that had been traveling in the pressurized hold.

As Brognola read the detailed analysis, the President rose to pour himself a coffee after his guest had declined. Sipping his drink, the President looked out the windows at the artificial horizon and impatiently waited. He desperately hoped that Brognola would have a different conclusion from the one that everybody in his cabinet had arrived at less than an hour ago.

Lowering the last page, the big Fed inhaled deeply, then let the breath out slowly. "Well, I'll be damned," he whispered. There were no bruises on the corpses. None. The dead passengers were laid out in a neat row on steel tables. Their clothing had been removed, and the bright halogen lights revealed every detail of the broken and twisted bodies in unforgiving clarity. No bruising meant the people had been dead before the aircraft hit the ground.

"When did the autopilot engage?" he asked, frowning.

"According to the black box," the President said, "somewhere over western Pennsylvania."

"Did the escorts report anything out of the ordinary in the vicinity?"

"Nothing unusual was reported until the 747 failed to start making course corrections over New York state. After that, they tried for a radio contact, then did a fly-by and finally got a visual of the dead bodies on the flight deck."

"And then what, sir?"

"They followed the plane, trying to contact anybody on board via the flight deck radio, cell phones, air phones, e-mail, pagers, you name it. Strategic Air Command and NORAD were still trying when the aircraft crashed into an escarpment just outside the town of Bouctouche along the Richibucto River in New Brunswick, Canada."

Brognola suppressed a whistle. Pennsylvania to Canada was a long ride on autopilot. He checked the photographs of the bodies again. "Not much fire damage," he noted thoughtfully. "The fuel tanks must have been bone dry."

"That's hardly surprising, since the original destination was Boston," the President said. "The aircraft was supposed to be dropping off the director of special projects to talk with me about a new weapon."

Brognola raised an eyebrow. "A neutron weapon?"

"See for yourself," the President said, lifting a slim laptop and passing it over.

Raising the lid, Brognola saw the machine was ready to play. He hit Enter and the video file began. The screen showed three different sections of the 747, the people laughing, sleeping and playing cards. A handsome Secret Service agent was chatting with a female flight attendant, and apparently the redhead liked what he was saying. Sitting all by himself, a middle-aged man in a rumpled suit was typing on a laptop. That could be the leak right there, Brognola observed. Aside from that, everything seemed normal.

But suddenly a flight attendant carrying a tray of sandwiches opened the hatch to the flight deck and fell dead. Almost immediately afterward, so did everybody else.

Watching closely, Brognola studied the bodies, then tapped the fast-forward button and went through several hours. Nobody stirred. Then there came a whining sound that rapidly built in volume, everything shook, loose items went flying, arms and legs of the dead people flopping around loosely. Then there came a horrible crunching noise. The picture went wild, more shaking, bodies lying on the deck were tossed about like rag dolls. There was more noise, a flash of fire, a metallic thunder and then blackness.

It was distasteful, but the big Fed ran the video one more time and turned the volume all the way up. The man rushing out of the lavatory seemed to be shouting something. But his back was turned away from the video camera, and the clatter of falling dishes garbled his words.

"The natural assumption is that whomever did this got the itinerary wrong, and thought I was on board," the President said, shifting in his chair.

"But you suspect otherwise?" the big Fed asked.

"Yes."

"I'll assume the Secret Service and Homeland Security have ruled out food poisoning and nerve gas— no, skip that." Brognola massaged a temple. Not even the best neurological agent could sweep an entire plane of people dead at the same time, along with the dogs in the hold. A massive electrical shock might do it, but there would have been visible arcing and sparks, plus small fires and a lot of charred flesh. The new air cameras hidden on commercial flights weren't very good, but the ones on Air Force One were top-notch, absolutely the best available, and the digital video had been crystal-clear. He could even hear the engines in the background. Everything alive on VC-25 had been killed without any mark of violence. And that could only be accomplished by a neutron bomb.

All too clearly, Brognola remembered reading about the weapons when he'd first taken the job with the Justice Department. A Dr. Cohen down at Oak Ridge had modified a nuclear bomb so that it would throw off a halo, a corona really, of neutrinos, ultrafast, subatomic particles. The blast of the bomb would destroy only six city blocks, it was pretty small. But the halo of neutrinos would radiate for a mile, killing every living thing it touched. Right down to the ants in the ground. Even microscopic dust mites died. Only plants weren't affected. With a neutron bomb, an enemy could kill all of the people in a city, but leave the skyscrapers, factories and farms intact for their invading forces to seize.

Brognola shook his head. A bomb that killed people, but not property. That was a thousand times worse than the dirtiest thermonuclear bomb ever made, because the neutron bomb had no downside. It let you capture the cities afterward. There was very little fallout from the quarter-kiloton ignition blast, and thus no downside to restrain the indiscriminate use of the weapon. There were countless international treaties banning the development of the doomsday weapon, and not one neutron bomb had ever been used in actual combat. Until today.

Thoughtfully, Brognola tapped a button on the keyboard and played the video once again. He had seen death before many times, but somehow this felt unclean. The people were slain in their seats, without even knowing that they died. There was no flash of heat, no tingle, no…nothing. Everybody just keeled over in perfect unison.

"Anything from the Watchdogs?" Brognola asked hopefully, playing the video again.

"NORAD reports no thermonuclear explosions over the northern hemisphere, if that is what you mean." The President sounded annoyed. "Or anywhere else, for that matter. And the halo effect of a neutron bomb has a limited range. Even without the uranium jacket. To reach a plane so low to the ground, the bomb would have had to be detonated within the atmosphere."

"Rather hard to disguise that."

"Absolutely."

"Yet these people must have been killed by a neutrino bombardment," Brognola stated.

"Yes."

"Only there was no explosion."

"Exactly."

Grudgingly, the big Fed was forced to agree with the President that the conclusion was horrifyingly clear. This was what the President had previously inferred about neutron weapons. For the first time in many years, Brognola felt his blood run cold. There would be no heat flash, noise, radiation, or anything else detectable. Just silent, invisible death. The ultimate stealth weapon.

"So somebody has finally done it," the Justice man muttered, crumpling the report in a fist, "found a way to build a neutron cannon."

"Unfortunately, that's also my conclusion." The President sighed, rubbing a hand across his face. "Some sort of a cannon, or gun, that can fire a focused beam of neutrinos, but without a nuclear explosion as a primer. How that can be accomplished is beyond anybody's guess. My scientific advisers don't even have a theory how the weapon could possibly work."

"So we check with other experts. Who is the top scientist in the field?"

"Dr. Sayar Himar," the President replied. "But he can't help us with the matter, because he's dead."

"And when did that happen?" Brognola asked, feeling that he already knew the answer.

"Yesterday. Dr. Himar was on VC-25 riding as the guest of the director."

Brognola bit back a curse. "This must have been what the director was going to talk to you about, sir."

"Obviously. He had mentioned something called Prometheus. He had wanted to discuss it."

"Hmm. Any other crashes reported?"

"None so far."

"Good." Brognola grunted. So this was why the President had sent the message to meet him down here in the bunker. If some terrorist organization had a working neutron cannon, all they would have to do was to aim the weapon at the White House and pull the trigger. Again and again, over and over, spraying the entire D.C. area, killing every senator and member of Congress, until America didn't have an organized government anymore, and the nation started to fall apart.

"Can a neutron beam penetrate this far down?" Brognola asked pointedly. "Are you safe?"

The President shrugged. "Unknown. There are no figures for a focused beam, and Himar isn't around anymore to take an educated guess. However, we're safe from a conventional neutron bomb strike. We're surrounded by massive tanks holding tens of thousands of gallons of water, the only thing that effectively stops a neutron halo. Whether this will work for a focused beam…" He left the sentence unfinished.

"Water stops neutrinos?" Brognola asked skeptically.

"Hydrogen, actually. Anything with lots of hydrogen atoms. Gasoline is excellent. All those big hydrocarbons."

"What about lead?" Brognola queried.

"Useless. And depleted uranium armor is even worse. In a neutrino halo, the DU plates in an Abrams tank begins to visibly glow as it throws off deadly gamma radiation. Anybody inside is fried in seconds. Anybody standing within fifty feet dies in two days, coughing out their major organs."

Yeah, radiation poisoning was a particularly bad way to die. "Is there anything, anything at all, totally resistant to focused neutrons?"

"Sadly, no." The President continued, "There is some experimental boronated plastic armor that might do the trick, but nowhere near enough to coat even a single plane, much less entire buildings. I've already put production into high gear, but it will be months before the first plates are available."

And we could all drop dead at any second, the big Fed thought.

"Hopefully the vice-president is in the Yukon," Brognola declared. "Or better yet, the other side of the world."

"He's in a Navy submarine at the bottom of the ocean," the President said with some satisfaction. "And the Speaker of the House is in Looking Glass, the flying headquarters of SAC. Only four people knew the exact location of the plane, and none of them would ever talk, even under torture." He paused uncomfortably. "The Secret Service has my double in Florida at the Miami Beach Open Tournament playing golf."

Laying aside the laptop, the big Fed understood the distaste in the man's voice. Having somebody else walk around in public to take a bullet for you seemed cowardly, but it made good sense from a security viewpoint. So far, the Man was on the ball, spreading out the targets so the enemy couldn't remove the entire echelon of the nation in a single shot...volley—whatever. Brognola glanced at the ceiling. If there was a satellite in orbit armed with a neutrino cannon, any city in America could be wiped clean of all life.

"What's our defense condition?" the big Fed asked, sitting straighter in the chair.

"As a precaution, I have moved the nation to Def-Con Two."

"Targets?"

"Everybody and nobody. But the missiles are ready to fly at a moment's notice."

Great, Brognola thought. A couple of hundred thermonuclear ICBMs armed and ready to go, but without targets. How could things have gotten this bad so fast?

"Now it is the belief of CIA that one of the nuclear powers must have created the weapon," the President noted, running stiff fingers through his hair. "Possibly China, maybe Iran. But in my opinion that's nonsense. If another government had such a weapon, they could never dare use it, because every nation in the world would instantly attack them out of sheer self-preservation. And if terrorists had such a weapon, the death toll would already be in the millions."

"Unless this was a field test," Brognola told him. Most weapons would be tested in the lab, or at a range. But with a neutron cannon, the only possible test would be a mass execution. Or taking down Air Force One, smack in the middle of a wing of jet fighter escorts.

"What can my people do to help?" the Justice man asked, getting to point of the meeting.

"Find the people responsible and gain control of the weapon. Now, I have every resource of the United States probing the sky for the satellite." The President paused. "If we can find them, then we'll blow the damned thing out of existence. Our F-22 Raptors can attack a military satellite even in a high orbit with their new missiles. However, if you remember the Sky Killer incident…"

"The weapon was in space, but the operators were on the ground," Brognola stated.

"Naturally, if we invented it, I would like the machine intact. Or at least a copy of the schematics. But stopping these people is more important than getting hold of the cannon. Kill these sons of bitches. No mercy."

CHAPTER TWO

Stony Man Farm, Virginia

The Black Hawk helicopter approached the Farm at a low altitude. Its unannounced arrival was unusual, so both the mission controller, Barbara Price, and security chief Buck Greene were concerned.

Pulling a radio from her belt, Price thumbed the transmit button. "Any ID yet?" she asked, watching the blacksuits move into defensive positions around the farm buildings. Several of them exited the farmhouse, slamming ammo clips into M-16 assault rifles. Another carried a Stinger antiaircraft missile launcher.

"Negative on the ID… Wait…correction, identification has been confirmed," the voice said without emotion. "Incoming is a friendly. Repeat, incoming is a friendly."

There was a crackle of static. "Should we stand down?" a blacksuit asked.

"Hold your positions," Price said into the radio, squinting at the sky. She could see the helicopter now. Hal Brognola usually used a Black Hawk whenever he visited, but he always let the Farm know when he was arriving. "Stay sharp, this could be a diversion."

"Or it could be a surprise inspection," Greene muttered, thumbing back the hammer on the Colt. "Haven't had one of those in months."

"Or somebody could be forcing Hal to land," she countered gruffly.

"Doubtful," Greene stated. "Hal would eat his own gun before betraying us."

"Agreed. It is highly doubtful, but not totally impossible," Price replied. "Let's go meet whoever it is."

Price led the way, her hands clasped behind her back to hide her Glock pistol from casual sight. In their line of work, surprises were always bad news. If this was indeed Hal, then the blood had really hit the fan someplace and the mess was about to be dropped in Stony Man's lap.

Rushing past the outbuildings, the pair reached the Farm's helipad just as the Black Hawk descended in a rush of warm wind.

The moment the landing gear touched ground, the side hatch opened and Hal Brognola hopped out carrying a laptop. Staying bent, he rushed through the buffeting hurricane surrounding the gunship from the rotating turbo-blades.

"Something wrong with your radio?" Price asked.

"Couldn't risk it," Brognola replied, pausing outside the cyclone effect of the idling Black Hawk and checking overhead one more time before finally standing upright. "My call might have been tracked. Are the missiles hot?"

"Bet your ass," Buck Greene stated, eyeing the gunship suspiciously.

"Good. Keep 'em that way," Brognola said, although he didn't know how effective they'd be against a satellite. It was unnerving to think somebody could be looking down upon them at the exact same moment he was looking up. "Come on, let's get the hell out of the open. We have a lot to discuss."

"Fair enough," Price told him. As they started for the farmhouse, Greene pulled out his radio and began relaying instructions to the blacksuits. Moments later, teams of men rushed to unload the equipment trunks from the waiting helicopter. Whatever was going down, the chief had a bad feeling that the Farm might need everything it could lay its hands on. There was no denying the obvious fact that Brognola was nervous. And that was more than enough to make the chief wary.

Stepping onto the front porch, Price proceeded swiftly to the door and tapped in the daily entry code on a small keypad. There was an answering beep and a green light flashed as the automated weapon systems guarding the portal disengaged.

Impatiently, Price waited until the three of them were visually scanned, then the door unlocked and the slab of steel swung aside with the soft hiss of hydraulics. As she entered, Brognola and Greene were right behind.

Stepping inside, Price headed directly for the elevator that would take them to the lower level. If the matter was too delicate to discuss over the radio, then it was too important to discuss in public.

"All right, now that we're out of visual range," Price said, hitting the bottom-most button, "mind tell us what's happening?"

As the elevator started to descend, the big Fed quickly informed the others about VC-25 and the scientist named Himar.

"A neutron cannon? Why didn't you call us about this?" Price demanded.

"These people have a level of technology we can't even guess about," he replied curtly, lifting the laptop slightly by the handle. "So there's no sense taking a chance on them being able to connect the White House to the Farm."

At first, Price thought he was overreacting, but then she considered the fact that they had neutralized an Air Force One 747 in midflight. That alone meant the enemy was extraordinarily capable.

"I don't think we have enough fuel cans to line the entire roof," Greene stated, running fingers through his hair. "And we sure as hell can't flood the place. Not with all of this electronic equipment. Only take one or two leaks and we'd go off-line."

"Even then, the blacksuits would be sitting ducks," Price agreed. "Not to mention all the visitors in the park. Chief, is there any depleted uranium armor on the Farm?"

"Sure. One of the SAM batteries is plated with it," Greene replied. "And Cowboy has a small arsenal of the stuff in his workshop, bullets and such."

Brognola didn't say anything, but he was impressed. When the hammer came down, these people moved at light speed. He only hoped it would be enough.

"I was afraid of that," Price said, leaning against the cool metal wall. John "Cowboy" Kissinger was the chief gunsmith for Stony Man. The tall, lanky man was a former member of the DGA, but more importantly, a master gunsmith. Kissinger was personally in charge of obtaining and maintaining all of the firearms at the Farm. He took pride in being able to supply the field teams with anything they might ever need for combat. From a crossbow to an O'Neil coil gun, the gunsmith was sure to have a couple in stock, primed and ready to go at a second's notice.

The elevator doors opened with a soft chime.

"All right, ready the blacksuits and set it on automatic," Price directed, stepping into the corridor. "And have Cowboy get those DU shells into a lead-lined safe and keep them there until further notice."

"Done," Greene said, and turned on a heel to stride away.

"Wouldn't make a difference." Brognola grunted. "If you're in the neutron beam, you'd be dead from gamma radiation long before any depleted uranium will start to visibly glow."

"True. But I'm thinking about the replacements you send in after we die," Price said, heading for the computer complex. "If the Farm gets contaminated with radioactivity, you'd have to abandon the whole place and start from scratch to build another Farm somewhere else. That would waste months, which could translate into lives."

"Not going to happen."

"Not on my watch anyway," Price declared resolutely. At the moment she knew everything depended on NORAD finding the neutron satellite and blowing it to hell. But if NORAD failed, the next strike could remove New York or London from the map. Thousands dead? Millions. It was time to activate the teams. She only hoped it wasn't already too late.

CHAPTER THREE

Moscow, Russia

Gracefully, the three MiG-29 jet fighters streaked across the clear sky. The weather was perfect for flying and visibility was unlimited. A thousand feet below, the city of Moscow was alive with traffic, the endless streams of cars, trucks and city buses flowing along the maze of streets like a smoky river.

The lead pilot of the MiGs scowled at the beautiful city, spread out like the dynorama at some science pavilion. Exhaust fumes, oil spills, gasoline fires…civilization had done away with horses and steaming piles of horse dropping, only to replace them with smog. Briefly he wondered if society really was advancing, or going backward. Suddenly a light flashed on the control board. Time for a react check.

"Sector fourteen, all clear," Major Alexander Karnenski reported into his helmet microphone, leveling the trim of his jet fighter.

"Acknowledged, Alpha Flight," a crisp voice from base command replied. "Maintain and report in ten."

"Confirm," Karnenski said, dipping the wings slightly to start the long curve around the bustling city. His two wingmen stayed in tight formation on his flanks. Another day, another air patrol. His team had to have circled Moscow ten thousand times in their careers. Still this was an easy assignment, if a trifle boring. Oh well, anything was better than flying combat missions in Afghanistan again.

Checking the radar, the Russian pilot saw several commercial planes in the distance, as well as a couple of news helicopters hovering above the noisy traffic reporting on the congestion near the construction. Thankfully, nobody had been foolish enough to go anywhere near the forbidden zone surrounding the Kremlin. Back in the bad old days of the Communists, the standing orders would have been to shoot on sight anything that dared entered the zone. The revolutionists had been terrified of another revolution. Then came democracy, and freedom, which was closely followed by waves of terrorists attacks, and the ancient orders had been grudgingly reissued. Kill on sight. It was a chilling reminder that hard days require harsh measures.

Their aft vectors thundering in controlled power, the three MiGs arched past the sports stadium, the river, an industrial park, a shopping mall and back toward the Kremlin. Another radar scan, another curve. With almost subconscious ease, the major's hands expertly operated the delicate controls, even though he was contemplating his girlfriend. Tatya was back in his apartment, waiting in a warm bed.

With a soft exhalation, Karnenski slumped over in his seat and died. Immediately the MiG began to drift off course as the limp hand on the joystick let go.

"Hey, stop thinking about your fat Czech woman," Captain Constantine Steloriv joked over the radio, from the right MiG. "She can't be that good in bed!" He knew the woman was Polish, and expected Karnenski to explode in anger over the slur. Czechs were considered fools, but Russians had great respect for the Polish.

Expectantly, Steloriv waited. But there was no reply. Only static.

"Alexander?" the captain asked in growing concern. Dead silence. "Major Alexander Karnenski, respond!"

Nothing. Only the hash of an open microphone.

"Alex, stop playing around, sir!"

By now, the lead MiG was starting to nose down toward the ground. Just a few miles ahead of the jet fighters rose the turrets and domes of the Kremlin, gleaming like gold in the bright sunlight.

"Sir, what should we do?" Lieutenant Ily Petrovich asked as the third MiG-29 pulled into sight.

Growling in ill-controlled rage, Lieutenant Steloriv swung his fighter dangerously close to the wallowing lead MiG. This was going to be tricky, and he had to stay sharp. A tiny slip at these speeds could make their wings tap, and Moscow would get a pyrotechnic display that would make the Rocket Brigade think World War III had started.

Maneuvering carefully, the captain got close enough to see Karnenski through the Plexiglas canopy. The major hung limp in his seat, held upright only by the safety harness, his head rolling around loosely. The man was clearly dead, or dead drunk. Either way, this was a disaster.

"Air Command, we have a problem." Steloriv spoke quickly into his helmet microphone.

"Radar shows clear," base replied curtly. "And why have you changed course without permission?"

"We haven't. Major Karnenski seems to be unconscious and will not respond." The captain swallowed hard. "I...I think he's drunk, sir."

"Checking," the stern voice replied. There was a short pause. "Negative. The on-board sensors show no trace of alcohol in the atmosphere of the plane."

Glancing at the surrounding array of controls, the captain was astonished. They had hidden sensors for that? Air Defense didn't miss a trick! But that didn't change the situation.

"Request instructions," Steloriv said in a tight voice.

"Under the circumstances we have no choice," the voice commanded tersely. "Our standing orders are clear. Authorization is given to fire. Shoot him down."

"My own commander?" Steloriv gasped. "But, sir—"

"We're over the city!" Petrovich added tersely. "The wreckage could kill hundreds of civilians!"

"We understand. You have twenty seconds to comply before we launch missiles," base stated harshly. "Nineteen and counting."

A salvo from the Rocket Defense would probably take out all three MiGs just to be sure of getting the right one, Steloriv realized. No choice then.

"Weapons systems armed," the captain intoned emotionlessly. He paused for a second, then engaged every missile on board. This was a one-shot deal. "Lasers have a lock."

"Captain, no!" Petrovich begged. "Surely there must be something we can try. Perhaps we could disable the MiG with our cannons…"

"Fire," Steloriv whispered with a hollow feeling in his belly. His hand tightened on the joystick as he pressed the trigger button.

The MiG-29 shuddered as all eight wing-mounted missiles dropped. When they were clear of the MiG, the solid-state rocket engines exploded into flames and they streaked away.

Pulling back on the stick, the captain banked his plane hard to get away from the blast. Even with the "iron bathtub" a MiG pilot sat in for protection from small-arms fire, shrapnel often penetrated a canopy to kill a pilot. Come on, baby, come on…he urged.

The third MiG stayed at his flank, and together they climbed for the sky, the turbofans screaming from the effort. On the radar screen, Steloriv saw the nine images move together just as a flight of missiles shot upward from the SAM bunker on the ground. Goddamn Rocket Brigade! he swore. A moment later the lead MiG vanished in a series of thundering explosions that grew in volume and fury as the ground-based missiles arrived a heartbeat later.

Strolling casually through Red Square, people looked up at the terror noise in the sky, then began screaming as flaming wreckage started to rain upon them only a few blocks from the mighty Kremlin.

"Alpha Flight, return to base," the voice on the radio commanded. "Beta wing has already been launched."

"Confirm," Steloriv said woodenly, leveling his trim and starting a sweep to the east. A million jumbled thoughts filled his whirling mind. Everything happened so fast. One moment they were joking about women and the next…

Casting a glance at the radar screen, Steloriv frowned. Could the major actually have died of a heart attack? It seemed highly unlikely. Their medical examinations were most through. Nobody with any weaknesses flew air patrol above a major city, especially Moscow! Even a slight heart murmur could get a fighter pilot grounded these days. But what else might have happened? What could possibly harm a perfectly healthy man inside an armored jet at a thousand feet above the ground? It was impossible, absurd, ridiculous, and had just happened before his very eyes. The idea of a heart attack, or perhaps a stroke, seemed to make sense as there was no other logical explanation.

Not unless somebody detonated a neutron bomb above Moscow, the pilot noted sourly, and we all forgot to notice.

Stony Man Farm, Virginia

PROCEEDING DOWN THE CORRIDOR, Price and Brognola passed several blacksuits, one of them working on an air-conditioner vent, another pushing a cart stacked with cases of shiny new shells, each about the size of a tube of toothpaste.

"When did we acquire a Vulcan minigun?" Brognola asked curiously as they got into the electric cart that would take them to the Annex.

"That's not for the Vulcan. Those are 25 mm rounds for the new Barrett rifle." ·

"Rifle?" Brognola repeated. "Barrett has invented a 25 mm rifle? How new is that?"

"Couple of months." Price almost smiled. "Cowboy is bench-testing one at a rock quarry a couple of miles from here. Our gun range was too small for this monster. If it passes his approval, then it will be added to the arsenal of both teams."

"A 25 mm rifle?"

"Cowboy says it shouldn't be harder to control than a Barrett .50-caliber." She paused. "Or getting kicked in the groin by a Mississippi mule. But you know Cowboy."

"Yeah," Brognola agreed. "He should know."

"Or so he says."

Reaching the entrance to the Annex, Price and Brognola exited the cart and proceeded on foot to the Computer Room.

Inside, the atmosphere of the room was cool and quiet. A coffeepot burbled at a coffee station and muffled rock music could be heard coming from somewhere.

Several workstations faced an array of monitors on the wall. One of the screens showed a vector graphic map of the world, blinking lights indicating the state of military alert for every major nation. Another monitor swirled with ever-changing weather patterns of the planet as seen from space. The remaining screens were dark.

Four people occupied workstations: a powerfully built man in a wheelchair, a young Japanese American wearing earbuds, a middle-age redheaded woman and a distinguished-looking black man with wings of silver at his temples.

"Aaron, where are the teams?" Price asked, heading for the Farm's senior cyberexpert.

"In the ready room checking over their equipment and weapons," Aaron "The Bear" Kurtzman said, turning to face the mission controller. "When Hal arrives without advance notice, I figure we're in deep shit."

"You figured correctly," Brognola grumbled, placing the laptop on Kurtzman's desk.

"Is Striker in trouble?"

"Everybody is in trouble," Price answered brusquely.

"Meaning?" Kurtzman demanded with a frown.

"Do you know about the crash of VC-25?"

He frowned. "No." The 747 had crashed? Obviously the President was okay because Hal hadn't called the plane Air Force One. "Was it shot down? Rammed in midair?"

"There's no mention that anything happening to the jumbo jet on the news services," Huntington "Hunt" Wethers announced. A pipe jutted from his mouth, but no smoke rose from the briarwood bowl.

"Nobody knows about the incident other than a select handful of people in the American and Canadian governments," Brognola stated, extracting a disk from the laptop. "And it's part of this mission to make sure that nobody ever learns the truth."

"Why not?" Carmen Delahunt asked.

"We'd never be able to handle the riots," the big Fed said, passing the disk to Kurtzman.

At the fourth console, Akira Tokaido vaguely heard the conversation. He was slumped in his chair, apparently sound asleep. Both Brognola and Price knew that the young man was hard at work. Tokaido would rather be running the massive Cray Supercomputers located on the refrigerated floor below than doing anything else in the world. Even breathing and eating. The Japanese American was a modern-day Mozart with computers, a natural hacker. There was very little Akira couldn't get done online, and he pushed the envelope further every day.

"Riots?" Kurtzman asked, taking the disk and sliding it into a slot on his console. The center screen came it life and Top Secret seals flashed by in a blur like a diesel-powered rotoscope.

"See for yourself," Price stated, looking at the wall monitors. According to the computerized maps, the world was at peace. There were a few scattered battles here and there, but nothing major. She wondered how long that would last if the news of the neutron satellite got out. That underwater arcology Japan was building would be overrun with people fighting and killing to get inside.

Kurtzman leaned closer to the monitor. The encryption on the disk was fantastic, the only data file he had ever encountered that had more was the dossier on the Farm. As the files grudgingly opened and slowly loaded, he grabbed a ceramic mug and took a fast swig of hot coffee. A neutron cannon in space? Sweet Jesus…

Running his slim fingers across the keyboard like a concert pianist, Akira Tokaido continued his Internet search. There were a lot of heavily encrypted transmissions going out these days, t-bursts they were called, and every one of them had a fake ID and source code. A t-burst was the newest scourge of the Internet, a computerized version of a blip transmission over a radio, a massive amount of information condensed into a small tone that lasted for only a second, sometimes even less. So far, the young hacker couldn't trace where they were coming from, or worse, where they were going. Obviously something big was going down in the cyberworld, and that was always trouble. Twice he had caught the garbled word "tiger" inside a picture code and logged it for further investigation.

"Everybody stop whatever you're doing and access these files," Kurtzman commanded. "And do it fast, people."

The members of the cybernetic team did as requested, their curious expressions quickly turning grim.

"Help yourselves to coffee," Kurtzman told them, reading the incredible material scrolling on the monitor.

"Ah…did Carmen make the coffee, or you?" Price asked warily.

"Me, of course."

"Pass," the woman snorted, crossing her arms. Strong wasn't the word normally used for Kurtzman's hellish coffee.

As they started reading the files, Wethers and Delahunt began to scowl deeply. Typing while he read, the former professor pulled up the passenger list of the crashed plane, while Delahunt fondled the air with the cybernetic gloves she wore, opening files. At the front of the room, one of the wall screens began to display reports on boronated armor, while another blossomed into a vector graphic of satellites orbiting Earth.

There were thousands of them, Price noted dispassionately. Needle in a haystack? she thought. Try a drop of water hiding in the ocean!

Skimming the pages, Kurtzman had trouble believing what he was reading. It would take a major world power to muster the resources to build a neutron cannon. The question was which one, and did it have control of the cannon now? If some terrorist group like al Quaeda, or Hamas, had control of the weapon, Washington would already be a death zone.

"A focused beam of neutrons," Wethers muttered, taking the pipe from his mouth and tapping his chin with the stem. "Amazing, simply amazing."

"And we have no idea who might be behind this?" Delahunt asked.

"Aside from the usual suspects, none at all," Brognola admitted honestly.

"I'll start a search for any other incidents of people dying without signs of violence," Delahunt said. "Now that they know the weapon works, the thieves will start using it."

Just then, a picture of Dr. Himar appeared on a wall monitor. A middle-aged man, short gray hair, black suit and a bolo string tie. The newspaper shot was of Himar receiving the Nobel Prize in Physics.

"Hunt, check the records of the public dossier," Kurtzman commanded, slaving his console to the others. "Find out who might have accessed any data about Himar under the *Public Information Act*."

"Over how long a period?" the professor asked.

"Ever."

"No problem," Wethers replied, his hands moving across the keyboard.

"Akira, get me his DNA and run a match on the remains in the morgue," Price directed. "Himar might not really be dead."

"On it," Tokaido replied, both hands busy.

"A duplicate?" Brognola asked in concern, coming closer. "You think that a Nobel Prize-wining physicist could be a traitor?"

"Let's see if we can find him and ask," Price stated roughly.

"Bear, how long will it take you to breech the firewall at the Department of Defense?"

"To get files on Himar, and—Prometheus? Is that what the President said?" the burly man asked. His monitor gave a beep. "They're just downloading now." The man scanned the scrolling images. "Okay, Himar has a home in Braintree, Massachusetts, but his DOD lab is on Wake Island. His research, code-named Prometheus, is based there."

The other side of the world. Price nodded. It was a smart move to keep his private and professional life as separated as possible.

"Wake Island," Brognola mused. "Isn't that an old missile testing range in the South Pacific?"

"North Pacific. Guess Himar wanted the laboratory isolated and far away from civilization in case something went wrong."

"Or else he wanted privacy," Price retorted. "All right, send Able Team to his house for any private files or papers. Phoenix Force will recon the lab. Send the details to Jack Grimaldi, and have Homeland Security tell the ground crew at Dulles to start warming up a Hercules and a Learjet."

Braintree was close enough for Able Team to use the Hercules so that they could arrive with their equipment van. But Phoenix Force had a long way to travel to reach Wake Island. The tiny landmass was so far away that it was only technically part of the United States.

"And remind our guys to be doubly careful," Brognola told her. "The only way to survive a neutron beam is to not get hit." With any luck, NORAD would locate the enemy satellite and the USAF would blow it out of the sky before a major city was destroyed. However, the top cop had a bad feeling in his gut that time was short, and that this was going to get real bloody, real fast.

CHAPTER FOUR

Calais, France

An unseen dawn arrived above the small coastal town. The overcast sky was dark with storm clouds and a torrential rain mercilessly pounded the sprawling array of homes, shops and hotels.

In spite of the early hour, the night's festivities were still going strong in Calais, the numerous hotels filled with drunken, happy tourists. Lining the old town's refurbished waterfront, hundreds of expensive yachts were moored at their slips against the inclement weather, and several cruise liners dominated the brightly illuminated public docks. Nearby restaurants were alive with colored lights and pulsating music. Old men and young women were laughing and singing, and the smiling waiters served a nonstop flow of steaming dishes from the kitchens to the tourists.

But on the outskirts of the city, the drab fishing docks

were filled with a different kind of excitement. There was no singing or dancing, but hearts were light as calloused hands moved ropes and nets, preparing for the day's hard work. The deep water report had just arrived and the sea bass were running.

Shouting orders, big men in yellow slickers moved around the sodden dock and trawlers, hauling ropes and nets. Powerful engines sputtered into life among the ranks of squat vessels, the dull exhaust pipes throwing out great clouds of rank diesel smoke. A bell clanged from the church tower in town, announcing the time. A man cursed; thunder rumbled. Somewhere a dog barked and oddly went silent. But nobody paid the incident any attention. Fishing was more than their business, it was their calling, the blood in their veins, and Frenchmen knew that the sea bass didn't care if it was raining or if there were tourists in town spending money as if it was the end of the world. The fish followed the deep water currents and the fisherman followed the fish. Nothing else mattered. Unless there was a hurricane blowing, the fleet went out.

Chains rattled as heavy anchors were hoisted. Radar swept the storm from a hundred ships trying to map the roiling clouds above the choppy waves. Trucks arrived from town delivering ice to the poorer vessels, while the others started refrigerators in their holds, making everything ready for the day's catch.

As the ice trucks pulled away from the docks, five large men appeared like ghosts from out of the torrential rain. Their boots thudded heavily on the damp planks, and the men appeared to be slightly hunch-

backed in their black overcoats. The wide brims of their
slouch hats drooped slightly from the unrelenting downpour, efficiently keeping the rain from their hard eyes,
and also masking their features from the busy crowd of
hardworking fishermen.

Marching in an almost military-like manner, the
group of strangers moved past the trawlers until they
reached the end of the dock. Moored at her usual place,
a brand-new catamaran, the *Souris,* was rocking slightly
from the force of the storm, her crew shouting through
cupped hands at one another as they tried to be heard
above the motors and thunder.

Lightning flashed in the sky as the five men climbed
on board the fishing trawler without a hail, or even the
common decency to ask permission. This was a major
breech of nautical etiquette anywhere in the world, and
a fighting offense in most French dockyards. Nobody
but a fool, or a lunatic, ever did it twice.

As the deck rose and fell to the rhythm of the waves,
two of the strangers stayed near the open gate of the
gunwale, while the others labored to extend the corrugated steel gangplank to the dock. They moved awkwardly, as if unsure of exactly what to do, but it only
took a minute before the task was accomplished.

Pulling a cell phone from his coat pocket, one of the
men hit a speed-dial button and spoke briefly. Immediately, there came a soft beeping from the land and a big
Volvo van began driving backward along the wooden
dock, the boards creaking slightly from the unaccus-
tomed weight.

Startled by its arrival, the angry fishermen scrambled

out of the way of the vehicle, vehemently cursing with their gloved hands as only the French can do really well.

As the beeping van rolled onto the gangplank, the strangers opened the rear doors and exposed a large canvas-wrapped object strapped tightly to a bright orange shipping pallet. The rest of the interior of the vehicle was filled with loose blankets and foam to cushion the bulky cargo.

On board the *Souris,* a young crewman raced up the exposed stairs to the bridge.

"Skipper, we have guests!" he exclaimed breathlessly.

Smoking a briarwood pipe, the captain didn't look up from studying a chart of the ocean currents. "Guests?" he muttered around the worn stem. "What the devil are you talking about, lad?"

"Them!" the lad declared, pointing down at the middeck.

"Them who?" the captain demanded, leaving the chart to stride over to the aft window of the bridge.

The front windows were equipped with wiperblades, but the rear weren't, and the captain squinted through the rain. Dimly, he could see people moving around. "Did we order anything?" he demanded suspiciously. "Extra ice, perhaps? In case the refrigeration unit breaks again?" The refrigeration unit was almost older than the trawler.

"No, sir," the lad replied, catching his breath. "Nothing out of the ordinary."

"Strange," the captain mumbled. "Maybe they have the wrong ship."

"I tried to ask who they were, Skipper…" the lad began.

But the captain had already slipped on his slicker and marched into the downpour. Time was short, the fleet would move out soon. As with anything else in life, it was always first come, first served. And after some unexpected repairs to the navigational equipment, he needed this catch to be huge. The sea bass were running exceptionally rich these days, and an early start held the promise of beating the corporate vessels to the day's catch. Timing was everything.

Keeping a firm grip on the railing alongside the perforated stairs, the captain clumped down to the deck and approached the strangers. He knew instantly they weren't sailors. The men kept trying to regain their balance, instead of moving with the motion of the sea.

Elegantly raising a single eyebrow, the captain crossed his arms and glowered at the landlubbers. "What is going here?" he demanded loudly. "Who are you people?" The man was furious at the interruption. He had no time for government inspectors or lost tourists.

There was no response from the strangers.

"I asked you a question!" the captain roared. "And this is my ship, so you damn well better answer fast, or by God—"

Turning slightly, one of the strangers pulled a Browning .22 automatic pistol from within his overcoat and fired. There was barely a sound from the acoustical sound suppressor, barely a muted cough. But the captain recoiled, a neat black hole in the middle of his forehead. He stumbled backward, and then tumbled over an electric winch to hit the deck. He shuddered once, then went still.

"Skipper!" the young crewman screamed from the doorway of the bridge, then started to rush down the stairs.

Looking up, the gunman fired again and the lad doubled over. Clutching his bloody stomach, he pitched off the stairs to hit the deck in a ghastly crunch of breaking bones.

"What was that, eh?" a crewmen shouted from the stern of the boat, his outline blurry from the combination of rain and salty spray.

Calmly, the rest of the strangers pulled out Browning .22 automatic pistols, the hexagonal shape of the sound suppressors giving the weapons a futuristic appearance.

"Is somebody hurt?" a different crewmen asked, placing a hand above his eyes to shield them from the blinding downpour.

Another of the strangers fired this time, and the sailor was slammed backward, crimson spraying from the ruin of his throat. The rain washed it away, but more kept pumping in a geyser of red life.

"*Zoot!*" a huge crewman shouted, dropping a coil of rope and pointing with a massive hand. The man stood well over six feet in height, and his slicker seemed barely able to contain his muscular frame.

The five strangers fired in unison at the giant, red blood puffing from his slicker as the barrage of .22 rounds hammered into him, forcing him constantly backward until he went over the side with a horrible scream and disappeared into the storm. But his death cry alerted the rest of the crew, and a dozen more men climbed from the hold and hatchways of the *Souris*.

Quickly reloading, the strangers opened fire, driving the fishermen under cover. Starting to realize that something was horribly wrong on board their beloved ship, the sailors frantically scrambled for anything to serve as a weapon: boathooks, an ax, a length of steel chain.

Two of the strangers took up defensive positions near the van, while the others spread out in an attack formation and advanced, their guns at the ready.

Shouting a rally cry, the fishermen charged, waving their weapons with grim intent. But they never even got close. The strangers gunned them down without a qualm, putting an additional bullet into the left eye of each fallen man to make sure he was dead. Nobody was spared.

The strangers began a systematic sweep of the deck, killing everybody they found. An elderly man raised his hands in surrender and was shot in the heart, his twitching body tossed over the side while he still gasped out his last breath.

Hearing a faint shout for help from above, one of the strangers near the van tracked the noise, then aimed his pistol high and emptied the clip. There came an answering cry of pain and a body fell from the crow's nest to impact on the main winches that operated the heavy nets. The results were ghastly.

Smoking a cigar, a fat man wearing a grease apron appeared in a hatchway holding a Veri pistol. At the sight of the bloody corpses sprawled on the deck, the cook raised the flare gun and fired. The magnesium charge shot across the *Souris* like a comet, but the strangers expertly dodged out of the way and the sizzling flare ricocheted off the van to disappear into the sea.

A man working on nearby trawler saw the flash of light and tensely waited for a cry for help. Had somebody fallen overboard? Was there a fire in the engine room? When nothing happened, the fellow dismissed the matter and went back to shifting bales of nets. Somebody had to have accidentally shot off the flare gun. That's how people get killed! Wasn't anybody concerned about safety anymore? The fisherman wondered.

On board the *Souris,* the strangers finished the reconnoiter of the catamaran, removing the last few crew members hiding in the bilge, then reloaded their weapons, smashed the radio just in case they had missed somebody and finally returned to the main deck. Time was short, and there was a precise schedule to keep today.

Now that they had some privacy, the five men started to release the chains from the trawler's boom arms normally used to haul aboard the heavily laden nets full of wiggling fish. Carefully, they attached the array to the orange pallet, and gingerly hauled the bulky mass out of the Volvo, and maneuvered it to the middeck. When it was in position, they pulled out pneumatic guns, firing steel bolts though the flanges on the pallet to permanently attach it to the wooden deck. Then the chains were removed and used to secure the pallet to the mast and several stanchions for additional security.

At last satisfied to the security of the pallet and its precious cargo, the men tossed the bolt guns overboard. In the heavy downpour, the canvas-covered pallet was merely a dark lump set among the other irregular shapes of the boat.

Checking his watch, one of the strangers went to the bridge and started the engines. Meanwhile, one man attached a strong rope to the bumper of the cargo van as the other rolled down the windows of the vehicle, released the hand brake and deliberately set the transmission into neutral.

Returning to the *Souris,* the strangers replaced the gate in the gunwale and started casting off the mooring lines. With a sputtering roar, the diesel engines came to life belowdecks and the little trawler began to move out to sea.

As the rope attached the van grew taut, the vehicle began rolling backward along the dock and dropped into the choppy waters with a tremendous splash. Ready at the gunwale, a stranger waited until the water started to pour into the open windows and the vehicle started to sink before slashing at the attached rope with a curved knife. The taut rope parted with an almost musical twang and the sinking van was soon left behind, the salt water efficiently removing the last traces of their presence from the stolen vehicle.

Dimly heard through the storm, shocked voices could be heard from the other trawlers, and people started running on the dock. Flares were fired into the sky, but their brilliant light was consumed by the torrential rain. Life preservers were tossed into the sea in the mistaken belief that people may have been in the van. But the only passenger was the dead owner, who had made the foolish mistake of stopping at the wrong parking lot in Paris and politely offering a stranger a lift.

Holstering their silenced weapons, the killers in control of the *Souris* gave no notice of the growing commotion while they pulled out assault rifles, the barrels tipped with bulbous 37 mm rifle grenades. Warily, the team watched the storm for any signs of the local police, or the much more dangerous French navy.

But the coastline was clear, and soon the frantic dockyard faded into the rain. Slowly building speed, the trawler chugged into the raging storm, heading across the channel toward England. Muttering curses, the big man at the controls tried to coax more speed from the old diesel engines. There was an important rendezvous to keep, and nothing could get in the way.

CHAPTER FIVE

Logan International Airport, Boston

The huge C-130 Hercules transport lightly touched down on the asphalt, the tires squealing at the contact. It rose slightly, only to touch down again, skipping along the runway until finally rolling along the pavement. Reaching a cross strip, the huge military aircraft paused, the propellers spinning with a subdued roar, then it turned and moved along the ground, heading for an isolated hangar at the extreme edge of the airport.

"Another one," Matthew Liptrot rumbled, lowering his binoculars. The Transportation Administration Security guard was frowning deeply. "I don't like unscheduled arrivals. They make my ass itch."

"Then get some salve, buddy," Jason Kushner replied gruffly, his voice rising in volume as a 757 thunderously took off into the sky. The two members of the TSA waited a few moments until the wash of the colossal jet dissipated. Dimly, in the parking lot, car alarms were starting to bleep and keen, their owners having set the sensitivity of the sensors way too high, in spite of the clearly marked posted warnings at the entrance kiosk.

"Every one of them is probably a BMW." Liptrot sneered in disdain, hitching back the cap of his blue uniform.

"Or a Lexus," Kushner agreed with a wan smile. "Chevy and Toyota owners know better."

"I hear that." The TSA guard turned to watch the Hercules disappear past the wind flags fluttering in the breeze. "Now, I know we were told to not bother the passengers on this flight, some sort of dignitary from D.C., but still…"

"Don't," Kushner warned forcibly. "The last person who violated an order like that is working at an airport concession stand in Alaska selling postcards to polar bears."

"Okay, okay, the Do Not Disturb order stands." Liptrot reluctantly relented. "But just the same, I'm gonna keep a sharp watch on the thing. Those 9/11 fuckers left from right here." He stomped on the pavement. "Our Logan International, and I'm not ever going to let that happen again."

"I hear that," Kushner agreed, raising his binoculars to study the massive Hercules. "Nothing wrong with staying alert."

Pulling out his 9 mm Glock pistol, Liptrot checked the loaded of armor-piercing rounds, designed to go through body armor as if it were soap suds. "Nope, nothing wrong with that," the man muttered, holstering the weapon. "Nothing wrong with that, at all."

THE C-130 HERCULES TRANSPORT rolled to a stop in front of the hangar. Jack Grimaldi set the brakes and killed the massive engines.

"All ashore that's going ashore," the Stony Man pilot announced over the PA system.

Down in the cargo hold, the men of Able Team unstrapped themselves from the jumpseats lining the curved wall and began to release the holding straps on their custom van.

"I still can't believe that anybody has a neutron cannon," Rosario "Politician" Blancanales said, freeing the buckles on the canvas straps wrapped around the rear axle. "How is that possible?"

"Something called induced magnetics," Hermann "Gadgets" Schwarz replied, doing the same to the front. "But exactly what that means I have no idea. The math is way beyond me."

Releasing the last of the locking clamps on the wheels, Carl "Ironman" Lyons grunted at the frank admittance. Schwarz was one of the leading experts in electronic warfare. Under a variety of pseudonyms, he wrote articles for every major scientific magazine and newspaper in the world. If Schwarz was unable to follow the mathematics, then few people could. Himar had to be a genius. And those were often disquietingly close to madness, Lyons thought.

Stowing the restraining straps, Able Team climbed into the equipment van and started the engine.

Watching from the open door to the flight deck, Grimaldi flipped a switch and the rear section of the military transport broke apart and cycled down to the ground with a hydraulic hiss.

"Stay in contact," the pilot said over their earplugs. "After I refuel, I'll keep the engines turning over, just in case you boys need some close-order air support." The civilian version of the Hercules was unarmed, but the one Grimaldi piloted was heavily armed with 40 mm Bofors cannons.

"Or a hasty retreat," Blancanales replied, touching his throat mike. "Stay frosty, Flyboy."

"You, too. Stand where they ain't shooting."

"Do our best," Lyons added, setting the van into gear. Carefully he drove the vehicle down the inclined ramp and out onto the paved landing strip.

Logan International Airport dominated their northern horizon, airplanes seeming to take off and land at the same time, passing within only a couple of hundred feet of each other.

A ballet of steel, Blancanales noted. If the neutron cannon attacked at just the right moment, a wall of dead jumbo jets would fly straight into the skyscrapers of downtown Boston. The death toll would be…unimaginable.

"Where did he live?" Schwarz asked, settling into his chair at the small workshop in the rear of the vehicle.

"An apartment building," Lyons stated, maneuvering onto a private access road. "Himar lived with his family on the top floor, the rest of the place was filled with relatives, cousins and such."

The scientist owned an apartment complex? Schwarz blinked. "Just how rich was this guy?"

"Not very. He used the money from the Nobel Prize to put a down payment on the place, and the relatives pay rent." Lyons frowned. "Or so the IRS and Massachusetts Housing Authority claim."

Blancanales frowned. "So this could be a hardsite."

"Exactly." Lyons growled, slowing in front of a wire fence, the top a curly profusion of concertina wire. The sensors in the gate read the electronic signature of the miniature transceiver in the Stony Man vehicle and the gate unlocked automatically, sliding aside.

"We don't know that for sure," Blancanales warned, opening a compartment in the dashboard. Nestled inside were rows of fake identification papers, permits and passports. "What do you want to be, FBI again or CIA?"

"NSA," Lyons suggested, driving through. "That will give us a free hand. Few people have any idea what the NSA does."

"Including the NSA," Schwarz quipped, opening a weapons trunk and extracting an M-16 assault rifle.

Behind them, the gate closed with a loud clang and locked.

"DID YA SEE THAT GATE?" Liptrot asked angrily, adjusting the focus on his binoculars.

"Well, I would expect the folks on that transport to have the exit codes," Kushner muttered unhappily, rubbing his chin. Sure, that was only reasonable. But the man still didn't like strangers moving so freely around Logan.

"How about we go have a chat with the pilot," Liptrot said with a hard grin, setting his cap straight.

"Whoa there, brother," Kushner cautioned, raising a restraining palm. "We were specifically told not to bother the passengers."

"Ah, but the passengers are gone," Liptrot replied, glancing at the retreating van. "Go check the regs, if you want. But pilots aren't considered passengers. They're crew. And nobody said anything about him."

"Well, maybe he left in the van."

"True. But perhaps we smell a fuel leak."

From this far away? Kushner thought, then smiled. "Son of a gun, I think I do smell a fuel leak. That could endanger the whole airport. We better investigate." Liptrot headed for their unmarked Jeep in the security parking lot.

Keeping pace with the other guard, Kushner checked his Glock, then his pepper spray and stun gun. Whenever possible, the TSA preferred to take troublemakers alive. However, Liptrot and Kushner enjoyed being the wild men of the TSA. They always pushed the limits on rules and regulations, and caught more drug smugglers and would-be hijackers than the rest of the TSA, on-site FBI and city blues combined. Half cousins, the grim men considered Logan their private property, and God help anybody stupid enough to try to harm the place.

"We talk first," Kushner stated, climbing into the Jeep.

"Naturally," Liptrot said, starting the engine. "However, if he—"

"Or she."

"Or she, refuses to cooperate, then the kid gloves come off."

"Yee-haw," Kushner muttered, turning on his radio.

"Unit Nine to Control, we have a possible fuel leak in area thirty-seven…"

MERGING WITH THE MADNESS of Boston traffic, Carl Lyons checked the digital map display on the dashboard and took a secondary road to head for Braintree. The land went from industrial to suburbia, and then stately homes with low stone fences and tall oak trees older than Columbus. The area looked like something out of a movie.

"You know, Braintree is the ancestral home of John Adams," Blancanales announced.

"I heard he was obnoxious and disliked," Schwarz said without looking up, thumbing HEAT rounds into a clip for his assault rifle.

Checking the house numbers, Lyons found the correct apartment building. It was a neat, five-story house that had been converted into apartments: brick walls, green shutters, a wooden porch with a swing. A dog slept on the driveway and a birdbath sat in the front yard.

Lyons drove past the building and parked a few houses down. He used field glasses to study the area to see if they were under surveillance. Nothing moved in the whole neighborhood. A television blared from across the street, and Indian music could be heard softly playing from inside the apartment building. That's right, Lyons remembered. Himar had been born in New Delhi. The tune was catchy, but the words were unintelligible.

"The place looks clean," Blancanales said, tucking the NSA identification into a breast pocket. Then he pulled a .380 Colt pistol from a shoulder holster and dropped the clip to check the load. Easing the clip back inside, he clicked off the safety and worked the slide to chamber a round. He wasn't expecting any trouble here. This was a simple data hunt. But no soldier went into danger without a loaded weapon.

"So let's get going," Schwarz said, tucking electronic items and plastique into a black nylon gym bag. There might be a wall safe to blow. But they had to stay low-key. These people might just be civilians. Unless Himar's "family" was actually his private army of mercenaries. Schwarz briefly inspected his own 9 mm Beretta and threaded on a sound suppressor. Better safe than sorry.

"Wait a second," Lyons advised, adjusting the focus on the field glasses. "Something's wrong here."

Instantly the other two men were alert and reached for the M-16 assault rifles hidden in the false ceiling of the van.

The Able Team leader surveyed the apartment building and lawn again, the hairs rising on his nape. Something about the area had triggered a warning bell inside his head, and the former L.A. cop was trying to spot what was wrong. A few of the windows were open, admitting the cool morning air. But New Englanders had a love of cold that the rest of the nation found puzzling. Just like getting a tan in California, it bordered on a mania. There was nobody moving in the bushes or in the backyard.... That's when it hit him. There was nobody moving at all. That dog wasn't asleep, it was dead. And there were tiny dark shapes floating in the birdbath. Wrens?

Turning, Lyons swept the whole block. Nobody was moving around any of the other homes, either. No leaves being raked, no mail being delivered, no dogs barking, no birds in the trees. Several houses away, a man was smoking while lying in a hammock. Focusing the field glasses, Lyons saw that the fellow had once been smoking, but now his shirt was smoldering. A cigar laying on the blackened ruin of his chest.

"Get hard, people," Lyons ordered, tucking away the field glasses. Reaching down, he pulled the Atchisson autoshotgun from the bag on the floor. "We're the only people alive on this street, possibly in the whole damn town."

"Why would Himar beam his own house?" Schwarz said, frowning, working the arming bolt on the assault rifle. "Unless…"

"Unless Himar really is dead, and somebody else also wants his files on Prometheus before we can get them," Blancanales conceded, thumbing a fat 40 mm round into the M-203 grenade launcher. "Mighty easy to rob a place if everybody is dead."

Just then the happy Indian music was cut off and a window on the fifth floor of the apartment house closed, a dark shape moving behind the curtains. In a house of the dead, somebody was still moving.

"Where did Himar live?" Lyons demanded, shrugging out of his suit jacket.

"Fourth floor, but his office was on the fifth," Schwarz said, passing out the NATO body armor. "I'd say that we've got hostiles inside."

"Could just be a street cop checking the place out,"

Blancanales warned, strapping on his light-weight bulletproof vest. "Or maybe a survivor who was taking a bath. You know, safe under the water."

Lyons clicked the safety off the Atchisson and stepped to the curb. "Let's go find out."

Moving across the lawn, the Stony Man operatives headed for the house, each trying not to think about the deadly satellite in space possibly pointing directly downward at their location. If the neutron cannon attacked, they would never know it, and so the soldiers banished the consideration from their minds and concentrated on the task at hand. Get in, get the files and get out.

"Stony Base, this is Einstein," Schwarz said into his throat mike as they passed the birdbath. "Our twenty may have been neutralized. If you don't hear from us in an hour, consider this a hot zone. Out." It took a moment for the message to be condensed, then the radio gave a short beep as the transmission was burst back to the Farm. Unless the enemy was listening to the precise frequency, at exactly the correct moment, Schwarz knew they would never be able to detect the microsecond radio pulse. Much less break the encryption created by Kurtzman and his team.

The world seemed unnaturally still to the Stony Man operatives. Traffic could be heard in the distance, and a jet liner rumbled overhead toward Logan International. But it was almost as if they were moving through a dream. No voices, no laughter, not even birds in the trees.

"We want them alive," Lyons whispered curtly. "But retrieving those files is more important."

The other men nodded, their eyes sweeping for danger.

Moving onto the brick porch, the Able Team leader saw a bearded man in slippers lying crumpled behind the laurel bushes, a folded newspaper still clutched in his hand. Lyons stopped and pried it loose. It was an afternoon edition. The attack had only happened a short while ago.

The front door was closed, but unlocked, and the three men eased inside, their weapons at the ready.

The foyer was empty. There was a grandfather clock softly ticking, and a coatrack with an attached bench that Schwarz recognized as an antique from before the Revolutionary War. A brass umbrella stand was in the corner and a ceramic bowl on a small table contained car keys.

Blancanales made a noise and gestured to the left.

In the living room, the shapely legs of a teenage girl stuck out from behind the couch in the living room. A cat lay lifeless next to a ball of yarn, a goldfish floated upside down in a glass bowl. But more importantly, there was a ten-gallon can of fuel sitting in the middle of the living room with a radio detonator attached to the side.

Tightening his grip on the autoshotgun, Lyons tried not to curse. The Prometheans, as Price had dubbed them, weren't here to steal the files, but to burn the place down to make sure nobody else got them! And they weren't going to take any chances on missing some papers hidden in the wall or under a floorboard. That firebomb would reduce the whole house to rubble. The neutron cannon could kill from space, but the deadly beams would have no effect whatsoever on computer disks and simple paper. Those had to be destroyed by hand.

Shouldering his M-16, Schwarz went to the colossal firebomb and pulled the wires free. As he turned, the electronics expert grimaced at the sight of a second firebomb in the kitchen. There was another firebomb at the foot of the stairs.

Fast and silent, the team moved through the first floor, deactivating the explosive charges. Reaching the cellar door, they paused for a wordless conference, but then heard footsteps upstairs on the wooden floor.

Separating into a one-on-one defense formation, the Stony Man commandos walked up the old stairs, carefully keeping to the outer edges where the wood would be the strongest and least likely to creak and betray their presence.

The second and third floors proved to be the same as the first, and the team quickly neutralized the bombs.

Reaching the fourth floor, Lyons paused alongside the railing. He could hear murmuring voices, and somebody was happily whistling. A fierce rage swelled within the man. The bastards were enjoying themselves!

"Hey!" a man shouted. "What the fuck are you doing, asshole?"

Able Team froze, swinging up their weapons for the expected attack. Heavy footsteps stomped closer.

"I wasn't doing anything, George," another man replied. But the man was cut off by the sharp smack of a slap, and a rustling sound was made by some small items scattering across the floor.

A glassine envelope went over the edge of the landing, and Blancanales made the catch. Opening his fist, he scowled at a tiny packet full of blue crystals. Interesting.

"You're a fucking liar, Troy!" the first voice snarled angrily. "I saw you stuffing packs in your pockets!"

"Hey, I only figured—"

Another hard slap sounded, then two more. "If Ravid sent us two pounds of crystal meth to sprinkle around the place, then we use every ounce!" George ordered brusquely. "That son of a bitch knew enough about our strongarm operations to send us to Wadpoole prison for the rest of our freaking lives!"

That caught the team by surprise. These were street toughs blackmailed to plant evidence of a drug lab in the house before burning it down. If the local police found traces of the deadly narcotic in the ashes, their investigation of the blaze would stop right there, assuming it was just case of the drug makers falling out over the business. *Ravid.* They would remember that name.

"Yeah, yeah, sure," Troy mumbled. "I was only just—"

"Shut the fuck up," George snarled. "Hey, Mike, you wanna remind me why we brought the feeb along?"

"Had to. He's my cousin," Mike mumbled. "And don't call him that word again, get me?"

"Go screw a rolling doughnut," George replied. "Okay, Troy, get the rest of this crap and meet us on the fifth floor. He said they were all to be strewed around the office."

"Sure, no problem, eh?"

"Did you put the tanks of ammonia in the basement?" a fourth man demanded. "Nobody's gonna believe this was a crystal meth lab unless there's lot of ammonia."

"Sure thing, Jeff, did that first off," Troy replied quickly. "Ah…do they really make meth from ammonia?"

"Oh, for the love of… Just pick up the envelopes!"

"Right away! Sure, no problem. Hey, you know me…"

The other men tromped away, and there came the sounds of somebody crawling across the floorboards, sweeping up the packets in their hands. Soon, a bald head appeared over the edge of the fourth-floor landing, and Troy gasped at the sight of the Able Team looking back up, their arms full of military ordnance. The man went pale and froze motionless.

Shaking his head, Lyons pressed a finger to his lips for silence, while Blancanales and Schwarz aimed their assault rifles.

"I surrender!" Troy cried, raising both hands, casting a deluge of packets upon the Stony Man commandos. "Don't shoot me!"

Muffled curses came from the fifth floor, and all of the arming lights on the cheap detonators strapped to the fuel canisters started blinking.

Furiously, Lyons charged up the stairs and fired. The Atchisson ripped off a short burst, and Troy stumbled backward from the barrage of 12-gauge stun bags.

"Freeze! This is the FBI!" Blancanales shouted, adding a long rip from the M-16 assault rifle into the ceiling. With any luck, the hardmen would simply surrender.

"Fuck you, cops!" George yelled, and a pair of black metallic globes sailed over the railing to hit the fourth-floor landing and bounce away.

"Grenades!" Lyons roared, diving aside, his teammates only a heartbeat behind.

The team was still airborne when the charges cut loose, filling the landing with thundering flame. Still kneeling with his arms raised in surrender, Troy was blown apart by the double explosion.

As they hit the floor, there came a sharp patter of antipersonnel shrapnel smacking into the doors and walls. In a bathroom, a plastic fuel canister ruptured, the pink fluid gushing out to spread along the wooden floor, heading dangerously close to the burning ruin of the smashed landing.

Charging into the bathroom, Schwarz tackled the canister, shoving it into the bathtub. Heading into a bedroom, Blancanales ripped the arming wires off a firebomb and went in search of another.

Rising up from behind the fire, Lyons dropped the drum of stun bags and slapped in a drum of fléchettes just as Jeff jumped down the stairs to land heavily on the splintery wood. Grinning fiendishly, the Boston muscle swept the entire fourth floor with an AK-47 assault rifle, the 7.62 mm rounds slamming into pictures, bookcases and the still bodies of the former occupants.

Ducking behind a wingback chair, Lyons fired a short burst from the Atchisson, the hellstorm of steel slivers tearing Jeff apart, arms and legs going in different directions.

Bracing against the recoil, Schwarz fired a 40 mm round up the stairs. The charge detonated against the ceiling, spraying down a hellstorm of plaster and wooden splinters. Somebody screamed, the noise becoming a demented howl as Mike staggered into view. His upper body was riddled with holes, red blood pumping out in a ghastly spray from the ruptured arteries.

Mouthing obscenities, he sprayed his twin Ingram MAC-10 machine pistols, the 9 mm Parabellum rounds hammering down the stairs in crisscrossing streams of glowing tracers and hot lead. From the bedroom, Blancanales peppered the banister, the 5.56 mm rounds chewing a path of destruction along the polished wood. Still shooting, Jeff retreated to the fifth floor. But just as he disappeared, George appeared and fired a line of tracers rounds directly into the pooled gasoline, dripping over the landing. With a whoosh, it ignited and wild flames raced along the floor going straight into the bathroom and up the wallpaper. Standing in the bathtub, Schwarz turned on the shower and angled the spray onto the walls, but the water did little to hinder the lashing orange conflagration.

"You men up there, get the hell out!" Blancanales shouted, slapping in a fresh clip. "The house is on fire!"

"Lead the way, cop!" George retorted from somewhere above. "I'm not going back to Wadpoole! I'd rather die here with you!"

Lyons shot his friend a hard look and Blancanales frowned from the doorway of the bedroom. It sounded crazy, but many men who had spent decades in jail swore death before returning to the rigid discipline of government cellblocks.

"We need those files," Lyons ordered, touching his throat mike. He burped a short burst up the stairs. "Think we can cut a deal?"

"No way," Blancanales replied, cracking the breech of the grenade launcher. He dumped the 40 mm stun bag and thumbed in an AP round. "We have to take them out."

Another grenade bounced down the ruined stairs and disappeared below. A moment later there came a muffled whomp and then a welling aura of hellish light. Lyons cursed. The grenade had ignited the canisters of fuel! The ground floor, maybe even the second, was on fire, and soon the flames would reach the other canisters. They only had a few minutes before the entire building was an inferno. *With us trapped on the top level,* he thought.

Turning the Atchisson upward, Lyons emptied the entire drum of 12-gauge fléchettes directly into the ceiling. The fusillade chewed open a gaping hole, and Blancanales and Schwarz instantly triggered 40 mm rounds. Once more, the shells exploded on the next ceiling, and men screamed.

Charging for the stairs, Lyons swept the room at waist level, blowing apart office furniture, computers, blackboards and both of the stumbling hardmen. But as they fell, a skinny blond man hit a radio detonator clipped to his bloody belt.

"Not going back…" George said, then went still.

A split second later, a muffled series of blasts erupted in the lower levels of the house, and the closet across the office was brightly illuminated from within, the door blowing off as the expanding fireball of the hidden incendiary charge cut loose. The only desk was coated with a sheet of flame, the DOD security documents vanishing into ash from the volcanic heat.

Rushing to a file cabinet, Lyons yanked the top drawer open, then quickly backed away as a secondary charge set the gasoline-soaked folders ablaze. In grudging admiration, Lyons was forced to admit that was exactly how he would have done it. They were amateurs, but not fools.

Ramming the stock of his M-16 into a computer, Blancanales smashed the machine into pieces. Using a knife, Schwarz pried loose the hard drive and shoved it into a pocket.

Flames licked out of the stairwell, and the crackling fire raced along the ceiling and walls, the updraft from the hole in the floor feeding the growing blaze.

"Let's go!" Lyons shouted as a thick cloud of pungent smoke rose up the stairwell. House on fire, files rigged, the book case empty of any technical journals, there was no place left to search in the scant time remaining. Besides, every soldier knew the danger of fighting in civilian homes. The carpeting often gave off toxic smoke that could kill a person.

However, Lyons had barely taken a step when his nose caught a sharp aroma. It was actually rather pleasant, and the man felt oddly good, almost drunk, his heart beating wildly.

"Don't breathe!" Blancanales cried, exhaling as hard as possible and slapping a hand across his nose and mouth.

With sleepy movements, the Stony Man commandos stumbled away from the hundred melted bags of crystal meth sizzling on the charred floorboards. The fumes were making them feel woozy, almost light-headed. A strange lethargy stole the strength from their bodies, their weapons suddenly feeling as if each weighed a million tons....

Fighting off the weakness through sheer force of will, Lyons aimed the Atchisson carefully, and triggered a long sustained burst at the flaming stairs until the smoky wood was torn into wreckage. It dropped away with a strident crash, and the heat in the office decreased slightly.

"Okay, that bought us a few minutes," Lyons said, coughing raggedly. He fumbled to reload the autoshotgun with clumsy fingers. "But we have to leave fast— or die."

More dull explosions sounded from below, the rising smoke becoming thicker, the floor growing hotter beneath their civilian shoes.

Snarling in rage, Blancanales fired from the hip, blowing out the rear windows. Rushing to the sill, he drank in the fresh air and momentarily his head cleared.

Firing to the left, then the right, a coughing Schwarz took out both side windows. The thick smoke thinned immediately, but the roaring fire noticeably increased.

Shuffling to the left window, Lyons saw only a gazebo on the ground five stories away.

Firing the M-16 nonstop, Schwarz blasted away at something outside the right window, then grunted in victory. "This way!" he shouted, slinging the exhausted weapon over a shoulder and hastily climbing through the opening.

Quickly joining their friend, Lyons and Blancanales saw Schwarz grab a dangling power line, a telephone pole at the corner of the property sparking and snapping. Wrapping the thick cable once around his waist, Schwarz rappelled down the side of the apartment building to land hard on the roof of the garage.

As he rushed along the sloping expanse of shingles, Blancanales arrived, then Lyons. Going to the edge, they jumped into the rosebushes, uncaring of the thorns, and fought their way to the front lawn. A heartbeat later, the roof of the garage collapsed, writhing flames licking at empty sky.

Returning to the van, the bedraggled Stony Man commandos piled inside and divested themselves of weapons before driving away. Oddly, there was no wail of incoming fire trucks, police or ambulance. The men solemnly realized that was because there was nobody alive in the neighborhood to report the mounting blaze.

Breaking out bottles of water, the men of Able Team drank deeply, clearing their sore throats, the clean air pouring through the vehicle slowly washing the stupefying effects of the cooking drug from their brains.

"At least we got this," Schwarz croaked, inspecting the hard drive.

"And even if that is blank," Blancanales wheezed, "we now have a name. Ravid."

"Any terrorists called that?" Lyons asked, lowering their speed as he headed for Logan International.

Tucking away the hard drive, Schwarz shrugged. "None that I know."

"I do," Blancanales said, pouring water into his open

palm and rubbing his face clean. He shook himself dry like a dog coming out of the rain. "Two, actually. There's a Ravid in Hamas and another in Tiger Force. But it couldn't be them. Neither group has resources to put a satellite into orbit."

"Unless they got some major-league assistance," Lyons returned, settling back into the seat. Anybody who hired thugs to do their fighting, might also have been hired as mercenaries in the first place. Hamas or Tiger Force, were they the real foe? Or was Stony Man facing a cartel of terrorist organizations this time? That would be a nightmare come true. And there was no way to know for sure until the hard drive was downloaded. Hopefully, that could be done on the Hercules.

Changing his mind, Lyons angled onto a highway and went straight past Logan to head for downtown Boston. If they could find the office where George and his crew worked before the word spread of their demise, Able Team might be able to find out exactly who Ravid was. Definitely a long shot, but worth the effort.

Merging with the thickening flow of honking traffic, the Able Team leader just hoped that Phoenix Force was having better luck at the Wake Island laboratory.

CHAPTER SIX

Wake Island, Pacific Ocean

About six hundred miles off the coast of California, Phoenix Force landed its Learjet on the deck of the USS *Kitty Hawk* aircraft carrier. Quickly transferring to a Black Hawk helicopter, the team continued its journey across the Pacific Ocean.

According to the U.S. Army records, the landing strip on Wake Island was too short to handle a Lear, and the helicopter gunship gave them the option of landing wherever they wished, possibly avoiding an ambush. Or worse, the deadly beam of the orbiting satellite.

Wake Island was an atoll, the crested rim of an ancient underwater volcano. The three curved islands barely covered one and a half square miles. But because of their position, the islands had been an invaluable refueling spot during World War II. In its time, the atoll had been heavily armed with anti-ship cannons hidden in the thick palm trees.

But these days the atoll was all but forgotten. The big guns were long gone, and all that remained of the refueling station was a small airfield for emergency landings that was used only once, or twice, a year. The only paved road was slowly returning to nature, the Quonset huts removed, the tiny jungle allowed to grow freely over the circular atoll. For a while, it had been a U.S. Army weapons research facility for an antimissile program, but the funding disappeared, and so did the Army. These days, two of the tiny banana-shaped islands were tangles of unfettered growth, while the third contained only the short, cracked landing strip, and a heavily fortified concrete laboratory. Code name: Prometheus.

The Black Hawk helicopter moved low across the Pacific Ocean, flying over some pleasure craft, a cruise liner and a fat oil tanker bound for Alaska. Halfway to the isolated atoll, it began to rain, soft and gentle. Wisely, the Black Hawk stayed below the cloud layer. What couldn't be seen, hopefully couldn't be attacked. Passive radar was clear, and the active radar revealed no hostile aircraft, only rumbling storm clouds and rain.

The five members of Phoenix Force were jammed into the jumpseats lining the walls, the open space in the middle filled with trunks of ammunition, explosives and assorted supplies. The team needed to be ready for anything.

"Anybody know a Ravid?" Calvin James asked, lowering the radio headphones. His accent was pure southside Chicago. Tall and lanky, the former Navy SEAL was the field medic for the team, and one of the best underwater demolitionists the soldiers had ever seen.

"The head of Tiger Force is Ravid something or other," T. J. Hawkins said.

"Tiger Force?" Rafael Encizo asked scornfully. "No way those backwater grunts could launch a bottle rocket, much less a freaking satellite."

A stocky man with catlike reflexes, Encizo was less than handsome, his face carrying the scars of too many battles. But the looks beguiled the razor-sharp mind inside. Slung across his chest was an MP-5 machine gun. Stun grenades festooned his web harness and a compact Walther PPK .38 rode in a high belly holster. A Tanto combat knife was sheathed upside down on his shoulder for fast access, and plastic garrotes dangled from a breakaway catch on his belt.

"Himar comes from India," David McCarter said from the copilot seat. "Was born there if I remember correctly, and now a south India terrorist group appears from the shadows."

The leader of Phoenix Force, McCarter was a former member of the elite British SAS. The Briton radiated controlled strength, and every man present owed their lives to McCarter a dozen times over. The bonds of friendship between the Stony Man warriors had been forged on the bloody fields of combat.

Hawkins grunted. "Hell of a coincidence."

"What kind of files do we have on Tiger Force?" Encizo asked, inspecting the razor-sharp edge of his combat knife for any feathering. Satisfied, he slid the knife into its sheath.

"Pretty sketchy," James admitted. "They're small-timers, not really on the world radar."

"So far," Gary Manning retorted, working the bolt of his titanic Barrett .50-caliber sniper rifle, then adding a drop of lubricant to the slide. "However, if these guys have a neutron cannon, then I'm really looking forward to meeting them."

Thunder rumbled outside the craft, the concussion buffeting it slightly.

"Fifteen minutes to the island, David," the blacksuit pilot announced crisply.

"Anything on radar?" Hawkins asked, checking the clip in his 9 mm Beretta.

"We're clear," the blacksuit reported from the front of the craft.

A moment later the blacksuit announced, "There it is."

McCarter looked hard through the rain-smeared window, but there was nothing to be seen below but endless ocean. "Better be sure," he demanded, unbuckling his seat belt. "The atoll has three islands, with a lot of water around them. We want the north island, just past the deep water cove."

"The instruments read dead center, sir," the pilot said confidently. "I'm on target."

"Fair enough." Strapping on a harness, McCarter went to the hatch, slid it back and stepped out of the helicopter.

A few yards down, the catch on his harness engaged and his descent along the rope rapidly slowed. With the downpour blurring the landscape, the leader of Phoenix Force couldn't see anything. It was like rappelling into an abandoned well.

A shiny refection swelled beneath his boots and McCarter braced for an impact into the ocean, then he caught the dim outline of a nearby building and quickly bent his knees.

With a hard thump, the Stony Man commando landed on a rain-slick parking lot. Immediately, McCarter slapped the release and saw the line swing free as he swung around his MP-5 and worked the arming bolt. A heartbeat later Hawkins landed, closely followed by Encizo.

Clearing the landing zone, the men flipped on their night-vision goggles and scanned for any possible dangers as Manning and James arrived. The Black Hawk promptly began to move away, the sound of the rotors lost in the storm.

Spreading out, the men swept along the parking lot, staying low to the pavement. There were no Hummers in sight, only a vague sensation of a fence to their left and a dark outline of something looming large in front of them like the side of a cliff.

"EM and thermal are clear," Encizo reported.

"Good. Okay, keep it tight, people," McCarter whispered. "Gary, you're on cover."

"Roger," Manning replied, stopping where he was and bringing up the long barrel of the Barrett.

The laboratory slowly came into view. A door to the left was situated under a small awning, while a set of large doors were to the right with concrete aprons jutting for truck deliveries. There was no light or movement.

Pausing in the rain just outside the clear area below the awning, McCarter studied the entrance. A drain in the pavement gurgled as the water from the parking lot trickled into it. The name of the project had been scraped off the door, the Plexiglas windows frosted white. There was no sign of a keyhole, but there was a palm lock on the jamb.

Warily, McCarter placed a hand on the sensor pad. It gave an angry buzz, nothing more.

"Stony Base, this is Firebird," McCarter said into his throat mike. "We need a knock-knock."

"On it," Aaron Kurtzman replied through a crackle of static.

"T.J., Cal, check for another way inside," McCarter ordered.

"On it," Hawkins replied.

Leveling his dripping MP-5, James went in the other direction and disappeared around the corner of the huge building.

The rest of the team waited patiently. A few minutes later the others returned.

"Found a loading dock, but the steel doors have been welded shut," Hawkins said gruffly.

"Same with the back door," James added. "Somebody really doesn't want people inside this building."

"What about the roof?" Encizo asked, glancing upward.

James snorted. "The access ladder is gone. Only the bolt holes remain."

"Firebird One to Stony Base, anything yet?" McCarter asked, shifting his grip on the machine gun.

Blowing their way inside was looking more and more likely.

"Not yet," Kurtzman answered from halfway around the world. "Whoever built the firewalls around these circuits really knew what they were doing."

Pulling out a wad of C-4 plastique, McCarter admitted he had half expected something like that. Walking under the awning, the big man pointed at the door frame. "Okay, I want a charge there and there," he directed. "Be sure to—"

"Wait a second," Kurtzman interrupted. "We might be on to something."

The team paused expectantly. There came a soft click from the door and it opened a crack.

"There you go!" Kurtzman said with a chuckle. "Anything else?"

"Sure," McCarter replied, sliding into the dark building. "Find the satellite in space, and make it blow up."

"I'll do my best. Stony Base out."

Careful of where they stepped, the Stony Man commandos moved through a dimly lit lobby. In the ghostly light from the goggles, they saw chairs for guests and a table stacked full of technical magazines, glass panels set into the wall for the receptionist and a couple of doors. An Army lieutenant slumped over the reception desk, a holstered Colt .45 on his hip.

"The poor bastard never even got off a shot," Encizo said in controlled rage.

"Check everywhere," McCarter ordered. "If the thieves were here, they must have left traces, a fingerprint, a cigarette butt, something we can use to track them down."

Nodding assent, the team spread out in a tight search pattern. Going to a closed door, Hawkins pushed it open with the barrel of the MP-5 and saw that it was a modern bathroom, toilet and bidet, plus a small sink. A sergeant lay on the floor, dried soap suds on his hands, the faucet still softly running. Hawkins turned it off with a hard twist. "Sorry, brother," he whispered.

Checking the closet, Encizo found only cleaning supplies, mops and buckets. Going into the reception area, James checked the video recorder for the security cameras, and wasn't surprised to find the disks gone.

Moving down a long corridor, McCarter saw a plump rat sitting on the carpeting eating something in its paws. How did a rat get on an island atoll? There was nothing indigenous to the islands but sand and surf.

Switching from UV to IR, the man saw a few more hot spots moving along the baseboards that turned out to only be more rats. The place was infested with them. That didn't bode well.

Pausing at the next door, McCarter inspected the jamb. There was a line of bullets holes in the thick wood and the lock was smashed apart. The thieves had shot their way inside. He looked around, but there was no brass on the carpeting.

On a hunch, the man took off his goggles and flicked on his flashlight. Something reflected the beam from behind a nearby potted plant, and McCarter bent to retrieve an empty brass cartridge. The thieves had obviously picked up their brass, but missed this one because it rolled away.

In the beam, McCarter could see no manufacture's

name on the bottom, just a lot number. There was a side strike mark for the ejector, so it came from an autofire, possibly an assault rifle. But the caliber was odd. The U.S. armed forces used a standard 5.56 mm round, as did NATO and a lot of other folks. But this was a just slightly larger, maybe a 5.8 mm. That would make it Chinese. The new QBZ-95 assault rifle used a 5.8 mm cartridge.

"Alert," McCarter said, touching his throat mike. "We may be facing the Red Star."

Everybody became more alert, if that were possible. Red Star was the counterintelligence group for Communist China. Stony Man had tangled with them several times, and the encounters had always been bloody. Especially that terrible incident at Hoover dam. The Chinese agents killed without hesitation and often tried to hide their escape under a mound of dead civilians. This sort of mass execution seemed just their style. It was even rumored that several KGB agents had found employment with their former enemy when the Soviet Union collapsed. The Chinese operatives were serious hardcases, and fanatical fighters.

The Red Star didn't give a damn if its covert missions were discovered. Hell, it seemed to McCarter that they welcome the publicity. On the other hand, all of the Stony Man ammunition, grenades, even their boots and MRE packs were totally without identification marks. There were no product numbers, bar codes, or anything that could be used to trace the items back to America, much less the Farm. The CIA did the same thing, as did MI-5 in the United Kingdom and the Mossad.

Pocketing the cartridge, McCarter moved past the swing door and into a vast open area that was a laboratory. Machinery and worktables were in total disarray, file cabinets and desks pushed against the walls in random order. Drawers had been pulled out of the desks, the computers smashed apart, the hard drives removed. The trash baskets were empty and blackboards were wiped clean. The lab had been looted to the bare walls.

That's when McCarter spotted the corpses, most wearing white lab coats over civilian clothing. Several had clipboards lying nearby, the papers removed from the spring clamps. The pockets of the corpses had been turned inside out, their belongings scattered on the bare concrete floor: keys, wallets, loose coins, pencils, chewing gum, lipstick, cigarettes and butane lighters.

"No cells phones, or anything else that could record data," Hawkins observed dourly. "Whoever these people are, they know what to do."

Making an inarticulate noise, James swung his weapon at a dead man whose shirt was moving. A second later a rat appeared carrying away a grisly morsel. His trigger finger tightened, but the Stony Man warrior withheld firing. That wouldn't help anybody at the moment. Dead was dead, and the rats were only trying to stay alive by doing their assigned role in nature.

Passing a bank of file cabinets, McCarter saw that all of the drawers were open and empty. Cleaned out completely. Himar's house had been burned to remove any duplicate files, but everything here had been taken by the attacking force.

Crossing a field of smashed electronic equipment,

the team's boots crunched softly on the ceramic chips and capacitors. There were more corpses here, and more rats. The men resisted the urge to crush them under their combat boots.

To the left was a loading dock, chains hanging from the ceiling girders like jungle vines. Softly, the links clinked in a gentle breeze of a broken window.

"Guess the rats couldn't find any place to go, so they came back," Hawkins noted, shifting his combat boot away from one of the scurrying rodents.

Plexiglas walls sectioned off a bank of electronic controls, and thick power cables snaked away to a hulking generator in the corner. Set into the concrete was a circular cradle of some kind, more power cables lying impotently on the floor.

McCarter scowled at the arrangement. He was no scientist, but it seemed logical that this was where the neutron cannon had been less than forty-eight hours ago.

"Now how could the thieves have stolen the cannon and gotten it into orbit fast enough to beam down the 747 above Pennsylvania?" Encizo asked.

"They couldn't have," James replied. "Unless they launched it from a mobile platform just offshore, but the Watchdog satellites would have spotted the launch in an instant." Something was wrong about this. Warily, he studied the equipment more carefully. There were a lot of meters and sensors behind sheets of metal and plastic. There was even a double-walled shield filled with what appeared to be gasoline. Small cages stood behind the barriers, several of them filled with the bony skeletons of dead rats. Test subjects. And the technicians stood behind the wall of gasoline for protection. Suddenly everything became crystal-clear.

"Himar wasn't building a neutron cannon," McCarter whispered, feeling the hairs rise on the back of his neck. "He was trying to invent a way to stop the beam!"

"Which means he must have been reporting to the President on some new development," Hawkins said grimly. "Maybe even a successful way of blocking the energy beam."

McCarter slammed the barrel of his machine gun onto an open palm. "Or his success—" he started. "We have got to find those files!" It all made horrible sense to the Briton. Himar invented the neutron cannon, and then tried to find a way to counter the hellish weapon. Guilty conscience? Maybe. But somebody stole the plans, built a functioning cannon, then took out the scientist to keep him from blocking their plans. Whatever those were.

"Firebird One to Stony Base. I think we have another Shklov incident here," McCarter relayed, adjusting the transceiver on his belt. A few years ago, a team of mercenaries had hit a Russian naval base, killed everybody and stolen the blueprints for a state-of-the-art torpedo. The aftermath had been catastrophic.

"Confirm, Firebird," Kurtzman replied. "Any idea who our mystery guests are yet?"

"Negative. But I have spent cartridge that could belong to them." He read off the lot number from the bottom of the shell. "Call me when you have something."

"Ten minutes," Kurtzman replied, and went off the air.

"T.J., get the lights," McCarter ordered, tucking away the shell once more. "Let's see what else we can find."

Going to the wall, Hawkins took off his goggles and flipped a switch. Bright lights flooded the spacious laboratory.

Instantly, the rip of a machine-gun fire exploded from the shadows above, and the riddled computer tower flew away from Encizo. The Stony Man commando dropped to the floor, a hail of bullets hammering the spot where he had just stood.

"Incoming!" the little Cuban shouted, his MP-5 spraying the darkness above.

The rest of Phoenix Force dived for cover and returned fire, their weapons seeking the hidden sniper. The MP-5 machine guns stuttered away, and the enemy's assault rifles boomed in response with a much heavier caliber. A rain of spent brass fell musically across the laboratory.

Suddenly another burst came from a different location, and then a third. In the strobing illumination of the cross fire, McCarter caught a glimpse of the snipers. Bloody hell, he thought, those were AutoSentries! It was a fiendish device composed of an automatic weapon set on a tripod and a computer. There was no human operator. Anything that came into range of the sensors was fired upon until the ammunition ran out. And these models sported double ammo drums set on top like mouse ears.

Spraying a long burst at the ceiling, McCarter bit back a curse. So the lab had been a trap after all! The

machines had to have been set to attack when somebody hit the lights near the loading dock. Where the
doors were welded shut, cutting off any possible retreat. The only way out of the lab was through the
swing door. Directly underneath the three hammering
AutoSentries.

Crawling to a better position, James fired upward at
a belly of a sentry, his bullets bouncing harmlessly off
the thick armor. Swiveling on a girder across the warehouse, a different sentry fired upon the man, the rounds
slamming into the concrete floor and ricocheting away.
James grunted as he took one in the chest, his body
armor feeling like it had been hit by a sledgehammer.

Returning fire, James saw that the disfigured bullet
lying on the floor was spread open wide, a soft lead flower
with a steel spike in the middle. Daisy cutters! That type
of ammo was illegal everywhere because it went in like
a finger and came out bigger than a splayed hand.

Rolling into view, Encizo whipped a grenade at the
ceiling. It clattered among the crisscrossing beams of
the girders and exploded. The high-explosive charge
shook the roof, blowing off a whirlwind of dust. But the
AutoSentries didn't even tremble.

Bloody bastards must be welded in place, McCarter
fumed, slapping in a fresh clip. Unless somebody got
in a lucky shot with a grenade, those machines were not
coming down. Time to call for the cavalry.

CROUCHING IN THE RAIN, Gary Manning adjusted the
collar of his poncho when he heard the crackle of gunfire coming from the laboratory. The man flinched, but

stayed as he was. His post was here, in case the others need any assistance.

"London to Toronto," Manning heard in his earbuds. "We have robos in the rafters! Bring the boom stick."

"On my way." Charging through the downpour, Manning was halfway to the laboratory when he slowed at the sound of a soft whistle in the rain above.

Sharply changing direction, Manning charged off to the side and hit the pavement just before there came a thunderous explosion a dozen yards away. Mortar shell!

Rolling over, Manning dialed his night-vision goggles for maximum enhancement and scanned the horizon. There was no way of telling where the shell had came from, and in this rain visibility was poor at best. Nothing could be seen outside the fence but dripping jungle and crashing waves. Had it come from the roof of the laboratory? There didn't seem to be anything up there.

A muted thump came from the right, closely followed by the steadily increasing whine of a descending shell.

Manning hit the wet pavement once more. The shell hit the dirt road just outside the entry gate, briefly illuminating the night. The gate sagged and fell over, covered with flames. The big Canadian ducked and a hail of hot gravel fell in a blanket across the parking lot. What was going on? Nobody had been near the gate. A few seconds later, a shell exploded in the middle of the lot, and then directly above the roof of the building, spraying the area with a deadly halo of shrapnel.

Shifting his grip on the Barrett, Manning watched the

night intently, straining to hear the telltale thump of the discharging mortar. There was only one possibility. A thump pulsed on a distant hilltop, and another shell hit the parking lot directly in front of the loading dock. Thunder rumbled nearby, and Manning waited for lighting. In the blue flash, he caught a brief glimpse of a squat machine on the hilltop across the circular lagoon.

It was another AutoSentry, but a mortar this time. Suddenly everything made sense. The team was pinned down inside by machine guns, held in place while the outside mortar worked a preprogrammed firing sequence, first taking out the helipad where a helicopter should be in the middle of the parking lot, then closing the gate to prevent any escape to the beach, and then clearing the rooftop of snipers. Next, it was going to hit the laboratory, blowing Phoenix Force to pieces, Manning guessed.

With a surge of adrenaline, he rushed through the downpour and knelt at the fence to thrust the long barrel of the Barrett through the woven links. Desperately, he put five shots in the direction of AutoSentry mortar with no results. The machine belched again, and the shell flew behind the laboratory.

Thunder sounded from the heavens above. Manning held his breath, his finger putting four pounds of pressure on the six-pound trigger. The next shell would finish the job. Come on, lightning… A blue flash from behind illuminated the landscape and he fired. Nothing seemed to happen.

A heartbeat later the mortar belched and something exploded across the lagoon, the flames revealing the machine now lying on its side. Working the bolt, Manning put another massive round into the exposed ammunition hopper, and the entire second island erupted, flames stretching in every direction.

Satisfied, Manning turned and charged back toward the laboratory. He had to move fast. If there were three AutoSentries inside, there could be another on the third atoll waiting for the signal to go into action.

Bursting through the front door, Manning hopped over a rat and charged down the hallway to stop at the swing doors. Risking a peek through the plastic window, he could see the AutoSentries in the girders firing down on the team, brass falling all over the place. Drawing his .357 Magnum Desert Eagle, the Stony Man commando blew out the Plexiglas window in the swing door and ducked low.

As expected, the door shuddered from a barrage of daisy cutter rounds blasting holes through the thick wood. The moment the firing stopped, Manning stood and stroked the Barrett. A foot-long lance of flame extended from the barrel of the titanic rifle, and the AutoSentry near the loading dock was smashed off the girder to violently crash on the concrete floor. Instantly, the other two machines concentrated their aim on the fallen sentry, tearing it to bits, the hanging chains dancing wildly from the ricochets.

"Light 'em up!" McCarter said over the radio link, and the rest of Phoenix Force concentrated their weapons on the jingling chains.

The shaking lengths caught the attention of the other sentries, and they blew flaming death in that direction.

Taking advantage of the distraction, Manning eased into the laboratory and took out one sentry, then the other, in swift efficiency.

The machines were still firing as they fell, and continued blasting randomly as they crashed onto the floor. Papers went flying, cabinets toppled over, the water cooler shattered, corpses shook and rats died in squeaking torment.

"End this," McCarter ordered, pulling a grenade from his vest.

Rings were yanked loose, arming levers flipped off and several lethal eggs rolled along the concrete floor to stop near the hammering Sentries.

The men took cover just as the interior of the laboratory was filled with the deafening triple blast, debris and bits of flesh from the corpses sailing away to smack into the walls. But as the smoke cleared, there was only silence. The AutoSentries were smashed, their circuits sparking and crackling from shorting.

Rushing over, James and Encizo pulled the power cords from the machines, then yanked out the ammo belts and stomped the sensor array on top.

"Incoming mortar fire!" Manning shouted, rising into view. "Get out now!"

Lurching into action, the team moved with a purpose and rushed from the building into the rain.

They reached the parking lot and moved a safe distance from the laboratory when the night ignited and a lance of stuttering flame reached out from the third atoll to hammer the building with strident explosions. The wall caved in, and the barrage of detonations chewed a path of destruction along the lab until cutting it in two.

Phoenix Force aimed its weapons at the third atoll and cut loose, the combination fusillade slamming the last sentry. Lighting flared, exposing a 35 mm mini-rocket pod just before it broke loose from the camouflaged nest in the palm trees and tumbled into the lagoon. Several flashes of light came from underwater, closely followed by a muffled blast and then blessed silence.

"Why such an elaborate trap?" McCarter snapped in dark harmony with the growing storm. "Why not simply beam us from orbit?"

"Maybe the cannon can't reach us through a rainstorm," Encizo suggested, brushing back his soaked hair.

"How the hell would they know it would be raining?"

"Okay, so the cannon is on the other side of the world."

"Maybe," McCarter relented, narrowing his eyes.

Then he turned. "Cal, get the Black Hawk back here. I want off this rock ASAP."

"On it," the man replied, then touched his throat to start talking to the sky.

Slinging the MP-5, McCarter adjusted the transceiver on his belt. Changing frequencies every other transmission was SOP. "Firebird One to Stony Base, do you read?"

"Roger, you're loud and clear, Firebird," Barbara Price replied. "Grizzly Adams is busy. This is Shady Lady, what do you need?"

"Any results on that trace?"

Dimly, there could be heard the steady beat of the helicopter starting to circle overhead.

"Good news actually," Price said, the smile audible in her tone. "The lot number on the cartridge came from a Chinese shipment hijacked a couple of years ago. We tried a cross-reference with Interpol and pulled out a winner. The rounds from that lot always surface in connection to mob-style executions for a Mohad Malavade."

Overhead, the dark shape of the Black Hawk appeared and began to descend, the rotor wash kicking out a spray of raindrops.

"Is Malavade a member of Tiger Force?" McCarter asked.

"Negative, no connection," Price said. Then lightning flashed and the radio crackled with static. "But according to India's Central Bureau of Investigation, Malavade is an arms dealer for the black market."

"An arms dealer would have easy access to AutoSentries and daisy cutters," Hawkins said with a hard grin, water dripping off his face. "Both of which are way out of the price league for the dirt-poor Tiger Force. They can barely afford knives."

The Black Hawk landed nearby, and the team started to board. In the distance, a small fire crackled in the ruins of the lab, and on the other atolls.

"And where exactly would we find Mr. Malavade?" McCarter asked.

CHAPTER SEVEN

Calcutta, India

Stepping out of his limousine, Mohad Malavade slid on his sunglasses and smiled defiantly at the blazing sun.

Short and fat, the man was dressed in an imported business suit made of raw silk, his shoes British Oxfords in two-tone leather. Silver rings flashed on his manicured fingers, and a gold Rolex watch adorned his left wrist. His black hair was slicked down flat with pomade, and his face was heavily scarred from childhood acne. More prominent, though, was the jagged scar that ran from his left ear and went down into his shirt where a would-be assassin had failed to cut his throat.

From the bustling crowd on the sidewalk, an old man dressed in rags limped forward, extending a weathered hand. "Please, sir, my family is starving and… Oh," the beggar began, then recoiled slightly. "My apologies,

Mr. Malavade! I did not see it was you, sir. My humble apologies." Turning, the beggar quickly hobbled away.

Glancing sideways, Malavade caught the attention of his chief bodyguard and pointed at the departing man.

Striding forward Bhoha Vinsara slammed a fist into the back of the beggar, sending him to the sidewalk, the crutches tumbling into the gutter. Immediately the other bodyguards converged on the old man and began to kick him with their steel-toed shoes.

As the beggar began to scream for mercy, Malavade smiled and turned away to start walking down the middle of the crowded sidewalk. All of the other beggars, and untouchables, quickly scrambled aside to make a clear path for the supreme crime lord of Calcutta. The wrath of Malavade the Mad was infamous. Man, woman or child, he simply didn't care. Anybody who he considered disrespectful to his authority paid a terrible price. The lucky were beaten; the unlucky begged for death.

Malavade ignored them all. The crime lord was repulsed at the very concept of claiming ownership to a section of sidewalk. Why didn't the fools stop breeding like pigs in the mud, save their money and get an apartment? The government actually offered cash rewards to any man who would get a vasectomy.

Glancing backward, the crime lord saw that Vinsara was almost done. He had a look of satisfaction on his face that always appeared after a killing.

A few years ago, a criminal group from New Delhi had tried to move in on the action in Calcutta. They hit a few drug drops, stole some cash and lifted a truck of

DVD players bound for Bangladesh. Malavade did nothing to stop them. Overconfident, the thieves took on more crew, only to discover that all of their new gunman were Malavade's men. The bloodbath lasted for less than a minute, and when it was over, only the Calcutta crew was still alive. That was when Vinsara went to work with a chain saw. It had been like watching a butcher take apart a chicken. Only these little birdies could scream. Malavade had videotaped the deaths, then sent a copy to every criminal family and gang in New Delhi. Nobody had ever tried to encroach on his territory again.

Across the crowded street, a policeman saw the crime lord and touched his hat in salute. Malavade paused to politely nod in return.

Turning away from the sight of the savage beating, the cop sighed in resignation. Life was life, and there was nothing a man could do about it. Most of the police officers were relatives of the men in the employ of Malavade. Or the crime lord had helped them pass the civil servants test to become police officers. If a policeman got sick, he received the finest medical care. If there was a legal problem, an army of lawyers came to his aid. And the officers received a fat weekly salary, from the captain down to the newest recruit.

Mohad Malavade didn't own the police in this neighborhood, he *was* the police. The crime lord could have used an ax to commit bloody murder in the middle of the public square and nothing would ever happen to him. Malavade was the feudal king of the city, and he ruled with an iron fist. Many people secretly called him

Little Shiva, the dark lord of the criminal underworld. But nobody said it very loud. Malavade's private spy, the Mongoose, heard everything, and he reported daily to his boss. Insult Malavade at 9:00 a.m., and by noon you lost your job. Anything worse than an insult, and you simply disappeared in the night.

Leaving the battered corpse on the sidewalk, Vinsara rushed to rejoin his employer.

"Dead?" Malavade asked, pulling out a silver cigarette case and lighting a slim cigarette with a gold lighter.

"If not, he soon will be," Vinsara replied.

Malavade exhaled a long stream of dark smoke. "Good," he whispered. "That thing almost touched me. The people seem to have lost their fear of me. Neuter the next one."

"Done." Vinsara smiled, flexing his oversize hands.

Puffing contentedly, Malavade strolled to the front door of a large warehouse and impatiently snapped his fingers. Immediately the heavy door rumbled aside to open a few feet. Vinsara went though first, and Malavade followed. The door closed promptly behind them.

The atmosphere of the warehouse was deliciously cool, the interior stacked high with thousands of crates and boxes in every size. Every bit of it had been hijacked from the cargo ships in the harbor or the nearby freight trains. All of the local business were used to paying graft; that was just a part of doing business in India. However, the international corporations had thought themselves immune from such things until a CEO vacationing in Switzerland had been found beheaded in his luxury penthouse suite. A rusty saw lay next to the mutilated corpse, fresh blood streaked along the array of blunted teeth. Ever since then, everybody paid Malavade for his invaluable "consulting services."

Going to a side room, Malavade stopped, and the door was opened by a hulking bald man.

"We have a problem with the delivery, sir," Nanravaska snarled, displaying a new gold tooth.

"You look like a clown," Vinsara said, sneering.

"Agreed. Have it removed," Malavade said, walking past the stunned giant. "I will not have my people appearing ridiculous. We rule by fear. Remember that."

Startled by the unexpected response, Nanravaska began to object, then thought better of it. The tooth had been a gift from his wife, and if it went, she would be furious. However, he could always get another wife. Hearts and lungs were much more difficult to replace.

The small room smelled of fish and sewage, and opened onto the Hooghly River, a curtain of thin plastic strips hanging down from the ceiling to offer a degree of privacy. Several small boats floated inside the room, their mooring lines lashed to cast-iron cleats embedded into the concrete. Standing at the water line was a thin man dressed in a white linen suit, surrounded by a gang of street toughs. The youths had shaved heads and were covered with tattoos. They also carried numerous handguns. They resembled young sharks ready to feed.

In front of the group was a rectangular wooden crate, wisps of fog seeping from under the lid.

"Well, here it is, sir!" Chandra Vubraman smiled broadly, gesturing at a the container. "*Dekho,* fresh from the Nile River, as requested!"

Two of the teenagers knelt on the damp concrete and flipped off spring latches before swinging up the lid. Nestled inside was a dark-skinned man wearing a burnoose and a turban. He was wrapped in clear plastic, and there was frost on his oily moustache. His dead eyes were as shiny as new coins inside the writhing fog.

"A corpse," Malavade muttered, hunching his shoulders like a bull about to charge. "You brought me a dead man? A corpse?"

Vubraman stiffened at the insult, but the street toughs didn't seem to notice. Their job was to protect the package, not engage in idle banter.

"Sure, why not a corpse? He's packed in ice, not dry ice, mind you!" the fellow hastily added. "Dry ice would burn the body. Leave marks the police could find. That's no good. So we wrapped him in plastic and kept adding ice. Fresh as a lily! Top notch!"

"And can a corpse sweat?" Malavade said slowly, raising his head to stare at the man. "Can I press his fingers against a steering wheel and leave fingerprints?" He advanced upon the others. "Perhaps I should dip his hands in olive oil first, eh? No, better yet, I could wipe the sweat off my brow to moist his fingers, and leave my DNA for Interpol to find? Is that your plan?" His voice rose to a shout. "Perhaps I could leave a photograph of myself, or my driver's license, you blithering *idiot*. That should do the trick, eh?"

Vubraman was sweating profusely now, and noting that more of Malavade's people seemed to have slipped into the secret dock in the last few moments.

"Look, Mr. Malavade, we broke him out of jail as

you requested, but the fellow hung himself before we reached Calcutta. These Tiger Force people are very tough. Very tough, indeed. So what else could we do?" Vubraman spoke nervously, feeling the sweat trickle down the back of his neck. "You said there was a schedule to keep, so I did my best. If he's no good to you, okay, no charge. I can always grab some untouchable off the street, eh? That should be even better, no charge at all for them. Always happy to make things right for a gentleman like yourself, sir."

Breathing deeply, Malavade stopped only a foot away from the grinning man. Nobody talked while a minute ticked by slowly, then another.

"Perhaps we can make a substitution," Malavade said quickly, narrowing his gaze. "After all, you're a Punjabi, just like me. We're brothers of the street. We should stick together."

Almost appearing bored, Vinsara said nothing. His boss was born and raised right here in Calcutta, not in some mud hole village a thousand miles to the south.

"Yes, sir." Vubraman beamed in delight. "And I didn't know that about you. So you're also from Punjab, eh? Well, well, small world."

"So what part of Punjab are you from?"

"Dulka, near the big wheat fields," Vubraman said proudly.

"Yeah, that'll do nicely." Vinsara chuckled, uncrossing his arms and flexing his hands.

"I believe it will," Malavade grunted. "All right, kill everybody else, but keep this idiot alive."

"No problem." Vinsara grinned as he stepped in front

of his boss and pulled out a Chinese QBZ 5.8 mm assault rifle.

Instantly, the teens dived to the sides, taking cover behind some packing crates. A startled Vubraman was left standing alone on the dock.

Vinsara raked the water with the bullpup-design machine gun, the 5.8 mm rounds stitching a line across the dock. A moment later the rest of Malavade's men pulled out INS 5.56 mm assault rifles and unleashed a storm of hot lead. One of the crates burst apart from the hammering, and a teen went tumbling into death, his pretty, nickel-plated, Heckler & Koch pistols sailing away unfired.

Dropping behind the wooden crate, Vubraman yanked out a .44 revolver and fired twice at Vinsara, a stiletto of flame stretching out from the hexagonal barrel. The bald giant grunted at the impacts, but didn't fall.

Dropping flat, Malavade came up with a pair of .357 Magnum Desert Eagle pistols and started firing. The heavy-duty combat slugs pounded the crate, knocking Vubraman into the river. The revolver went flying and disappeared into the dirty waves.

A popcorn crackling sound erupted as the huddle teens returned fire with their 9 mm pistols. Two of them died under the concentrated barrage of the professional gunmen, and one teen threw down his gun and raised both hands in surrender. Malavade shot the kid right in the face with his twin Desert Eagles, the head exploding in a grisly spray of bone, brain and blood.

Snarling in rage, the remaining teens went after the crime lord directly. Vinsara staggered from the incoming lead, and Malavade felt the hot wind of death rush past his cheek.

Rolling sideways, Malavade fired both guns for cover, as Vinsara sprayed the Chinese QBZ at the street toughs. Blood sprayed everywhere, and another body splashed into the river.

The door to the loading dock slammed open. Nanravaska and a dozen more men armed with assault rifles rushed across the concrete to take positions behind heavy pieces of equipment. Their weapons chattered fiery flowers from the shadows, as the other men crawled among the packing crates snapping off shots whenever possible.

The teens pulled back in a group and tried to maintain return fire. But attacked from three sides, they soon went down, torn to pieces.

Diving into the river, Vubraman started to swim for the open water past the dangling plastic curtain. In the distance, a tour boat floated by, loudly blaring its horn.

"Get that asshole back here," Malavade ordered, rising from the dirty floor.

"Yes, sir!" Grinning wickedly, Vinsara started to fire at the curtain, making the clear strips jump and dance. The rest of the men started firing into the water, the surface churning from the hail of high-velocity lead. Only halfway to his goal, Vubraman paused to dogpaddle in the greenish water.

"Die now, or die later," Malavade said in a conversational tone. "Your choice, Punjabi!"

Lowering the angle of his weapon, Vinsara started burping the Chinese assault rifle into the river, slowly swinging back and forth, each time the 5.8 mm rounds coming closer to the trapped man.

"Please!" the man begged, trying to stay afloat. "I only—"

"Kill him!" Malavade shouted.

"No!" Vubraman cried, turning to swim back to the dock. "No, please!" Wearily, the man rose from the reeking waters and shuffled along the bloody concrete to stand helpless in front of the smug crime lord.

"Now, get in the box," Malavade ordered.

Pausing only for a second, Vubraman lifted the lid and started to haul out the dead terrorist.

"There's room for two," Malavade said, pulling out a cigar and applying the flame of a gold lighter to the tip.

Trying not to weep, Vubraman climbed into the crate and laid down on top of the icy corpse, then pulled the lid shut from the inside.

"Wrap that tight with rope and haul this moron to the Tower," Malavade directed. "We'll deal with him later. Let's go."

While Malavade and Vinsara got back into the limousine, the men carrying the crate loaded it into the back of a waiting van, then climbed inside themselves. Crouching in a pile of garbage, an old beggar dressed in layers of rags watched carefully from the mouth of an alley.

As the vehicles drove away, she began muttering to herself for several minutes, then rose to slip into the shadowy darkness and disappear from sight.

CHAPTER EIGHT

HMS Edinburgh, North Atlantic

Stooping slightly to get through the hatchway, Captain Edward Caruthers walked into the destroyer's busy control room.

"Captain on the bridge!" someone called, standing at attention.

"At ease, gentlemen," Caruthers said, nodding politely. "Back to your posts. This is going to be a busy day."

With appropriate nods and murmurs, the crew returned to their consoles and continued preparing for that morning's exercise.

Taking a stand near the wheel, Caruthers couldn't help but remember when ships still had wheels, or at least yokes, to steer them. Real sailors were needed back then, and you could always tell a wheelman by his colossal arms. Now it was a teenager in a cushioned chair operating a joystick, as if the 5,000 ton destroyer were a video game.

"How is she handling, Mr. Norton?" Caruthers asked, looking over the man's shoulder.

"Fair sea, and smooth, sir," Norton replied promptly. "We're on course and time."

"Very good, Mr. Norton. Carry on."

"Yes, sir!"

Walking to the forward window of the control tower, the captain made sure the men on deck could see him watching them. A little taste of big brother always helped to keep them on their toes. The British navy was conducting missiles tests again, some new antisatellite, and the job of the *Eddy* was to track the experimental rockets to see how well they behaved in combat. Blowing up a spy satellite was only half the job, Caruthers knew. The first part was hauling itself into space, often while being fired upon. After the first went up, he was supposed to try to shoot down the next. Caruthers allowed himself a small grin. Bit of fun there, sort of like duck hunting out of season. Every dark cloud had a silver lining, and all that.

"The *Grafton* is starting the countdown, sir!" a wireless operator announced. "T minus sixty and counting."

"Antimissiles, guns?" Caruthers asked loudly.

"Sea Darts armed and ready, sir. Cheese Whix is ready."

Caruthers hated that nickname. The Vulcan 40 mm Gatling minigun operated by CISW was the proper designation. But a captain needed to be tolerant. He clasped both hands behind his back. "Radar?" he asked, over a shoulder.

"Clear, sir. There are a few civilian ships on the horizon, but they're all far beyond the danger zone."

"Excellent. But keep watch on them anyway," The

captain smiled, knowing it was time to ease the tension with a joke. "We don't want to appear on BBC Four explaining why we blew up a ship full of Welshmen, eh?"

The crew gave a brief chuckle as expected.

"Time, Mr. Norton?

"T minus ten seconds, sir. Eight…six…four…two… Ignition!"

Everybody braced for fire and smoke. But nothing happened on the *Grafton*. The ship coasted along serenely in the ocean.

"Has the launch been delayed?" the captain demanded, feeling a tingle at the back of his neck. Something was wrong. He knew it. Bloody hell, was it a technical glitch, or sabotage?

"No reply from the *Grafton,* sir," the wireless operator said, twirling dials and pushing buttons. "No reply from the control room, or the XO, or anybody! Yet I'm getting a carrier wave, so I know their set is hot."

"Try the deck mikes," the captain ordered brusquely.

Sitting at the board, Norton looked up with a strange expression. "I have, sir. I can hear the engines and the sea…but nothing else. No voices, no footsteps."

"Red alert!" Caruthers barked, climbing into his chair. "Engine room, give me full speed! Chief Surgeon, get a medical rescue team to the helipad double-quick."

Horns sounded across the destroyer as the engines surged and the vessel began to head directly toward the small missile frigate.

Frantically, seamen scrambled on the aft deck, readying the Lynx helicopter and tossing in supplies. The sailors at the bow armed the 40 mm Vulcan miniguns, ready to defend the *Edinburgh* in case there was more to this than some monumental gaff.

Taking a pair of binoculars from a stanchion, Caruthers adjusted the focus and checked the control room in the tower. There wasn't anybody at the wheel that he could see through the windows. Curious and unnerving. Swinging the binoculars down to the deck, his blood went cold at the sight of men hanging over the safety railing. Dozens more lying supine on the deck.

"Counter that medical team!" Caruthers stated. "Get an ABC team suited up."

The crew paused at that. An Atomic Bacteriological Chemical team? What had hit the *Grafton?*

"Mr. Danvers!"

"Sir?"

"Check with Command to see if the *Grafton* was carrying any nonstandard weapons on board, aside from those missiles."

"Aye, aye, sir."

"And have the XO arm an assault team," the captain added in a husky growl. "We may have to board and storm the *Grafton* to take her back."

The bridge crew shared shocked looks, then went to work. Take her back? Were enemies of the crown in control of the frigate?

Taking a hand mike from a clip, the captain started to give caution to the forward deck crew when he saw the XO stagger over the railing and disappear into the foamy brine.

"Man overboard!" Caruthers cried out, then gasped as the other seamen on the deck toppled over.

"Seal the ship!" the captain bellowed. "We go air-tight in one minute!"

"Sir?" a crewman asked, turning. But the man kept moving and fell to the deck in a heap as if his bones had been removed.

The captain stared in growing horror as the crewmen at their stations slumped over in their chairs and collapsed at their control boards. Grabbing the hand mike, Caruthers held his breath for a moment to marshall his thoughts. There was only one thing that he knew of that could this. Nerve gas.

"Alert all decks!" Caruthers exhaled, knowing it was probably his last act. "Gas attack! I repeat gas—"

Suddenly he felt prickly all over, there was a split second of warmth, then blackness filled the universe.

Less than a minute later, the HMS *Edinburgh* held only corpses. Plus, a lone sailor down in the bilge calmly working on a jammed petcock located far below the waterline, just behind the main fuel storage tank.

With nobody at the helm, the autopilot engaged and the massive destroyer continued heading straight for the lolling *Grafton* at full speed. The vessels hit with a strident crash that threw a thousand corpses wildly around. Tortured metal screamed as the destroyer shoved in the side of the frigate, sparks flying everywhere as steel scraped steel. Fuel gushed from broken feeder lines, and soon flames engulfed both vessels, spreading rapidly. Fire alarms howled, then died as the electrical systems shorted. A minute later, the stores of munitions exploded, blowing sections of both ships into the sky.

In a stuttering cacophony of destruction, the warships violently tore themselves apart, black smoke and orange flames filling the sunny sky.

By the time a Royal Air Force recon wing of Harrier jets arrived, there was barely a sign in the water that either of the noble warships had ever existed, aside from a few tattered bodies floating in the oil-slick water. Everybody in charge of the experimental project was dead and gone, as well as the only existing prototypes.

In the far distance, a French fishing trawler moved away from the ghastly maritime disaster, taking a new heading across the Atlantic toward the Middle East.

Boston

LEAVING THEIR VAN parked in a garage, Able Team started along the crowded streets of Boston. This area of the city was infamous for its numerous sex shops, strip clubs, singles bars and brothels. The windows of the passing shops were either painted a solid yellow to hide the delights within, or were jam-packed with electronic devices of dubious medical use.

The team had stopped at a gas station to wash as best they could, and change into casual clothing, sneakers and windbreakers. Dark suits were perfect for pretending to be FBI or NSA. But down here, they were more likely to get a person shot in the back more than anything else.

"Hey, stud," a platinum blonde called, smiling at them all. She opened her coat to show she was wearing nothing underneath. "Looking for a good time?"

"Always, do you have Nintendo?" Schwarz asked politely.

The prostitute recoiled, then snarled a vulgarity and walked away to offer herself to other potential customers.

"Nintendo?" Blancanales asked, cracking a smile. "Hermann, you are an odd man."

Schwarz shrugged. "Maybe I should have asked for Xbox?"

"There it is," Lyons said, indicating the direction with his jaw. "The Golden Hind."

"Droll." Politician sneered. "Very droll."

A quick call to Kurtzman had gotten them the dossier on all the top leg-breakers in the Zone. George Suda was the cream of the crop. George was their man. According to the Boston police department, Suda ran a thug-for-hire business out of the rear of a strip club in "the Zone." If somebody owed you money and wouldn't pay, simply hire George and he would beat it out of them. Want some revenge? Need to make a competitive business go away? The same. The skinny man had formerly operated an empire of brute force from the very heart of the great historical city.

"I wonder if Suda has any Mob connections?" Blancanales asked as they waited on a corner for the light to change.

"He never received a marksman medal, if that's what you mean," Lyons replied, starting across the street. The traffic moved slow, the drivers lustfully ogling the prostitutes.

"Jamaicans? Yakuza?" Schwarz asked, shrugging the shoulder holster under his coat. The M-16 combo was much too large to wear under the short windbreaker, so the man was only armed with the silenced Beretta and a few grenades.

"Suda is strictly small time," Lyons said. "Which raises the question, why did the Prometheans choose him?"

"Expendable," Blancanales suggested. "Fire and forget."

Lyons nodded. It made sense, and added a sense of urgency to their mission. If the Prometheans were planning to dispose of Suda after he burned down the Himar property, then somebody could already be at the office burning files and deleting e-mails. Pausing for a moment, he glanced at the cloudy sky. Hopefully, burning the place down was all the enemy had planned.

"Okay, same plan as before," Lyons directed, checking the draw on his.357 Magnum Colt. "Get the files and get out. The farther we are from this place, the better I like it."

"I hear that," Politician said in agreement, straightening the collar of his windbreaker.

The strip club covered half a block, with the front door on the corner to help hide the fact that a customer was slipping inside. Lyons opened the door, and hot smoky air flowed over Able Team, along with the reek of cheap cigars and stale beer. Leather booths lined the walls, the floor space filled with tiny tables jammed with drunk men and a couple of somber women. The air was a thick haze of smoke, and the thumping rock music blaring from the cluster of wall speakers was a tangible force, beating on their skin. A swirling disco ball on the ceiling filled the club with animation, and neon signs offered lap dances for a reasonable fee. There was a small bar with stools, but the people there were all drinking coffee or reading the newspaper. No one was watching the show.

In the strobing light, Lyons at first registered them as the staff taking a break. But then he noticed their posture, and realized every man at the bar was armed. An establishment like this would have a bouncer or two, but not a small army carrying major firepower. These had to be more of Suda's boys waiting for the boss to return from Braintree. Or additional thugs hired by Ravid to blow away Suda when he returned from the arson job. Either way, with this many civilians around, things could get nasty fast if the numbers fell.

On stage an amazingly busty blonde wearing only boots and a g-string was dancing around a steel pole, while the customers hooted and cheered, offering fistfuls of dollar bills.

A waitress approached carrying a serving tray. "Hi, table or a booth?" she asked, flashing amazingly white teeth. The voluptuous redhead was dressed in high-heeled shoes and a fishnet bodystocking that hid nothing.

"Don't those hurt?" Blancanales asked, glancing downward.

The waitress blinked for a second, then laughed. "Like a bitch," she said, shifting her feet on the floor. Then her smile faded. "And when I'm in this outfit, nobody straight notices my shoes except cops." She paused. "And I'm betting you're not gay."

"If you mean filled with joyous merriment, sure," Schwarz replied smoothly. "But otherwise, no."

"And we're not the police," Lyons said truthfully, stepping out of the way of a Japanese woman hurrying for the stage. "Just…business associates of Suda."

As the long-haired Asian scrambled up a ramp and onto the platform, the music from the wall speakers swelled in volume and she immediately ripped off her sequined vest, exposing a wealth of tattoos. The crowd roared in approval.

"I see," the waitress demurred, nodding in understanding. "Well, the office is upstairs, through the dressing room."

"Through?" Schwarz asked. "Not around, or past?"

She shrugged. "Suda owns this club, and he likes to catch a glimpse when going to his office. He grabs more when possible, but we're all pretty nimble around here."

"So I noticed." Blancanales smiled politely.

Grinning, she studied the middle-aged man. There was some gray in his hair, but he seemed nice and radiated physical strength the same way a furnace did heat. His clothes were clean, and he was clearly packing heat. "I'm Kiki," she said, smiling for real. "Kiki Daire. And just to let you know, I don't dance here. I'm a waitress, nothing more."

Having been in strip clubs around the world, Blancanales knew the difference between a waitress and a showgirl. One was on her way down, the other had already hit bottom.

"Trouble, Kiki?" a burly giant asked, swelling into view from the smoky darkness. The bouncer was a rippling mass of muscle, his sleeveless T-shirt clearly chosen to show off his impressive physique. Prison tattoos decorated his arm from knuckles to neck. Bar fights were bad for business, so a good bouncer always tried to intimidate any trouble-makers into leaving before things got broken and the cops arrived.

"Just talking to my friends," she said, laying a small hand on Blancanales's arm.

The Stony Man warrior smiled politely and gave it a pat.

"If you're not drinking, then you're walking," the bouncer snarled menacingly. "No free shows."

Pulling out a wad of bills, Lyons thumbed a hundred loose, showed it to the man, then laid it in the serving tray. "Beer," he said. "Keep the change."

Grunting in satisfaction as if he had just won a battle of some kind, the bouncer lumbered away to his booth in the corner.

"Thanks, he's always trying to keep other men away from me." Kiki sighed. "They usually run away. But you didn't." The smile she gave would have lit up Atlanta for the next century.

"Weak ankles," Blancanales joked. "Keep that beer cold for when we come down. Business first."

"Sure," Kiki purred, moving sensuously under the bodystocking. Her excitement was visible, even in the strobing disco light. "Anything you say, Daddy."

As the men headed for the beaded doorway, Lyons tried not to snort a laugh, and failed miserably. Then Schwarz nudged Blancanales with an elbow. The man shrugged. Just because there was snow on the roof, didn't mean there wasn't fire in the furnace.

Going past the curtain, Lyons saw that the dressing

room was filled with young women in scanty outfits, and older women in fancy costumes. The air smelled of sweat, hairspray and perfume. Lighted mirrors covered a wall, the table below filled with cosmetics, curling irons, electric shavers and an endless array of cosmetics and makeup. A couple of wigs rested on foam heads and feathered boas seemed to be hanging from everything in sight. Incredibly, a topless woman was holding some kind of a template to her breasts and using rouge to enlarge the size of her areolas. A line of green metal lockers covered the rear wall, some of them open showing street clothes and the pictures of movie stars. There was a fire escape to the left, stairs to the right. From somewhere came the sound of a shower, barely discernable above the thumping dance music.

"Who's getting arrested?" a mature redhead asked without looking up from her magazine.

"Where's the office?" Lyons asked.

"Follow your nose, cop," a petite blonde snarled, tightening the leather corset around her tiny waist. Her black boots had five-inch steel spike heels, and she still barely crested five feet tall.

Taking the stairs, Able Team saw the fortified door on the next level. It had four hinges, a sheet of steel bolted over the exterior, and a Vishy lock. Schwarz frowned at that. The lock was almost impossible to trick. The advertising brochure said the easiest way to get past a Vishy lock was with dynamite. Unfortunately, it was true.

Outside the formidable door was a large man with a shaved head, dressed all in black, sitting in a wingback chair that had seen better days. As the team came close, the guard removed his headphones and turned off the small CD player clipped to his belt. There was also an electric stun gun holster on the belt, and a mini-Uzi machine pistol in a black shoulder holster.

"Yeah?" he snarled menacingly, rising from the chair. "What do you want?"

Without a word, Lyons drove his fist directly into the man's groin. In an explosion of breath, the guard doubled over and Lyons hit him again in the belly. Groaning softly, the bald guard fell to the side and slumped unconscious.

Placing the guard back in the chair, Schwarz put the man's headphones back on, trying to arrange them into a natural position. Going through the pockets of the unconscious man, he found a ring of keys. One of them was shaped like the eighth letter of the alphabet, and was covered with ridges and convoluted indentations. Schwarz slid the key into the lock and heard the sound of bolts disengaging from all four sides of the door. He pushed it aside with fingertip pressure.

The team stepped inside and closed the door behind them. The office was silent, the soundproofing of the walls and floors obviously of top-notch quality. Several leather chairs were scattered around, and a small but well-stocked bar stood in a corner. To the side was a gun rack full of AK-101 assault rifles with wooden stocks. A photographic mural of Boston spanned the far wall. Underneath was an antique cherrywood desk with a very modern computer. A vidcam sat on top, and there was a blinking icon for incoming video e-mail on the screen. There were no files cabinets and the desk held only ink cartridges for the printer and blank paper.

Taking the chair, Schwarz started searching for files, but the computer was clean. No e-mail or data files, RTF, PDF or anything useful. There were a few games, a couple of pornographic screen savers, but nothing of importance.

Taking a jewel case from his equipment bag, Schwarz extracted a disk and slid it into the computer. A data recovery program loaded automatically and started searching every inch of the hard drive, buffer and memory cards.

"Damn, no hidden files," Schwarz muttered, reading the results. "Nothing masked, nothing in any subfolders or buried in a screen saver…" The program came to an end and he tucked it away. "Shit, this machine is clean. How can Suda run a major criminal operation without keeping track of his deals?"

"Can you recall the data?" Lyons asked, leaning over the chair.

Schwarz frowned. "There is no data! Suda didn't keep anything on this machine except a worksheet for the club employees."

"Well, the police report said SID believed Suda had a photographic memory." Blancanales sighed in annoyance. "Guess they were right."

"He got his messages here," Lyons noted, rubbing his jaw, "but kept all of his records inside his head." Damn the man. That was the only type of security that couldn't be beaten.

"No choice then," Schwarz said, cracking his knuckles.

Swiveling the vidcam on top of the computer so that it was pointed at the ceiling, the Stony Man warrior used the mouse to click on the blinking icon.

Instantly the vidcam came alive and the on-screen icon swelled into a upward view of a plump man in a very expensive suit, his hair slicked down flat. The picture bounced with irregularity, and traffic noises could be heard in the background.

"Report," he said impatiently, then looked downward with a scowl. "What is wrong with your video?"

Lyons leaned past Schwarz. "This is my office, so I ask the questions, asshole," he snarled.

The fat man's eyes narrowed at that. "Watch your mouth, fool, or I'll fry your ass," he muttered in barely controlled rage. "Who the fuck are you, and where is George?" His diction was perfect, but the English carried the singsong rhythm of modern-day India.

"Suda's dead," Lyons said on a hunch.

"Is he?" the other man murmured with a frown.

"Burned alive. Terrible thing. It seems that one of his radio detonators…accidentally went off early."

"Ah. Understood. Which now puts you in charge of the Boston operation." The fat man didn't phrase it as a question. "A bad move on your part. I do not deal with strangers. Goodbye."

The window closed, the icon vanished, the vidcam went dark.

"Damn," Blancanales cursed, lowering his cell phone. "You weren't on long enough for Aaron to run a trace."

Schwarz started to speak when he felt a growing wave of heat radiating from the computer.

"Run!" he cried, shoving back the chair and diving away from the desk.

The Stony Man commandos hit the floor and a split second later the computer exploded on top of the desk. There was a familiar hissing in the air and the office shook with a hard pattering. Pictures shattered on the walls and liquor bottles crashed behind the small bar.

As the smoke cleared, Lyons warily rose to a knee and saw the shotgun pattern of shrapnel from the antipersonnel charge circling the room at waist level. Son of a bitch, Suda had armed the computer with a Claymore mine! Or was it the fat man?

Suddenly heavy footsteps could be heard thumping up the stairs. There came a jingle at the lock and the door was slammed aside.

"What the fuck is going on here?" the bouncer demanded, racking the pump-action of a Remington shotgun.

Moving from behind the door, Lyons smacked the man with barrel of his Colt Python. Dropping the shotgun, the bouncer groaned mightily and fell to the floor. He stayed there, but the slow rising and falling of his chest showed the man was still very much alive.

"There's nothing here to harvest," Lyons stated. "Time to go before we get targeted from orbit."

Rising from behind the desk, Blancanales and Lyons raced to the doorway with their pistols in hand. Looking down the stairs, the Stony Man team saw armed men duck out of sight into the dressing room, but nothing could be heard above the pounding music from the stage.

"We're cut off," Blancanales snarled, looking at the fire-escape door just past the entrance to the dressing room. "And there are too many civilians to try to blast our way to the street."

There was a brief pause in the music as the club DJ changed songs.

"So we clear the way," Schwarz said, taking a stun grenade from his windbreaker and pulling the pin.

His teammates did the same, and the men threw in unison. The grenades bounced down the wooden stairs and ignited. The fulminating guncotton charges sounded louder than doomsday, and magnesium flared brighter than the sun. Anguished cries came from the dressing room, and two men stumbled into view, dropping their handguns and cursing wildly as they rubbed stinging eyes.

Flicking a butane lighter alive, Lyons played the flame across the sprinkler set into the ceiling. A moment later there was a gush of water and a fire alarm started to howl.

Down in the club, frightened people began shouting, and there came the sound of trampling shoes as the music abruptly stopped. A mob of partially dressed women rushed screaming for the exit door and out into the street.

Charging down the stairs, the Stony Man commandos joined the escaping throng and hit the sidewalk running. Maneuvering through the thick Boston traffic, they took a corner, then another, before allowing themselves to finally slow down.

Watching the strip club from a safe distance, Able

Team tried not to hold its breath in nervous consternation. A slow minute passed, then two. People were still milling around directly in front of the club.

"Unless the Promethean has incredible control of the cannon," Blancanales said slowly, "and they only beamed the office, then nothing is going to happen here."

"Yeah, it's clear," Lyons agreed, easing the tension in his shoulders. "Let's get back to the Hercules to see if there is anything at all on that hard drive."

"Hopefully the name and address of the fat man," Schwarz said, starting for the van. "Think that was Ravid?"

"Don't know," Lyons said, watching a fire truck come flying around the corner, the traffic parting like magic for the emergency vehicle. "But these assholes like traps too much for my taste. Before we hit their headquarters, wherever it is, we're going to need a can opener." He gave a hard smile. "And I know just the thing."

CHAPTER NINE

Batticaloa, Sri Lanka

Disguised as tourists, the heavily armed NATO troops lounged around the luxury hotel sipping nonalcoholic drinks and pretending to read magazines. Gardeners carrying silenced pistols moved among the lush plants, the radios in their ears maintaining a constant report on the surrounding landscape.

Trying to ignore the arsenal of weapons carried by the guests, the hotel staff of the Blue Coral went about its daily chores, watering flowers, ferrying luggage, setting up chairs in conference rooms and cleaning the trash out of others. But wherever the staff went, NATO security forces were always right alongside, EM detectors sweeping for illicit listening devices, what the Americans and the British called "bugs," and chemical sniffers hunting for a wide array of explosives.

On the rooftop, a squad of soldiers stood guard over

the water supply, binoculars and portable radar sweeping the sky for any possible incursion. Antiaircraft and antitank missiles lay nestled in the gray foam cushioning inside military cases nearby, the weapons primed for instant action. However, none of the soldiers was in uniform. They were dressed in casual clothing, slacks and flowery dresses, baseball caps and turbans. A few were swimming in the pool, a commando squad lounged on the patio overlooking the beautiful Bay of Bengal, hollowed-out books containing grenades and automatic pistols.

Out on the ocean, heavily armed speedboats skimmed along the surface, paratroops gliding in the air above in colorful para-sail gliders. Expert scuba divers splashed playfully in the shallows, and laughing commandos at the beachfront bar drank colored water, pretending to be drunk.

Three hundred miles directly over the hotel in a geosynchronous orbit, a NATO Watchdog satellite studied the Sri Lanka coastline, watching intently for any unwarranted shift in the direction of commercial air traffic or the telltale heat flash of a missile launch.

Created to be an oasis of paradise, the luxury hotel was now a hardsite to protect the hundreds of people inside the conference rooms.

Driving along the winding road, a Heron sedan approached the hotel, but a smiling man in a blazingly white hotel uniform blocked its entrance.

As the car slowed, the driver rolled down the window as the hotel employ walked casually over, his smile nailed in place.

From the nearby trees, sniper rifles focused on the Heron sedan, and the vehicle was painted by a dozen ultraviolet laser beams. At the first sign of trouble, the driver and car would be torn to pieces by a hail of armor-piercing rounds.

Sitting prominently in the crosshairs, the puzzled driver scowled at the employee.

"Hi, what's going on?" the fellow demanded in heavily accented Singahelese.

The man dressed as a hotel employee shrugged, keeping his hands below shoulder height. If they rose above that for any reason, everybody on the road would die.

"Sorry, sir, the hotel has been blocked for the weekend," the NATO operative said apologetically.

"The whole hotel?"

He shrugged. "Some crazy American is throwing a party. Perhaps it is their Fifth of July, or John Wayne's birthday, who can say?" He deliberately got the date wrong to check for any reactions. But the man in the car seemed oblivious to the mistake.

"Is it that Paris girl?" the driver asked.

"Oh, I really could not say, sir. Did you have a reservation?" He knew that nobody had a reservation on this weekend, or for the whole week before or after. The hotel was the temporary hardsite for a special UN Anti-terrorism Conference.

"Well, no, not really," the driver admitted sheepishly, unknown that his words were being recorded on a dozen audio devices.

In the basement of the hotel, a Norwegian major was

handed a brief report on the intruder. The license plates had been run, and the driver identified by his photograph. Just a dentist from Colombo who usually took this weekend to go fishing in Kalmunai. However, with the Blue Coral commandeered, the regular patrons had gotten lodgings elsewhere, and his usual hotel was fully booked.

High in the sky, a small plane dropped out of the clouds and moved along the horizon, keeping far away from the hotel.

"Sir, I found him a room fifty miles down the road," a lieutenant crisply reported into a microphone on her console. "The Grotto is much more than he can afford, but—"

"Cover the difference and get him going," the major snapped, tossing the report aside. "I want the perimeter clear at all times!"

"Sir!" the woman replied crisply, and rushed to comply.

"Have you considered the Grotto, just down the coast?" the guard asked, resting a friendly arm on the roof of the Heron. The metal was warm under his bare arm.

"Kind of pricey, isn't it?" the driver said hesitantly.

"Normally, but our special guest has made arrangements for her friends there in case additional people arrived. Rock stars, movie actors... I am most certain that I can find you a room, and a discount price."

"That would be splendid!" the driver told him. "This is my only weekend to go fishing and—" He slumped onto the wheel, setting off the horn.

In a flash, the guard stepped back and a small .22 pistol appeared in his hand.

"Alert," he said, feeling the answering tingle from the miniature throat mike taped to his skin. The hair-thin wire connecting the microphone to the transceiver on his belt under his shirt was virtually invisible.

"Report!" a voice demanded in his ear.

The guard started to speak when there was a warm feeling along his spine, the sensation spreading through his entire body and rising into his brain until the world went black and abruptly ended.

"Man down!" a rooftop sniper reported just before he died.

Throughout the hotel, people dropped in their tracks, tumbling off balconies and falling down stairs. In the main conference room, a hundred special representatives collapsed at the table, copies of the international treaty falling from their limp hands.

Opposite the Blue Coral Hotel, a small truck surged from behind a wall of hedges, the engine backfiring noisily.

NATO operatives on the patio fell over as the truck rushed by, their weapons unfired.

Watching the deaths from the beach, the NATO commandos rushed onto the shore, and grabbed assault rifles hidden underneath blankets. Charging onto the access road, the soldiers formed a ragged line and hammered the fleeing truck with heavy fire. Riddled with bullet holes, the truck veered wildly off the pavement and crashed through a safety barrier to plummet straight down into the rocky sea. The vehicle hit with a crash of glass and metal, then erupted into a strident fireball as the gas tank promptly ignited.

It took almost an hour before the NATO soldiers could reach the wreckage, and by then there was little remaining of the complex electrical equipment filling the rear of the crashed truck, or the lone driver. Only one arm was undamaged, found several yards away floating in the sea where it had been throw by the violent crash. The limb was covered with cryptic tattoos unknown to the commando.

The fingerprints from the arm, along with photographs of the tattoos and samples of the DNA scraped off the bloody rocks, were all sent to NATO headquarters and Interpol. A few hours later the results came back from Brussels.

The driver had been Chandra Vubraman, believed to only be a small-time criminal. But the tattoos proclaimed him to be a secret member of the brutal Punjabi terrorist organization, Tiger Force.

CHAPTER TEN

Bombay, India

Returning to the USS *Kitty Hawk,* Phoenix Force had reclaimed the Learjet and taken off immediately for Bombay. The intelligence community didn't know Mohad Malavade's exact location inside India. The man lived in the shadows, and rarely surfaced to expose himself. But Kurtzman and his team had unearthed a couple of slim possibilities in Bombay, and they were going to quickly track down the ghostly leader of organized crime in India before the Prometheus cannon spoke again.

The flight across the Pacific was long, and the team was well-fed, rested and itching for some action by the time they landed in Shara Airport. They had also traded field reports with Able Team and were going to be extra careful about booby traps. The Prometheans liked misdirection: false leads, mercenaries, traps and such. That meant they were either weak or cowardly. Possibly both. A bad combination for folks who controlled the greatest weapon in the history of the world.

In spite of everything, McCarter was pleased to see India again. The place was alive as few nations in the history of the world ever have been, or ever will be. The staggeringly ancient mixed freely with the ultramodern on every street. Affluence and poverty lived side by side. India was orderly chaos and tumultuous peace. The traffic was terrible, but the pedestrians freely mixed with the moving vehicles in a total disregard for safety regulations that would have been the envy of any seasoned New Yorker. Sparkling skyscrapers of steel and glass rose amid sandstone mosques, and cool marble homes rubbed elbows with tarpaper shacks.

Even on a clear day, a blue haze blanketed the city, a thick mixture of gasoline fumes, incense, tobacco smoke, perfume and unwashed bodies. Beggars in rags lived beneath steel-encased security cameras. Dancing eunuchs sang and rang silver bells in front of a new department store for good luck. Religious chanting mixed with Muzak music and car horns. Crowds were everywhere, an endless stream of humanity ebbing to and fro, living, loving, fighting, dying.

Over the past few decades, Bombay had become a major center of advanced technology, the electronics plants and computer centers sprouting like mushrooms. Whatever the Indians did, they did wholeheartedly. War, sex, religion. The people of India seemed to have one setting, full throttle. Born and raised among the more languid British, McCarter rather liked that. Too many folks were complacent these days, unhappy with their lot in life, and not willing to go out and try to change it. But not these people. When a nation had few resources but a lot of people, they got smart, or withered and died. India got smart, and now had some of the best software engineers in the world.

Sitting in a stolen car parked across the street from a small café, the men of Phoenix Force checked their weapons below the windows and watched for the target. This was the fifth place they had hit today in a blitz through the Bombay underworld. Unfortunately, it was also their last. If this man couldn't help them, then the long flight to India had been precious time wasted. There was nowhere else to go.

The first man had known nothing about Mohad Malavade. He sold bombs made in his basement. Phoenix Force left him down there forever. The other three, a drug dealer, bookie and fence, were all found with their throats slit. Somehow, the crime boss knew that he was being hunted, and was trying to remove any possible link to his unknown whereabouts. Everybody on the street seemed to know who Malavade was, but nobody had any idea how to contact him. Nor did they have any desire to. The reputation of the fat little man was formidable. An orphan from the streets, he had reached out with both hands to shake the very pillars of Heaven.

"Yarma," McCarter said out loud.

"What was that?" Manning asked. "Did you mean karma?"

"No, yarma. Karma is your unchangeable destiny."

He grinned. "But yarma is the ability to change your destiny through intelligence. Not forces of arms, or money, but sheer smartness."

"Smartness?" James chuckled. "Is that a word?"

"It is now."

The morning rain had been brief, and the air of the city was crisply clean. The streets were shiny with moisture and children played in the puddles, splashing happily.

With the end of the storm, the square filled with tents and stalls, forming a market around the parked car. The Stony Man commandos got a few nasty looks from a couple of the dealers, as if the foreigners should know better than to park here, but the team was ignored.

As the market opened, India arrived in all her glory. Young women wrapped in a variety of saris, their flashing eyes highlighted by henna, every finger and ankle jingling with jewelry. Proud businessmen with severe haircuts were talking urgently on their cell phones, a laptop tucked under their arm like the rifle of a grenadier. A beggar limped by singing his ancient song. A rickshaw raced by, the running coolie almost hitting the children in the street. Bicycles were everywhere, bells ringing, people shouting.

Traffic slowed as it went through the market, the trucks and cars moving at a stately pace through the milling throng. The locals were dressed in a riot of colors, the tourists in white linen outfits as if this were a hundred years ago and air conditioning hadn't yet been invented. The locals tried not to laugh behind the backs of the sweaty visitors. It would have been very bad manners.

Flowers were everywhere, and exhibition stands were being erected for some upcoming event. People began haggling with the vendors, buying, selling or just sharing gossip. Rich, poor, young, old, scientists, lawyers, thieves, holy men, Bombay was a city of life, brimming with humanity in all of its tragedy and splendor. Bombay had four times the population of New York, but a lot of the people were Buddhists, and there wasn't much crime. Begging was pandemic, but very little mugging and shooting. If a person didn't mind the sight of abject poverty wherever they went, India was a lovely country, filled with delightfully friendly people.

Stopping at a flower cart, a young man bought a pretty girl a necklace of marigolds, and they walked off arm in arm. Until her mother appeared and whacked the boy with a broom, wailing away madly. Ducking and running, the lad was hit several times before barely escaping alive.

"Now that's good technique," Hawkins complimented as the woman shouted threatening things in Hindi at the rapidly retreating boy. "Smooth motion, efficient use of leverage. Give me a month to teach her, and she would be a lawnmower with a katana."

"I don't think that would help Romeo very much." Encizo chuckled, resting both arms on the steering wheel. The Walther PPK .38 lay in his lap, the hammer already cocked for instant response. Every split second might count when approaching Sanjeev Bharah. They wanted the man alive, and Malavade needed him dead. It would be a race that had no second place.

"Hate or love it," McCarter said. "But nobody is neutral about India."

"Heard the same thing about Los Angeles," Manning added, checking his KGB Special. The windows were down and the cool air was unexpected. India was always shown as steaming-jungle hot in the movies. But in October, it was quite pleasant.

"Los Angeles?" McCarter snorted, sounding scandalized. "Nobody there but lunatics, and more lunatics."

"Ironman is from L.A.," James reminded him.

"See? I told you."

The clean air was becoming rich with the smell of the thousands of flowers being delivered, the perfume mixing into a heavenly miasma.

"Get hard, people," Hawkins said, drawing his Beretta pistol and snicking off the safety. "Here comes our boy."

Strolling around the corner, Sanjeev "Sandy" Bharah smiled politely at the milling people. Everybody grinned in return, or quickly turned away hoping they hadn't been seen. But in his wake, many spit upon the ground or made vulgar gestures toward his back.

Flanking the man were two hulking bodyguards, large-caliber revolvers tucked into belly holsters, so the weapons were in plain view. Apparently brothers, the men were badly scarred, and one walked with a slight limp. But both had quick eyes and a loose stance. They spotted Phoenix Force immediately, and watched them carefully, keeping between the strangers and their boss.

Thumbing live his personal digital assistant, McCarter reviewed the Interpol report retrieved by Kurtzman. On the surface, Sanjeev Bharah was a loan shark. But in truth, he was a blackmailer on a grand scale. When clients couldn't pay the soaring interest rates, the man often suggested they pay with information about friends or colleagues. A photograph of something tasty often brought the client a week of reprieve. But only a week, unless more and better was provided the next week, and then the next. In a matter of years, Bharah had an army on informants throughout every level of society in Bombay, from the street sweepers to bank presidents. With affluent people now under his thumb, McCarter knew, the man moved among the elite, helping them against business rivals or financing a questionable deal. Half of Bollywood was in his debt, and a delicious stream of starlets ebbed and flowed into his bed. Drug dealers, CEOs, judges, politicians and millionaires. Bharah knew them all, including international arms dealers.

McCarter turned off the PDA.

Taking a seat at the café, Bharah snapped his fingers in a friendly gesture and a waiter hurried over with a glass pitcher of iced tea and a folded newspaper.

"Thank you, cousin," Bharah said with a chuckle, handing the man a ten thousand rupee note.

"Oh no, thank *you,* cousin," the waiter said proudly, fanning the wealth for all and sundry to see. But nobody on the street was looking, their backs turned from the viper sitting in their midst.

As his poor relative went to serve other customers, the blackmailer sipped a glass of iced tea and ignored the newspaper. He tried to smile at the passing people, but nervously kept glancing at the bodyguards standing stoically nearby.

"I think he knows Malavade is cleaning house, and that he might be next," Encizo snorted. "So why is the bastard sitting out in public?

"The greedy fool is trying to conduct business and stay alive at the same time," McCarter stated. "Multitasking isn't a good way to keep your ass intact."

"I hear that," Encizo agreed.

"And there they are," Hawkins whispered.

Two big men stepped out of the crowd, dressed in white linen suits, Panama hats hiding their faces.

Surging from the car, Phoenix Force moved through the market square, weapons at the ready.

The bodyguards clawed for their guns and the hit men took them out with silenced pistols, the weapons yielding hard coughs tipped with flame. With a scream, Bharah ducked below the table, and the hit men flipped it over just as Phoenix Force attacked, their weapons slamming the killers against the white stucco wall, cracking the plaster, blood pumping from the black holes in their clean white suits.

It was over in a matter of seconds, the danger gone. Slowly realizing what had just happened, people were starting to react to the attack, screaming and running around.

"Where's Malavade?" McCarter demanded, towering over the cringing blackmailer. He had hoped to get there before the hit men. The incident seriously cut their time short. The police would be arriving soon.

Wide-eyed in amazement, Bharah stared at the bodies lying in the spreading pool of red. "I really didn't think anybody could take down the Hajal brothers," he whispered in shock. "But you treated them like infants!"

"They were slow and overconfident," McCarter said. "Now where is Malavade?"

"Fuck Malavade, the big bastard," Bharah panted. "Come work for me, and I'll pay you a thousand dollars U.S. every week."

"That wasn't our CV," McCarter growled, using the British term for résumé, curriculum vitae.

"This is," Hawkins said, patting the gun. "Now answer the question before we let the next team of assassins finish the job."

"Two thousand a man," Bharah offered, straightening his rumpled coat. "But I only need two of you. Okay, three, but no more than that."

Since this was going nowhere, McCarter grabbed one arm, Hawkins the other, and they dragged the unprotesting man inside the empty café. There were a dozen tables in sight, meals abandoned, chairs flipped over, drinks gurgling onto the tiled floor. Even the waiter was gone, the back door partially ajar, admitting a slice of sunlight into the dim interior.

The rest of Phoenix Force took defensive positions near the door and watched the street. The market was mostly empty, leaving a field of trash and the dead bodies.

Slamming the criminal against the bar, McCarter and Hawkins knocked the wind from his lungs.

"Four thousand a week," Bharah wheezed. "And I take all of you. Deal?"

Drawing his Browning Hi-Power, McCarter fired. The man jumped as a bottle of whiskey exploded on a shelf behind the bar.

"You owe me two hundred dollars for that," Bharah said nervously, wiping his mouth on a sleeve. "But it can come from your first paycheck, eh?"

"Last time," McCarter said, laying the hot barrel to the blackmailer's cheek. "Where is Malavade?"

"Mohad Malavade?" Bharah asked in surprise as if hearing the name for the first time. "Are you mad? If I knew where he lived, I would have retired by now. I'm sorry, gentlemen, but I do not know where Malavade can be found."

"Wrong answer," Hawkins said, pulling out a wad of rupees big enough to choke a water buffalo and stuffing the money into the shirt of the frightened man.

Totally confused, Bharah stared at the money, then McCarter placed the gun right alongside the man's head and fired again, the muzzle-flash brushing his throat. Crying out in pain, the blackmailer grabbed his neck and hunched over, his icy resolve finally broken.

"Malavade," Hawkins said, shoving more money into the shirt. Punishment and reward at the same time. It was an old Mafia trick that worked on almost everybody.

"Really, gentleman," Bharah stated, holding his blistering flesh. "I really do not know—"

Hawkins fired, shattering a pitcher of iced water on the counter, the fluid gushing over the trembling man. In cold deliberation, McCarter laid a medical kit on the counter, pulling out bandages and antiseptics.

"Shoot him in the knee," McCarter said, placing aside a tourniquet. "That hurts the most."

"How much money do we have?" Hawkins asked, holding his gun on the man.

"About a million rupees."

"Then I have another target in mind," Hawkins said, placing the sizzling barrel of the Beretta between the man's quivering legs.

"I cannot help, you!" Bharah shouted, tears trickling down his pudgy cheeks. "Honestly, I cannot!"

Hawkins thumbed back the hammer.

"But here is a man who can!" the blackmailer added in a rush of words. "But even he is of no help. Nobody can visit him. Kantin Hu is in jail for life, maximum security, no visitors!"

It sounded like the truth, but McCarter waited a few moments as if debating the matter. "Which prison?" he demanded. "Arthur Road?"

"Thane!" Bharah wept. "North wing, cell block four."

Hawkins let the man stew for a moment, then eased down the hammer of the Beretta and holstered the weapon.

"We'll be back," McCarter said, tucking away the medical items. "If what you say is true, there will be a reward. But if it is a lie…"

"No, the truth!" Bharah whimpered. "I swear!"

Hawkins smiled. "Or if you place a phone call to anybody…"

"Nothing! I will do nothing!"

Without further comment, McCarter started toward the back door, the rest of the team close behind.

"How soon do you think he'll start talking?" Manning asked, his hand tight on the KGB special inside the pocket of his jacket.

"Tomorrow, after he's had a good night's sleep," McCarter replied gruffly. "So time is against us."

"Always is," Enciso snorted, leading the way to their second car parked a few blocks away.

SLUMPING TO THE DIRTY FLOOR, Bharah just breathed for a while, savoring the feeling of life still pounding in his veins. Those weren't men he would ever want to cross. On the other hand, Malavade might just pay a hefty sum to know who was after him. And then he might kill me anyway.

Frowning, Sanjeev struggled to his feet and dropped heavily into an empty chair. No, there was nothing he could do to make a profit this time. His shirt was full of cash, but the café was ruined, and his cousin would demand a fortune for his compliance. Sadly, silence meant life. That would have to be profit enough for today.

Police sirens were starting to bleat in the distance, when a small boy entered the café, his sandals crunching on the broken glass. He was hugging a bundle of old newspapers and looking around timidly.

"Go away, child, I have no errands to run today," Bharah snapped, soaking a cloth napkin in a glass of bottled water and gingerly moistening his throbbing ear and neck.

"Mr. Bharah?" the boy asked. "I am Hakim, the son of Hassan, the shoemaker."

That caught his interest. "Did your father send that package for me?" the blackmailer asked, adding more water to the cloth.

"No, sir. I wanted to tell you that my…." Hakim swallowed with some difficulty. "My father took his life last night."

Bharah scowled darkly. What a day! A rich vein of potential funds lost. He'd have to reveal the shoemaker's secret to make sure none of his other clients decided to take the coward's way out from under his thumb.

"Well, you have delivered the message, boy," Bharah snarled. "Go away."

"I—I wish to take over the payments," the child said.

That caught the blackmailer totally by surprise. That was unique. "And how are you to pay me such a large amount every month?" Bharah inquired gently. The boy was small, but healthy-looking. If he was sent to work in a brothel, this would reap a windfall down the road twenty years from now. A man had to plan for the future.

"I have the first payment here, sir," the boy whispered, starting to unwrap the newspapers.

"Did you steal a neighbor's DVD player?" Sanjeev asked jokingly. "I do not handle stolen property, boy, just hard cash…" His voice faded at the sight of the sawed-off shotgun, the dirty barrel matted with tufts of hair and blood.

As the barrel swung up, Bharah knew it was the weapon the boy's father had used to end his life. Then it had to be empty! No mere child could know how to reload such a weapon!

The blast completely removed the blackmailer's head from his body.

A few minutes later when the police arrived everybody on the street blamed the gruesome murder on the five big Europeans. Nobody seemed to notice the little boy sitting at a nearby stall, an old woman carefully wrapping his broken arm.

CHAPTER ELEVEN

United Nations, New York

"Lies!" the ambassador from Albania shouted, hammering his desk with a fist. "All lies! Tiger Force does not have the resources to build a satellite weapons system. This is just another trick from the American CIA!"

"I agree, it must be the CIA," the Laos ambassador added, smiling.

"The CIA has nothing to do with the matter," the American ambassador retorted. "This is monstrous slander!"

"You are the only monster!" Albania retorted hotly. "Do you really think that we would believe your outrageous lies? If terrorists have control of this magical 'neutron gun,' then why haven't they attacked civilians?"

"I have no idea," the American ambassador admitted honestly.

"Well, I do!" Albania shouted. "Because the weapon was made by the CIA!"

"You're insane." The American sighed, raising both hands in dismissal.

"Admit the truth!" Albania shouted.

"Please! Will the representative of Albania, please sit down and relinquish the floor!" the Secretary-General demanded, leaning into the microphone attached to her podium.

"No, madam, I will not." The translated voice spoke softly in her earplug. "Let us cease to play games. We have all heard from our spy networks about the destruction of Air Force One and the MiG war plane near Moscow, the British fleet…"

"Two frigates hardly compose the bulk of our fleet, old chap," the British ambassador muttered, completely unruffled. "Perhaps it does for you, but we, on the other hand…"

"…and now the ruthless slaughter of our Special Commission on international terrorism in Sri Lanka!" Albania continued unabated. "There can only be one possible cause." He paused for a breath. "Once more, the American CIA is trying to seize control of the world."

With that pronouncement, most of the delegates leaped to their feet and began shouting for recognition.

"Order! I will have order!" the Secretary-General demanded, banging her gavel. When silence wasn't forthcoming, she stoically flipped a small switch on her podium. Instantly, every translator relay was killed, and suddenly nobody could talk to anybody. It still took a few minutes, but eventually, order was restored. Or, at least what passed for order in the United Nations.

"Has the European Space Agency found anything in orbit above Earth?" Spain asked.

"No," the Secretary-General replied. "Nor has NORAD or NASA."

"Nor have we," Japan added calmly.

"All puppets of the CIA," Cuba stated forcibly.

Japan faced Cuba and raised an eloquent eyebrow in response.

"However, we aren't the puppets of anybody," Australia declared, standing. "And Port Woomera has found nothing that suggests the United States is involved in these attacks via an orbiting satellite or platform."

"More lies," China said smoothly. "I demand that the United States confess it is illegally using nuclear weapons in space."

"Then submit its Nebraska silos to UN inspection, and total disarmament!" Bulgaria roared, brandishing a fist.

"That will never happen," the U.S. ambassador stated in a voice carved from ice.

"So you willfully defy the edicts of the assembly, and admit this new weapon is under your control?"

"Of all the convoluted… No, the weapon is most certainly not under our control."

"So you have lost control of the CIA?"

"You, sir, are a total moron," the U.S. ambassador exhorted.

With that, the delegates broke into a uproar once more.

"Gentleman and ladies, please, calm yourselves!" the Secretary-General demanded from the podium, banging away with her gavel. "Does anybody have any proof, any demonstrable proof that they can, and will, share to show the culpability of the United States?"

There were a lot of angry murmurs, but nobody came forth, and nothing was relayed to a page for general distribution.

"Then if there is nothing further to be discussed on the matter," the Secretary-General said in relief, "this session is closed." She sharply banged the gavel twice. "Good day."

As the delegates broke into groups to continue to discuss that matter, the Secretary-General watched from the podium. Personally, she understood their feelings. Invisible death from the sky. The delegates were terrified, and needed something to report back home to the leaders. And every word said in anger brought the world closer to the brink of total war.

Many years ago, during the cold war between America and the Soviet Union, the leader of the USSR had declared that the Communists would bury America. Now, in Russian, the phrase meant that the Communists would see the Americas die by their own foolishness. But in the U.S., the phrase was heard as "We're coming to kill you." A single slip of the tongue, a garble phrase, and a war could erupt. With a few of the nations, the wrong expression could trigger an preemptive attack. Diplomacy was more a matter of what not to say, than relaying the truth.

And to be honest, she couldn't think of any way these mass deaths could have been accomplished aside from the detonation of a neutron bomb, and only America and China had those. So, either one of them was lying, and this was a prologue to global warfare, or somebody has invented a neutron beam weapon.

That would be too terrible to even contemplate.

Stony Man Farm, Virginia

THE MONITORS ON THE WALL of the Computer Room were alive with activity, while the cybernetic team was almost motionless, typing away at their keyboards.

At the front of the room, a map showed the military status of every nation on Earth, along with the location of the two field teams, Able Team in Boston, Phoenix Force in India. There was no known location for the crime lord of India, so McCarter was going to flush the man out of hiding the only way possible. By brute force.

A submonitor on the wall was filled with a vector graphic of Earth surrounded by thousands of tiny dots, every known satellite that moved above the world. One by one, each was being cataloged, investigated, double-checked, probed and finally removed from the screen. When there was only one left, they should have located the neutron cannon satellite. In theory, at least.

Watching the satellite monitor, Barbara Price saw a dozen more dots disappear from sight, then a whole swarm. The hunt was progressing swiftly, but there were still thousands of satellites remaining.

Suddenly a monitor showing weather patterns changed to a Most Secret report from the British navy sent to the Pentagon about the destruction of the two missile frigates.

Reading the report, Price started to frown. All right, that seemed to directly connect to the murder of Dr.

Himar. The Prometheans were removing any possible threat to their plan. But what did they want? World domination, or simply mass murder? The strike on the MiG didn't seem to fit with the other two incidents. And why hadn't the terrorists hit the new F-22 Raptors in California? The ultra-high-altitude jet fighters could easily strike any target in orbit. Did that mean the Raptors weren't considered a danger? The enemy was clearly working toward a specific goal, but what was it?

Going to the kitchenette, Price poured herself a half mug of coffee, then added a lot of milk, filling it to the brim. Taking a wary sip, she found the diluted mixture barely drinkable.

"Anything on the Boston hard drive?" Price asked.

"No," Kurtzman said as if it was a curse word. "Just personal correspondence and such. Apparently he kept all Prometheus files on a removable zip drive. Carmen double checked the wreckage and we found it near his smashed laptop."

"And it was blank." Price sighed.

"Hell no." Kurtzman grinned. "It had the full technical reports on Prometheus for the President. McCarter was right. He wasn't trying to build a neutron cannon. Apparently he had done that years ago."

"What?"

Kurtzman waved a hand. "Some secret project for the Fortress."

Price knew that Red Fort was the Indian government version of the Pentagon located near New Delhi. However, the Fortress was two hundred miles off the east coast of the subcontinent on a secluded island. It was their doomsday redoubt and carried half of their nuclear arsenal. Every missile pointed at India itself. The nation had been invaded and conquered many times, but never again. If the government ever fell, and a foreign power invaded the subcontinent, the Fortress would release its nuclear missiles to burn the nation to the ground. No foreign potentate would ever rule over the people of India again. If an enemy conquered India, they won only radioactive wind.

"So India has the cannon," Price muttered, deep in thought.

"Not anymore," Kurtzman said incredibly. "They canceled the project and destroyed all of the satellites while they were still on the ground. They were just too afraid of this very scenario, a terrorist group gets hold of the weapon and starts waging silent war from above." He frowned. "Besides, they only want dirty weapons for the Fortress, the dirtier the better. If they can't have India, nobody can."

"Live free or die," she whispered. It was what the colonial troops from New Hampshire had shouted as a battle cry during the Revolutionary War. Apparently, the Indians felt the exact same way. "They are gusty bastards, and that's the truth."

"So what was Himar working on at Wake Island? Price demanded, not sure that she wanted to hear the answer. "The DOD wasn't financing research into a weapon that already existed."

"Shielding for the weapon," Kurtzman answered incredibly, casting a sideways glance at a monitor on his console. "He was trying to find a way to block the deadly beam."

"Anything we can use?" she asked hopefully.

Rubbing a hand across his tired face, Kurtzman sighed all the way down to his shoes. "Nothing. There is no protection aside from deep water. The focused beam has ten times the penetration of a halo from a neutron bomb."

"How did India destroy the cannons Himar built for them?"

He shrugged. "Hunt is working on that, but India has some of the best hackers in the world. And the best of the best are in COIN, the counterintelligence. Their firewalls and coding are impressive."

She drained the coffee cup. "Great. Any good news? Anything on the Internet?"

"Nothing about the weapon being offered for sale," Carmen Delahunt said from behind her VR helmet. She was getting closer to the source of those annoying t-bursts, but wasn't quite there yet. "And if anybody knew about the attacks before the incidents occurred, they're not talking about it online. So either we're dealing with professionals who know better, or the operators are dead and we're facing a runaway."

Still locked in deep thought, Price went for more coffee. A battle satellite running on automatic with nobody at the controls. There was a chilling thought. If that was the case, there was nothing they could do until they found the satellite.

"Now this is strange," Akira Tokaido mused, studying a scrolling monitor on his console. "Has anybody double checked the metallurgy reports of the crash in Canada?"

"Not yet," Kurtzman said, turning his way. "Why? Find something?"

Turning down the music on his headphones, Tokaido blew a pink bubble, then chewed it back inside his mouth. "Well, I used a software program from the FAA to reassemble the plane," he said. "Just wanted to make sure we hadn't missed anything important. Then correlated it against the metallurgy analysis to make sure the lab hadn't been sloppy and tested everything on board."

"And?"

"Some of the 747 isn't radioactive."

"Impossible," Price said. "When a neutron beam passes through metal, it leaves a faint radioactive signature. Not much, it would barely make a Geiger counter tick, but still enough to be detected if you were looking for it. The entire plane, right down to the filings in the people's teeth should be ever-so-slightly hot."

"Which part are we talking about?" Kurtzman demanded, resting an arm on his console.

"The top of the wings."

"But if the plane was fired upon by a satellite, then the bottom of the wings should be clean because of the fuel shielding…" Delahunt frowned from behind her VR helmet. "Are you saying this was a ground attack?"

"Looks like," Tokaido said, reaching out to choose a new CD and insert it into the stereo on his console.

On the wall monitor, a dozen more satellites blinked off the screen, and the Most Secret report had an addendum that the flight of rescue helicopters sent to search for any survivors of the crashed British frigates mysteriously dropped off radar and didn't answer a hail. Additional helicopter gunships had been dispatched, along with full wing of Harrier jets.

"Show me," Price demanded, leaving the kitchenette to walk over to the young man.

"Sure," Tokaido said, flipping a switch.

Standing rigidly behind the lounging hacker, Price watched as the monitor came alive with a graphic image of the crashed plane reassembling itself, a side bar scrolling with the name of every nut, bolt and flange. Then came the people, and anything metallic they were carrying, rings on their fingers, braces on the teeth of a flight attendant, titanium plate in a Secret Service agent's head, shrapnel in the hip of a news reporter, the springs in their ballpoint pens...everything had been analyzed.

"So this was a ground attack," Price said, staring off into the distance. "And all this time, the thieves have been trying to make it appear that the weapon is in orbit!"

"So that we would go searching in the wrong direction," Kurtzman said, his brow furrowing. "Clever bastards."

"Maybe the plane was turning at the time—" Hunt Wethers started, then scowled. No, the data recorded in the black box of VC-25 should have been correlated with everything else.

"But this can't be right," Price muttered. "There wasn't enough time for them to steal the cannon, then chase down a 747..." Her voice faded, only to come back strong. "Unless they already had a cannon in position."

"The Prometheans have two?" Kurtzman asked, shaking his head. "But then the attack on the lab was to steal the prototype of any shielding Himar had created. They already had the weapon!"

"Only there is no shielding. They killed a lot of people just to find out they already had the ultimate weapon."

"Yeah, better safe than sorry."

"How do we know there are only two?" Wethers asked grimly. "Perhaps the cannons from India weren't destroyed, but simply disassembled and put into deep storage. We do that with a lot of our defunct weaponry, why not them?"

"Only somebody found the storage facility, and stole the cannons?"

"Exactly."

Scowling darkly, Price was forced to agree the idea had considerable merit. And who better to find a secret stash of government weapons than the biggest arms dealer in Asia?

Striding to a secure phone on the wall, Price grabbed the receiver and tapped in a code. If they were right, the Prometheans didn't have a satellite; they were just thieves in trucks. It should be all right to use standard communications again. The Farm wasn't contending with a cadre of scientists, but just a bunch of guys with crowbars. It was the first lucky break they had gotten so far.

There was a fast series of clicks as the call was relayed through a dozen different satellites, then halfway across the world, before returning to D.C. only a few miles distant.

"Hal, tell the Man we believe the item in question is

not in orbit," she reported crisply, then paused. "No, damn it, we're not positive. But every indication is pointing that way. And there may be more than one." She listened for a minute, then hung up.

"Okay, let's find those cannons," Price said, returning to her chair. "Check the angles of the strikes. Were they from the land or air? I also want a full breakdown of each strike—time, speed and distance. Are we facing two of these things or a dozen?"

The trio of hackers nodded and bent to the new task.

"If the neutron cannon is on the ground," Kurtzman said slowly, worrying his chin, "then it must have been in Braintree. Maybe it even passed Able Team on the highway. Yet they sent in hired muscle anyway to burn the place down."

"Red herring?"

"Looks like."

Price wondered where Kurtzman was going with this. "They're very good, if not professionals, then highly talented amateurs."

"Yeah. Now so far, the Prometheans have been ahead of us every step of the way, constantly leaving false trails and conflicting clues. So they must have spent a great deal of time and trouble in careful, detailed, planning."

She got the idea. The Prometheans weren't fools, and they already had the cannons, a weapon worth billions on the black market. Money clearly wasn't the goal. So what were the bastards after? Obviously, something more important than money. Or at least, more important to them. The only thing greater than greed was love. But you didn't kill out of love. You killed because of love.

"Revenge," Price whispered thoughtfully. "The Prometheans want revenge against somebody that they couldn't kill with the cannons." Which logically meant somebody they couldn't find. They were stirring up the entire world to drive their enemy into the light.

"Bad move, guys," Price said harshly. Because Stony Man was going to blitz them out of existence.

CHAPTER TWELVE

Victoria Towers, Calcutta, India

Sitting in a chair in the restaurant, Mohad Malavade sipped a glass of chilled red wine and contemplated how everything seemed to be moving along smoothly. Himar was gone, Suda was dead, along with his usurper, and the advance work for his plan was almost finished. Soon, he could begin the heart of the project, the final stage and true purpose. Revenge.

Finishing the drink, Malavade stood and dropped a few hundred rupees for the waiters. He had worked as one in his youth, and considered it the hardest work in the world. Which was why he stopped as soon as he purchased his first gun, he mused in grim amusement.

Turning away from the table, Malavade glanced out the nearby window to scowl at the bustling city below. The traffic generated a low din through the supposedly soundproof glass, and the air outside was hazy from the car exhaust and diesel fumes. The current census listed a billion people living in India, and sometimes to Malavade it seemed as if they all were clustered around his skyscraper. Born and raised in a local orphanage, Malavade hated Calcutta with a rage that would have driven a weaker man insane. Instead he had rallied and conquered the city, until it bent to his will. Calcutta was a hole, but it was his. And soon enough, he would be free to leave and never return.

That thought put a smile on his face. Malavade already owned a small island off the coast of Tasmania, where he planned to retire. He'd never see another human being aside from his family and servants. The crime lord grinned. Peace and quiet. What a wonderful life that would be!

Almost tenderly, Malavade reached out to pat the cool marble wall. But until then, the Victoria Towers was his oasis and home. His wife and children lived far away, safe from his line of work, but Malavade stayed at the Victoria, the secret ruler of all he surveyed.

Built in the business boom of the 1990s, the skyscraper rose above the scuffling, scurrying mass of humanity on the busy streets, as clean as a mountain of ice. Covering most of a block, a ten-story-high apartment complex formed the base, then from the middle rose a blue stone tower for fifteen more stories. For several years, Victoria Towers had been the tallest building in India. But then it had been surpassed by others, and some of the soaring goliaths in New Delhi dwarfed the meager twenty-five-story building into insignificance.

But like a favorite whore, the Victoria had secrets that only he could appreciate, Malavade thought, strolling through the restaurant.

Two of his bodyguards lounging near the bar immediately left their drinks and took flanking positions behind their employer.

Barely noticing the civilians, Malavade walked directly toward the crowd of patrons waiting to get into Victoria Ten. Wisely, they parted for the man and maintained a respectful distance until he was gone.

"Now who the blazes was that fellow?" a British tourist demanded hotly. "The Rajah of Bangalore?"

"You really don't want to know, old chap," the head waiter replied in an exaggerated English accent. It was an open secret who truly owned Victoria Towers, no matter what the name on the lease said.

Waiting at the elevator bank, Vinsara nodded in greeting to his boss and pressed the button for the private car. The doors opened with a sigh, and Vinsara got in first to make sure it was empty before gesturing for his boss to enter.

"How was your lunch?" Malavade asked as the elevator started toward the penthouse.

"Same as always. It was food, I ate it. What else is there to say?" Vinsara said, checking his hair in the security mirror. "Made any decisions yet?"

"Of course. The next target will be my old friends on 46th Street," Malavade said. "A little thank-you gift for all of the trouble the fools have caused me over the years."

With a musical ding, the elevator stopped at the twentieth floor, but the doors remained closed.

Pulling out keys, Malavade and Vinsara both inserted them into notches in the wall, and turned in unison. There was an electric hum and the doors opened onto the lobby of Malavade Enterprises.

The spacious area was lined with marble and filled with beautiful flowering shrubs from the northern region. A mural of Mt. Everest covered one wall, and a couple of armed guards stood behind the stainless-steel reception desk, AK-101 assault rifles slung across their backs.

The men murmured greetings as Malavade walked past them and straight into a hallway lined with glass walls. These were the offices for his business concerns. Weapons here, drugs there, smuggling, blackmail, and so on. Serving some time in jail for armed robbery, Malavade had spent his two years reading everything in the prison library. When he came out, he rebuilt his organization along the lines of a regular business. Money was money, whether you were selling soap or heroin, and the tactics always remained the same. Crush the competition, seize control of the market, then gouge the consumer for every rupee he or she had.

Malavade stopped in an open doorway. "How are we doing?" he asked, leaning on the jamb.

"Beef is up again," the clerk replied, looking up from her small computer. "Do you wish a market brief?"

"Send it to my desk," the crime lord said, turning to leave. One of his earlier investments had been a cattle ranch. Cows were sacred to the Hindus, but everybody else in the nation wanted a steak occasionally, so Malavade supplied that forbidden delicacy, for a price. Oh, every now and then some religious fanatics would find the ranch and storm the fences, in spite of the presence of armed guards. Incredible, but true. The lunatics valued the lives of a cow more than their own. It was beyond madness! But still the fools tried. And when they did, the guards would gun them down.

Straight ahead was the ornate double doors to his private office, but Malavade turned left instead and walked to plain wooden door at the end of the hall. There was a sign hanging from the latch showing the picture of a nuclear bomb blast and the legend Do Not Disturb printed in large letters.

Yanking off the sign, Vinsara crumbled it into a wad and threw it away while Malavade went inside.

The air was cold, so cold the crime lord could almost see his breath, and the room was full of computers of every type, size and shape. Some of them were scrolling binary code, others were defragging or playing the start-up screen for some game. Another computer was splayed across a worktable, the naked guts held together with duct tape and alligator clips, while the hard drive was downloading into an Indian Army Palm-Comp.

The walls of the room were a wild compilation of American science-fiction movie stills and Bollywood starlets in outrageously flamboyant costumes. A large whiteboard was filled with overlapping equations, the sequence corrected so many times it was impossible to detect what was old data and which was new. A bonsai tree covered with Christmas lights sat on top of a small vault, the door partially ajar revealing a box of rainbow-colored data disks and a Uzi machine pistol. A stereo on the shelf was playing the soft sounds of the sea, waves cresting on a sandy beach.

"Morning, sir," Hasuraya "Mongoose" Metudas said without looking up from the triptych computer monitors positioned around him in an arch. The young Indian man was wearing a backward cap bearing the name of a local soccer team, and a heavy sweater that moths seemed to find particularly delicious.

"Try afternoon," Malavade said, closing the door. "Must it be so cold in here? The computer is in the next room."

"Computers, we have three Cray supercomputers," the young man corrected glibly, using a laser pen to open and close files on the central monitor. "The cold keeps me alert."

Malavade controlled his temper. He detested being corrected by anybody, especially someone like Metudas. But the hacker was the best in the country, possibly the world. And nothing was free. Loyalty had to be paid for in tolerance.

"Have you ever tried coffee?" the crime boss said, crossing his arms for warmth.

Turning off the laser pen, the hacker grinned wolfishly. "I prefer cocaine, but—"

"No drugs on duty," Malavade snapped irritably.

Ending one program and starting another, the hacker shrugged. "Thus I live in a refrigerator. Now wait just a second…" With a flourish, the young man tapped a key on an ergonomic keyboard. The monitor to his left flashed binary code for a moment, then went back to a kaleidoscope of scanning e-mails across the globe. Part of the hacker's job was to identify theft and spamming. He earned the organization ten million rupees a day selling bogus products, and emptying the bank accounts of people who foolishly stored their credit card numbers and passwords on the family PC. Stupidity was its own reward.

"That was the last one, sir," Metudas stated. "I bundled the last bunch of t-bursts in a cascade of—"

"No details," Malavade interrupted. "Just let me know when they responded."

"Of course."

"Is everything else under control?"

"Sure, no problems. Our neutron cannon in America is already at the next target waiting for your command to strike. Our trawler in the Atlantic is tracking a liner filled with European dignitaries on a holiday cruise to the Bahamas. And—" A screen blipped, and the hacker smiled. "Good news! I just e-jacked a shipment of kiddie porn from a sex studio in Japan. We'll make a fortune selling it on the Net."

"Burn it," Malavade snarled. "I do not deal in such filth."

"But, sir," the hacker said hesitantly, tilting back his soccer cap. "I've seen you crucify people."

"That is business. This is a pointless waste of time. Children must never be harmed." For a brief second, the crime lord remembered his adolescence on the street and the things he was forced to do to stay alive. "Burn it all," he stated savagely. "Then send the address of the studio to the Japanese authorities."

Seeing that the man was serious, Metudas stroked a mouse pad with a finger and redirected the shipment to a waste disposal plant in Luxembourg, then sent an anonymous e-mail to the Tokyo P.D. from an Osaka retirement home.

"Done," Metudas reported nervously. "Oh, and I've also been sending out reports of strikes that we haven't really done, to help confuse things and maintain the idea that the weapons are in orbit. A factory here, village there…"

"That wasn't in the original plan," Malavade muttered, scrunching his face. "But I like it. Well done. Keep it going."

"Our fourth neutron cannon is returning from Sri Lanka by seaplane." Metudas shook his head. "Those dumb cops bought the whole thing. They're positive the cannon was in the trunk, and that Tiger Force is actually behind the killings. NATO has issued a search and destroy order."

Malavade said nothing, but a smile played across his lips. Excellent. Misinformation was the heart of his plan. Somebody had to take the fall for these attacks, so why not use known terrorists? His parents had died in a bombing by Tiger Force. Their idiotic politics sent him to hell for fifteen years. It took Malavade three long decades, but finally he was getting revenge. I become a billionaire, and my enemies die. What could possibly be better? If a few million people had to die, that was a small price to pay for justice. But if all went well, he would be on his way to Tasmania by this time tomorrow.

"And that's the lot of them, sir," Metudas said, tapping a monitor showing the six locations. "The dummy was in the wrecked truck, we have one airborne coming home, and the other four are all safely in position, ready to strike at your command."

There were seven, Malavade noted, rubbing his Kali watch fob. But that wasn't the hacker's concern.

"Well done," the crime lord said, slapping the man on the shoulder. "After this is done, there will be a substantial bonus for you."

"Thank you, sir," Metudas said warily. He started to tell his boss about some unusual activity he had detected in the eastern United States, but decided against it. He couldn't quite seem to pinpoint where the other hackers were. Probably Langley, or Quantico. However, he knew better than to show any weakness. One wrong move around here and a man would disappear.

"I'll be in my office," Malavade said, turning to leave. "Let me know when the auction is ready to begin."

"Of course, sir."

The crime lord paused in the open doorway. "Oh yes, and one more thing, Hasuraya."

The use of his first name startled the hacker. "Sir?"

Malavade gave a smile that sent chills down the hacker's spine. "If you ever offer me child pornography again, I'll have Vinsara remove one of your eyes." Slowly, the door closed behind the crime lord and locked with a soft click.

Swallowing hard, Metudas crossed the room and peeked outside to make sure the man was gone. Then he went to the safe and lifted the dead bonsai tree from its pot to remove a small glassine envelope. Replacing the tree, he took a hard sniff of the cocaine inside and went back to work. This was going to be a very long day.

FINISHED WASHING his hands, Vinsara dried them on a towel of the finest imported Egyptian cotton. Tossing it on the floor for the maids to retrieve, the enforcer left the lavatory whistling a tune.

Almost immediately, there came a whining sound from behind the last door in the row of private stalls. The noise briefly stopped as Nanravaska rushed into the room heading for the urinal. But when the man departed, the noise returned again, rising and falling in pitch. Then it stopped again, and there came a soft crunching noise, like somebody crumbling corn flakes, then a sharp crack, followed by a prolonged silence.

Easing open the door, a hulking giant wearing body armor stepped out of the private stall. The intruder was covered with drywall dust, and carrying an INS 5.56 mm assault rifle.

Suddenly, there came the sound of running footsteps, and the intruder ducked into a different stall.

A moment later, the guard walked into the tiled room and laid his AK-101 assault rifle on the counter. Starting to unbuckle his gunbelt, the guard turned and the intruder was upon him, one hand slapping across his mouth and the other thrusting forward with a slim stiletto. The narrow blade went deep in the chest of the guard, and he died with hardly a noise.

Dragging the corpse into a stall, the intruder laid it carefully on the floor, then reclaimed his blade. Going to the first stall, he knocked twice, paused, then twice more.

Immediately, the door swung open and out came another armed man from the small stall, closely followed by a third, fourth, fifth, sixth...

CHAPTER THIRTEEN

Stony Man Farm, Virginia

Hunched over her desk, Barbara Price was studying the wealth of reports delivered by Aaron Kurtzman and his team. The Chinese government wasn't being cooperative with the reports involving stolen shipments of their experimental QBZ assault rifles. She guessed the Communists didn't like to admit failure. Some the rifles and ammunition had been recovered from terrorist attacks in Beirut and Angola, which implied that Malavade had stolen the shipment, kept a few of the rifles for himself and sold the rest.

However, India's Central Bureau of Investigation, and Interpol, had nothing on the man. They didn't know his address, true name, associates, or much of anything else. Only that his parents were dead and he had been raised in an orphanage. Aside from that, Mohad Malavade was an enigma. Almost a ghost. Which seemed to indicate that he was crooked. Honest people had post-office boxes, credit cards and ISP accounts.

On the other hand, Malavade might be clean. Lots of businessmen skirted the edges of the rules, but never actually crossed over into criminal activity. And maybe he just liked his privacy. No law against that. There simply was no hard data either way.

Unfortunately, the UN General Assembly was nearly rioting over the existence of the neutron cannon, and the Security Council was holding a clandestine meeting somewhere they hoped was safe from attack.

A brief from Kurtzman showed that Carmen Delahunt had ripped through the records of the Atomic Energy Commission, and the Department of Defense, but there wasn't a single square yard of boronated plastic armor left in existence. Every scrap of it had been destroyed at Wake Island. Now what? Were they supposed to start living underneath swimming pools full of gasoline?

. Laying the reports down, Price ran stiff fingers through her hair. This matter was getting worse by the hour. Tensions were high in D.C., and people were running scared. Worse, the news reporters smelled blood in the water, and were hounding the politicians for a comment about all of the mysterious goings-on. If somebody—some clerk or assistant—cracked and spilled the beans, there wasn't an army in the world that would be able to contain the spreading riots.

The intercom buzzed on her desk, and Price hit the button. "What is it?" she asked wearily.

"You might want to come down here," Kurtzman said. "I think we have something hot."

"On my way."

A few minutes later, Price walked into the Computer Room slightly out of breath.

"What did you find?" she demanded.

"Do you know what a Faraday Cage is?" Kurtzman asked, pushing his wheelchair away from his workstation to face the woman.

Price nodded. "Yes. What about them?"

"We know that Dr. Himar had been working on some sort of a shield to try to stop a neutron beam." Kurtzman frowned. "But from the descriptions of the lab by Phoenix Force, there seemed to be a lot of Faraday Cages there. Those are utterly useless against a neutron beam. So he must have been using Faradays as protection from intense magnetic fields. Perhaps those induced magnetics he talked about in his earlier work."

"How is this good news?" Price asked impatiently.

"I think we can track the neutron cannons from space," Kurtzman said. "Pinpoint their locations to within a square yard."

Price raised her eyebrows. "Show me," she commanded, taking a chair set aside for visitors.

"Akira, have you got that NASA satellite yet?" Kurtzman asked, wheeling around.

"No problem," the man replied, flipping a switch.

The map of the world changed to a blurry image of red and black splotches.

"What's this?" Price asked.

"That is an electromagnetic view of Earth," Kurtzman announced, waving a hand. "For a long time, NASA has been studying the magnetic fields of the planet, ferreting out oil deposits, iron, sunken ships and lava flows."

"Lava?"

"There often is a lot of ferric oxide in lava," he explained. "As it forces new channels underground, it alters the magnetic fields on the surface. Not enough to change a compass, or anything—microscopic changes— but still enough to be registered."

"From space?" Then again, nobody had ever claimed NASA was staffed by fools. But this was incredible.

"Six years ago, no. But nowadays, absolutely."

Pensively, Price's forehead creased. "If this satellite can track minute changes in the magnetic fields, how can it find a neutron cannon?"

"It can't," Kurtzman stated. "But it can find the Faraday Cage the operators need to protect themselves from the induced magnetics that powers the weapon." He pointed at the screen. "See those gray splotches in the red and black? Those are natural dead zones. A Faraday Cage would register as a blank area, a dead zone."

"Exactly how small an area can it register?"

"We can pinpoint a dead zone the size of a shoebox," Hunt Wethers said from his workstation. "And based upon the observations of Phoenix Force, our guess is that a neutron cannon should be about the size of a refrigerator."

"Are there a lot of natural dead zones?"

"Sure, but they're all irregular in shape. These Faraday Cages would show as perfect square."

"Then you've already tried it?"

"Of course," Kurtzman said, going to his workstation and tapping the keyboard.

The red and black splotches on the wall were overlaid with a vector graphic of Pennsylvania. There was a gray circle directly on Route 80 outside of Reading. "That's where a neutron cannon was located exactly when VC-25 was destroyed."

"Incredible. What are those other gray areas?" Price asked. "Those circles and rectangles?"

"Government buildings, military installations, NSA listening posts, and such," Wethers announced, concentrating on his monitor. "The White House and the Pentagon have Faraday Cages built into their walls as protection from microwaves."

"As do we." Kurtzman grunted.

"So we really can track the bastards wherever they go," Price mused. "This is fantastic! Get me a precise location, and I'll have the teams—"

"Ah, that's the problem. We can't give a precise location," Kurtzman stormed. "It takes NASA a while to process the massive amounts of data reaching their satellite. After all, they're scanning the whole planet. That's over 197,000,000 square miles."

A huge amount of ground to cover every minute of every day, she admitted grudgingly. "Okay, how long is the lag?"

"Two hours."

"Hours!"

"Give or take a few minutes."

"Are our computers any faster?"

"Lord no, the ones at NASA are the best in the world for this sort of precise scientific analysis."

"And the NASA satellite can only register the Faraday Cages when they're activated," Wethers finished apologetically. "The dead zones only appear when the weapon is turned on for an attack."

"Okay, it's still better than nothing," Price relented. "What are the most recent locations?"

"We have done an overlay of the mag-field recordings from the time of the attacks," Kurtzman said, fiddling with the controls on his console. "They appear and disappear, probably from testing the equipment, or from killing people who got too close to the weapon. A street cop, customs inspector, and so on."

The map changed again, showing a gridwork of the world. The red and blacks splotches fading out, the gray areas remaining to now become blinking red dots. There had been a neutron cannon moving along a train track from Russia to Ukraine. It seemed to still be on board. Braintree appeared for a moment, then vanished. Another dead zone was in the Atlantic Ocean moving away from England toward South America along the commercial shipping lanes. A third had briefly appeared off the coast of Sri Lanka.

"I thought that attack was made from a truck on dry land," Price muttered, changing her position in the chair.

Draining his mug, Kurtzman went to the coffee station for a refill. "Maybe they sent the truck as a backup," he speculated. "It was an important target. Half of the top cops in the world are dead. It'll take us years to recover from that hit."

"Maybe they sent two, maybe not," Price noted thoughtfully. "They haven't sent two for any other attack, why there?" There was something very odd about that. Was their nameless enemy trying to pull some sort of trick? They already had the nations of the world hunting for them in space. So why not a second diversion to fool any hunters into…what? Exactly what were the terrorists trying to hide? Their identity, or location? But the identity of the driver was already known as an operative for Tiger Force. But if that was a fake…

Suddenly a new dead zone blinked into existence on the Manhattan harbor, then disappeared.

"They're in New York," Delahunt said from behind her VR helmet.

"Give me a time check!" Price demanded, standing.

Frowning deeply, Wethers checked the digital readout. "Two hours, one minute ago."

"Any reports from New York?" Kurtzman called, wheeling back to his station.

"Nothing on the radio or television," Delahunt reported crisply. "And we'd certainly hear about it if everybody in the greater New York area dropped dead all at the same moment."

"Send Able Team to Manhattan," Price commanded, making a decision. "Give them the precise location of the dead zone two hours ago. Maybe they'll get lucky."

"On it," Kurtzman replied, both hands moving. "What about Phoenix Force?"

"They're still trying to track down Malavade," she said, "He may be our best chance to find the people behind all of this." If he wasn't the man in charge himself. They had a name, but didn't know if it was the right one, yet.

"Hunt, we need a diversion," Price said, going over

to his console. "Contact the Citadel in London, and give the British navy the last-known coordinates of the neutron cannon in the Atlantic. After those frigates, I'll bet they're itching for some payback. Then inform NATO about the cannon in the Ukraine. Have them board the train, and try to take the operators alive."

"Is that wise?" Wethers said slowly, his hands poised above the keyboard. "Even with the element of surprise, these are tantamount to suicide missions."

"A soldier's burden," Price said emotionlessly, staring at the map of New York on the wall screen.

It took the professor a moment to realize that the woman was talking about herself, not the troops. She had just ordered men to their deaths in order to save millions of civilians, who would never know about the sacrifice. A soldier's burden. It was heavier than any rucksack and more vital than ammunition. It was a heartfelt oath that kept their souls clean and prevented them from ever becoming the people that they fought.

The professor got to work. This dirty little war had only just begun.

CHAPTER FOURTEEN

The Atlantic Ocean

The control room of the nuclear submarine was large, cool, and brightly lit by a hundred twinkling lights on the complex controls panels, a military rainbow of indicators showing the detailed status of the billion-dollar war machine.

Bent over the navigation table, the captain and first mate of HMS *Vanguard* were studying the charts of the undersea canyons they were planning to travel through in a few days. At the moment, the *Vanguard* was safe at the bottom of the ocean more than a mile beneath their hull.

Suddenly the radio operator appeared in the hatchway, looking around anxiously. Then he rushed toward the captain.

"What is it, Sparks?" Captain Richard Danvers asked, straightening and putting aside the compass and ruler.

"Message from the Citadel for you, sir," the man replied, passing over a folded piece of paper.

"From where?" the captain asked with a frown, opening the sheet.

"Direct from the Big C, sir," Sparks whispered, as if afraid to invoke the dreaded name. "I decoded it twice to make sure this wasn't a garbled transmission, or anything."

"I see what you mean," Danvers muttered, reading it again himself. "That will be all, Sparks. Carry on."

"Yes, sir," the radioman answered, obviously disappointed that there wasn't any additional information forthcoming.

"Trouble, sir?" Executive Office John White asked, tilting his head.

"I should say so," Danvers said. "NavCom, prepare to change course!"

"Aye, aye sir!" the man at the navigation control replied.

Checking the paper, Danvers read off the coordinates.

"Sir, that's going to put us in the commercial lanes," the executive officer said with a worried tone, as the boat began to tilt slightly.

"Yes, I know. Full speed, helmsman, if you please!"

"Aye, sir," the man called. "Full speed!"

Everybody in the control room began to exchange puzzled glances, but withheld any comments.

Reaching upward, the captain took down a hand mike and pressed the transmit switch with a thumb. "Red alert," he said, the words echoing throughout the entire submarine. "Red alert. All hands to battle stations! Prepare for surface action!"

A Klaxon started to sound.

Releasing the switch, the captain pressed it down again. "Torpedo room," he demanded.

"Torpedo room, here, sir," a voice replied.

"Load all tubes, Tigers to the port, Sharks to Starboard."

"Sir?" the man gasped. "That is, I mean…aye, aye, sir!"

Clearing the line, the captain pressed the switch once more. "Arms master, prepare an Away Team."

"Aye, sir." There was a pause. "Is this a drill, Captain?"

"Put some heat into that, mister!"

"Yes, sir!"

"Helmsman, up bubble seven degrees. Blow all tanks."

"Aye, aye, sir! Prepare to surface!"

As the *Vanguard* started to angle for the surface, White moved close to the captain. He could see the controlled anger in the commander's face.

"What the bloody hell is going on, Chuck?" the XO whispered urgently. "Are we at war?"

"Read for yourself," the captain said, passing over the paper. "We have a seek and destroy order from the Citadel."

Unfolding the paper, White read the short message, then read it twice more.

"I thought the *Edinburgh* blew up from a fuel leak," the XO said softly, returning the radio message.

"Apparently not," Danvers rasped, tucking the slip of

paper into his uniform pocket. "And the cheeky bastards are right in our backyard, ripe for the plucking."

With a hard lurch, the *Vanguard* reached the surface and the forward speed of the craft nearly doubled.

"Passive radar only," Danvers ordered as a sailor delivered a gunbelt. Quickly he strapped on the weapon and checked the clip.

"Jefferies to the diving tower," White ordered, buckling on his own gunbelt. "Report any surface ships immediately."

"Aye, sir," the man replied, sliding on a rain slicker and starting up the ladder to the top hatch.

"You know, the message doesn't say what kind of a boat they're on," White said carefully. "I assume that's why you want a boarding party ready. In case there are several in the area, and we have to do a hard recon."

"Board and storm, a British tradition." Danvers smiled without any humor.

"And when we find them?"

Placing both hands behind his back, Danvers frowned. "You read the orders, XO. We blow them out of the water."

AN HOUR LATER, there was a crackle on the intercom. "Top watch to control room," Jefferies said over the sound of rushing spray. "Fishing trawler on the horizon. Estimated nine kilometers, south-by-southeast…" He stopped talking.

A clatter sounded from the ladder and a moment later Jeffries crashed limply onto the deck.

"Medical to the control room!" White barked into a hand mike.

"Radar, active sweep, please!" Danvers ordered.

Rushing over to the still man, a sailor checked for a pulse, then for a heartbeat.

He's dead, Captain," the man said hesitantly.

"Where did they shoot him?" the XO demanded with a grimace.

"Nowhere, sir," the sailor replied in confusion. "There's not a mark on the man."

"Good God, are you saying an experienced sailor fell down a ladder and died?" White demanded hotly. "Check the body again."

"I did, sir! He's clean."

Glancing up the diving tower, White set his jaw and grabbed the ladder to start climbing. He reached halfway when the man went limp and plummeted straight down the tower to noisily crash on top of Jefferies.

Moving to the periscope, Danvers swept the surface and soon found the other vessel. It was a French fishing trawler. Pretty far out at sea for such a small craft. She seemed to be hauling some cargo on the top deck…then he saw the men on deck wave assault rifles. Fury welled within the officer, only to be replaced by confusion. Maybe the bastards shot poor Jefferies, but White was still inside the boat! He had to have barely cleared the water line when he died of… There his line of reasoning petered out. What could kill a man behind four inches of reinforced steel?

"Mozart, anything near us?" the captain demanded.

"Just that surface ship," the sonar operator reported, one hand holding a massive set of earphones to his head. Then the man shuddered, then fell over, his face cracking the glass of the sonar screen at his station.

In growing horror, the captain saw everybody else at the bow collapse in their seats. Then the control room seemed to get warm. A strange tingle prickled Denvers skin and he toppled over, along with everybody above the water line.

With nobody at the helm, the submarine charged blindly across the Atlantic Ocean.

IN THE FORWARD LAUNCH bay of the *Vanguard,* rows of sleek torpedoes rested in cushioned cradles lining the curved metal walls. A few were sonar probes, a couple were "cold fish," dummies for practices runs. But the bulk of the weapons were deadly Tigerfish and Sharkfish, long-range, armor-piercing torpedoes. The Tigers were steered by sonar, the Sharks wire-guided. The only visible difference between the two was that the Tigers had yellow rings on the collar and the Sharks had red. These were the fastest torpedoes in Her Majesty's arsenal, traveling at over 100 kph.

"Control room, this is the torpedo room," the sailor said again. He waited for a reply but nothing could be heard.

He clicked the switch clearing the line. "Security, there's something amiss in the control room," he reported.

"You don't know the half of it, mate!" came the terse reply. "Stay right where you are! Hear me? Right where you are! Anybody who steps above the water line dies."

"What a hot steaming pile of—" the boson started.

"God's truth, mate!" the officer in Security interrupted. "I have no idea what's happening, but we're obviously under some sort of attack and I just have no bleeding idea what it is!"

"Is…is it nerve gas?"

"Gas? How the bloody hell should I know? But the moment that damn trawler got in sight, people started dying. We're trying to seize control of the main computer and regain control of the boat. We'll let you know when we do."

"And what should we do in the meantime, sir?" the boson asked, turning authority over to the unseen lieutenant.

"Follow your last orders," he directed, "and pray."

"Aye, sir, torpedo room out." Breathing hard for a few moments, the boson turned to look at his men. They weren't frightened, or anxious. They seemed pissed, every man jack of them.

"I don't know about you lot," the boson said slowly, attaching the mike to a clip, "but I clearly heard the captain give the fire order before he died. Are you with me, lads?"

The sailors broke into a cheer and rushed to their tasks. The tubes were flooded, and pressure checked. They didn't have a heading or range, but the boson remembered the captain saying that there were no other vessels in sight. Fair enough.

"Fire one," the boson commanded with a dry mouth. "Fire two!"

"Firing one," a sailor repeated, hitting the launch button. "Firing two."

With a gurgling hiss, the Tigerfish and the Sharkfish

left the boat and streaked away. Instantly, the sonar speaker on the wall started pinging.

"It's in God's hands now," the boson muttered, making the sign of the cross.

ON BOARD the *Souris,* the hijackers had shrugged off their heavy overcoats and worked the trawler openly dressed in shoulder holsters and ammo belts.

Seated just outside the humming Faraday Cage, the slim man operating the neutron cannon carefully watched the radar screen, keeping the distant submarine squarely in the center of the crosshairs on the digital scope. Their orders from Mr. Malavade had been clear. If any military vessels got within range, burn them down.

"Anything in the sky?" the gunner asked, licking the salty spray from his dry lips.

"Radar is clean," muttered the man nearby, checking the India Army PalmComp unit in his hand. The device was linked to the radar array above the ship's bridge. He switched to the next function. "And sonar reads— Hot fish! We have hot fish in the water coming our way!"

"Use the Sea Darts," the slim gunner commanded, his voice rising in fear.

At the stern, a canvas sheet was dragged off an emplacement and the aiming mechanism was connected to the sonar. The stanchion holding the four sleek antimissiles swiveled around automatically, then two launched two rustling firebirds, then two more.

Even before the smoke had cleared the deck, the men were rushing forward with a wheeled cart to reload the launcher.

Naturally, Mr. Malavade had expected situations like this, and the weapons dealer had armed his men with everything they needed to stay alive.

Streaking across the surface, the missiles dived into the water and exploded.

"Well?" the gunner demanded anxiously.

"Got 'em!" The fat man chortled. "I thought NATO would be much tougher than this."

"They are, trust me," a bald man shouted from the rigging, scanning the sky with binoculars.

The sonar pinged, then did it again.

Instantly, another salvo of Sea Darts launched.

There were multiple torpedoes in the water coming in from different directions! the gunner realized in growing horror.

"They're tracking our sonar!" he shouted. "Turn it off, you fool. Turn it off!"

"But then the Sea Darts can't track them!" he objected, shaking the PalmComp.

"Do it!"

"Done!"

"Well?"

"Still on course…" the fat man announced.

The gunner at the neutron cannon twitched, sorely tempted to swing the weapon at the sea even though he knew it would have no effect on the deadly machines.

Incredibly, there was a double explosion in the water a hundred yards away, and the sonar went silent.

"Got 'em!" the fat man cried, and the crew cheered in victory.

Just then, several water spouts appeared on the horizon, the tiny columns rising to become fireballs that flashed into the sky.

Lord Shiva, there had to be somebody alive on the sub and they managed to launch a flight of antiship missiles! The gunner checked the instruments on the cannon, but everything was in the green. The supposed superweapon was operating perfectly. Then why weren't those sailors dead?

The pings got louder, the Sea Darts launched and flashed away.

"How many are there?" a short man standing at the gunwale asked, loading a 30 mm round into the grenade launcher of his AK-101 rifle.

"Four," the fat man replied

And they had four Sea Darts, the gunner noted sourly. One miss and they'd die. Their fate was sealed.

Skimming the ocean surface, the Darts disappeared into the distance, never rising toward the sky.

"They can't lock on the missiles!"

"Switch from sonar to radar, you fool!" the gunner snarled.

The man hurriedly changed the feed, then he frowned. "Hey," he said slowly. "The incoming missiles…they're gone."

"We got 'em!" the short man cried triumphantly.

The fat man went pale. "Maybe," he said hesitantly.

"Look!" shouted the bald man in the rigging.

Six foaming wakes could be seen in the surface of the Atlantic, heading straight for the trawler.

The gunner felt his heart stop beating. Those hadn't been missiles that the submarine launched, but rocket-assisted torpedoes! They flew above the Sea Darts, and then dived into the ocean to strike from below.

Rushing to the gunwale, several of the men worked the arming bolts of the AK-101 assault rifles, and started wildly firing into the shimmering expanse of ocean. When the clips emptied, a couple started tossing grenades into the water in a desperate hope to distract the incoming torpedoes.

"Call them!" the gunner said, turning off the cannon. "Tell NATO that we surrender!"

Realizing that they were facing death, the fat man rushed to comply. No amount of pay was worth this. "Attention all ships, this is the fishing trawler *Souris*. This is the *Souris* calling the NATO submarine. We surrender. Repeat, we—"

"Coward!" the bald man in the rigging cursed. "Traitor!"

Pulling a machine pistol, the furious man racked the deck, accidentally killing the radar operator. Abandoning his post, the gunner dived over the side and started swimming for his life.

The heavy slugs tore into the men a split second before the trawler shuddered and the bow exploded from the sea, wood fragments and dying men flying everywhere. The call was too late. The torpedoes had arrived.

Two detonations hammered the trawler, breaking the hull apart. Covered with short circuits, the neutron cannon exploded in electrical sparks, just before the ship vanished in a thundering fireball.

When a recon patrol arrived a few hours later, they

found only floating bits of wreckage and the gunner. Taken into custody, the street tough from Calcutta folded easily and started spilling his guts.

CHAPTER FIFTEEN

Manhattan, New York

During the drive to New York, Able Team read up on everything it could about Himar and neutron bombs. There wasn't much.

"Any chance of rain?" Lyons asked, looking at the cloudy sky. If a neutron cannon was sitting off the docks of Manhattan, they'd have to be double careful. One wrong move and seven million people could die.

"None," Blancanales sighed. "And those are the wrong kind of clouds to try seeding."

"Don't know if that would have helped much," Schwarz said, sweeping the cityscape with the dish antenna of the oscilloscope.

"Couldn't have hurt us any."

"Agreed. Nothing on EM," the electronics expert said, adjusting some delicate controls. Bolted into place, a large oscilloscope was humming away, the sine wave pattern on the gridwork screen smooth and evenly spaced. If the terrorists were using induced magnetics to power the cannon, Schwarz hoped there might be leakage, some sort of a secondary magnetic field he could detect.

In frustration, he boosted the machine to its maximum setting. New York had too many broadcasting television and radio stations, microwave relays, satellite uplinks, and the cell phone traffic was off the chart. An EM scan here for a portable power source was pointless. He might as well try to find a specific grain of sand on a beach. Schwarz knew the mission would have to be done the old-fashioned way, by brains and balls. Thankfully, the team had plenty of both. He just hoped it was enough.

Taking Interstate 95 into Manhattan, Lyons headed toward the Henry Hudson Parkway. Twenty years ago the elevated road had been dropping chunks of concrete on the vehicles below, and actually killed one poor woman in a convertible. Now the rebuilt road was smooth and safe, and covered with graffiti.

As per instructions, Jack Grimaldi had taken the Hercules and flown to Teterboro Airport in New Jersey in case the team needed to go somewhere else quickly.

"I heard he left them a card," Lyons said out of the blue, swinging around a rusted-out Chevy and a Lexus sedan.

"Who?" Schwarz asked. "You don't mean those two TSA agents in Boston, do you?"

"Sure."

"A contact card. He wants to recruit them?"

"Why not? We can always use a couple more black-suits," Blancanales said pragmatically. "Besides, Jack said they actually got inside the Hercules through a locked door before the alarms tripped and he flooded the cargo hold with sleep gas." He smiled. "That's pretty good in anybody's book."

"I wonder if they're awake yet," Schwarz said, taking another bite.

"I wonder if they're out of that locked closet yet."

Leaving Henry Hudson, Lyons took an inclined exit, accelerating to merge with the traffic pouring out of the Lincoln Tunnel. Cutting across the Bowery, he passed city hall, the infamous Flatbush Bridge and finally parked at a public lot facing the East River. In Manhattan, the term public only meant that you didn't have to be a member of a business club to park your car there, just well-funded. New York wasn't Tokyo yet, with parking spaces being sold by real estate agents, but it was definitely headed in that direction.

Choosing a spot closest to the water, Lyons killed the engine and set the brake. Behind the team, the streets were busy with honking cars, the sidewalks endlessly flowing with pedestrians, talking, shoving, complaining. Ahead of them was the river, a wide lazy expanse of muddy blue water. Which was a vast improvement over the open sewer of industrial sludge the river had been a couple of decades ago. These days, aquatic life had started to return to the river, and occasionally some bold fisherman actually pulled a wiggling trout out of the water.

From their location, the team had a pretty good view

of the mile-long dockyard. It was truly colossal. But then, New York never did anything halfway in business or pleasure. Dozens of massive cargo ships were moored along the city docks, with hundreds of people moving around, shouting, waving, driving fleets of forklifts. Soaring high overhead, cranes were lifting metal boxes from the holds of ships and swinging them over the dockyard to deposit them in a fenced storage facility. Even sealed containers didn't leave the Manhattan dock without being thoroughly inspected first. And the New York City customs inspectors were some of the most diligent in the world.

Taking out a pair of binoculars, Lyons checked over the array of big ships and easily found their goal, the *Delta Sue,* a 100-ton cargo ship from Lisbon. The last NASA scan put the weapon on board, in the aft hold. The *Delta Sue* was moored by itself, well away from the other ships, which placed the Able Team leader in a quandary. He flexed his hands on the steering wheel. The most logical tactic would be to have the Air Force bomb the ship out of existence, killing several hundred civilians, but saving seven million. A good exchange. If the cannon was still on board. If not, the terrorists would sweep the city clean in retaliation. There was no choice. They were going in.

Suddenly the fax machine in the rear of the van came to life and yielded a sheet of paper covered with an alphanumeric code.

"Hmm, good news," Schwarz said, mentally translating the report. "The crew of a British sub took one of the terrorists alive in the Atlantic. He said the man in charge is a Mohad Malavade, a weapons dealer from India."

Lyons grimaced. At last, the enemy had a name. Malavade. It was interesting that the weapons dealer and the inventor of a weapon both came from the same country. How closely did their two worlds touch? he wondered. One wrong word from an assistant of Himar, a clerk, a janitor, and Malavade might have learned about the new weapon before it was even assembled.

"He say from where in India?" Blancanales asked, checking the clip in his M-16.

"Sadly, no. Claims to have been hired by somebody named Mongoose over the Internet." Schwarz frowned slightly. "Barbara and Bear think it's the truth. Apparently the Indians killed half the crew of the HMS *Vanguard* before being taken out by torpedoes, so the Brits were a tad, shall we say, enthusiastic in their questioning of the prisoner."

"He still alive?"

"Yes, but not taking any solid foods for a couple of months."

"Good," Lyons growled, lifting the Atchisson from the floor and checking the ammunition drum. "Gadgets, get me an update on the NASA scan for this area."

"Already coming through," Schwarz replied, checking his U.S. Army laptop. "Okay, two hours ago the Faraday Cage came on line for a short period, swinging back and forth, until moving in long arcs over the side... Son of a bitch, the blasted thing was being hoisted off the ship with a crane!"

"I had hoped that it was leaving the country." Lyons'

tone gritted, his temper starting to flare. With an effort of will, he forced it back down. This wasn't the time or the place.

"When did the Brits blow up the fishing trawler?" Blancanales demanded.

Schwarz checked the monitor. "An hour and a half ago."

Then this wasn't some form of retaliation for the Navy strike, Lyons realized. The cannon had been safely on board the cargo ship, but Malavade hauled it off for some reason. Had he discovered the NASA scans, or had the arms dealer chosen a new target for the weapon, one that he couldn't reach from past the underwater cargo hold of the ship?

"He can't be planning to hit all of New York," Blancanales thought out loud, rubbing his chin. "Or else the city would already be gone. Where did the crane deposit the weapon?"

Activating a zoom function, Schwarz scrutinized the satellite scan. "Holding facility," he said slowly. "But it turned off before setting on the ground. The shipping box could be anywhere."

"Or long gone."

"Yep."

"So let's find it," Lyons said, starting the engine and backing out of the parking spot to head for the exit.

Paying their way to the street, the team drove a few blocks. Illegally parking next to a fire hydrant, the team donned windbreakers, Homeland Security caps and went to the customs office located outside the high-security fence. Upon showing their Homeland Security identification to a pretty young clerk behind a counter, they were immediately escorted to the office of the division manager.

"How can I help?" the middle-aged man asked, rising from his desk to shake their hands. Homeland only showed up when something bad was going to happen. "Is it drugs again?"

"Has anything left the facility in the last two hours?" Lyons asked, ignoring the question and tucking away the commission booklet. "Better make that, three hours."

"No, sir," the division manager said in relief. "Nothing has gone out since noon. One of our men is sick, and we're way behind schedule. People are screaming for their stuff, but, well, you know how it is."

Forcing themselves to stay outwardly calm, the men of Able Team felt adrenaline flood their bodies, and they looked out the dirty window to the holding facility. The neutron cannon must still be here, hidden somewhere in the cubist mountains of painted steel boxes.

"Is…anything wrong?" the manager asked nervously.

"Nothing you need to be concerned about." Lyons smiled. "Just a routine check."

"Really?"

"Sure."

"Got a manifest?" Blancanales asked, crossing his arms.

"Sure, no problem," the division manager muttered, riffling papers on a overfilled clipboard and easing one out from under the spring clip. "Here ya go."

Taking the sheet, Blancanales checked the list from the *Sea Haven*. There was nothing listed.

"Is this everything?" he demanded sharply.

"Absolutely!" the man replied, sounding insulted. "I hope you're not insinuating that I would ever…"

"Of course, not," Lyons said smoothly. "We know your reputation."

The division manager licked dry lips. "You do?"

"Sure. Why do you think we came to you instead of…" Schwarz gave a wink and didn't finish the sentence.

Trying to hide a smile, the man preened under the implied compliment.

In reality, Able Team knew nothing about the man, but there wasn't a government clerk in existence who didn't think they were overworked, under appreciated and had a mortal enemy out to steal their thunder.

"We will, however, want to take a look around?" Lyons said as a question.

"No problem!" The division manager beamed. "Just drive your car around to the gate, and I'll have Susan give you a pass to get inside."

Thanking the man, the Stony Man operatives left the office and headed for the exit.

"Smart," Lyons said in grudging admiration. "Malavade doesn't bribe the clerks or inspectors, but the crane operator. Who's going to notice one box moving in the wrong direction among all of the others swinging overhead?"

"So it could be anywhere," Schwarz said. "This is going to be like searching for a needle in a haystack."

"That's easy enough to find," Blancanales replied. "Just burn down the hay and shift the ashes."

"Sounds great if you don't mind a half-melted needle," Schwarz retorted. "And in this case that translates as seven million dead."

They stopped at the front counter and Susan already had the pass ready for them. As they exited onto the sidewalk, a blue Dodge van rolled to a halt at the gate and sounded its horn. The rear of the vehicle was closed, the windows tinted a reflective blue.

Leaving a brick kiosk, a frowning guard walked over to the Dodge, stopped and keeled over limply. Throwing open the passenger side door of the vehicle, a dark-skinned man with a Jackhammer shotgun slung across his back hopped out and raced into kiosk to start working the controls. With a ratcheting sound, the gate unlocked and started to rumble aside.

Instantly, Able Team drew their weapons and started to fire on the vehicle. The windshield of the Dodge made wet smacking sounds as the rounds embedded into the bulletproof plastic. Turning his Colt Python on the man in the kiosk, Lyons blew him away, red blood splashing against the corkboard covered with Wanted posters.

Schwarz fired his 9 mm Beretta along the body of the Dodge van, the rounds ricocheting off the armored chassis, and Blancanales aimed for the left rear tire. The .380 hollowpoint rounds of the Colt pistol blew off chunks of material, but the tires were solid rubber, impossible to deflate.

Mouthing curses, the driver threw the Dodge into reverse and drove backward into the holding facility, disappearing around a tall stack of painted metal boxes.

Casting away their entry permit, the Stony Man commandos scrambled into their van. As Lyons started the engine, Blancanales leveled his M-16/M-203 out the window and fired. The 40 mm shell hit the partially open gate and blew it aside, flames and shrapnel flying everywhere.

On the sidewalk, a man cried out, clutching his shoulder, and everybody else in sight began to run away, screaming.

"Civilian down!" Schwarz yelled, donning his throat mike and earpiece. "Send EMTs now!"

"On the way," Kurtzman replied in a crackle of static.

Revving the engine, Lyons barreled through the gate, the headlights smashing and metal scrunching.

Throwing open the rear doors, Schwarz tossed out a couple of canisters. As the van drove into the facility, the canisters violently exploded, searing flames expanding from the military charges of white phosphorous.

With the exit securely sealed for twenty minutes, Lyons accelerated into the facility, briefly wondering if he would even notice if the neutron cannon took his life.

Taking a corner on two wheels, they caught a brief glimpse of the blue van, and Blancanales emptied a clip of 5.56 mm AP rounds into the rear hatch. The glass window shattered, and a man shouted in pain, or perhaps anger. It was impossible to tell.

A moment later, two round spheres flew out of the window and bounced along the pavement.

Grenades! Twisting the steering wheel, Lyons shot into a small passageway between two stacks of crates. A split second later the grenades detonated, shrapnel zinging back and forth between the metal boxes. The van was hit several times, but the ricochets never penetrated the armored chassis.

As the van swung around a corner, Lyons felt the vehicle scrape the edge, leaving behind the chrome trim and hubcaps.

"Aw shit, I have an EM spike," Schwarz cursed, glancing at the oscilloscope. "They're powering up the cannon!"

"Just give me one shot," Blancanales stormed, leveling the M-203 out the window, his finger on the trigger. An AP/HE round was in the breech. "That's all I need!"

"Get ready!" Lyons snarled, rocketing down a passage. Then he slammed on the brakes at the sight of a couple of startled workmen in hardhats.

"Hey," one of the men shouted angrily.

Sifting gears, the Able Team leader moved away from the civilians and took a dark side passage. The space was narrowing quickly, and he feared the van might become jammed when they shot into sunlight. They were on the east side of the facility, the river flowing directly past the dented security fence.

"Stony Base, this is Senator," Blancanales said into his throat mike. "We are at the Manhattan docks, cargo holding facility. The prize is in a blue Dodge van conversion. Repeat, the Indian curry is in a blue van. We are in pursuit."

He paused as Lyons took a corner at fifty miles an

hour, the tires squealing in protest. The Dodge could be seen weaving between the tall stacks for only a moment, then it was gone from sight once more.

"I'll leave the mike live," Blancanales continued, pressing his cheek to the M-16/M-203 combo. "If we stop talking, send in jet fighters and bomb this place off the map!"

"Copy, Senator, will comply," Kurtzman said. "Jets are on the way. And JG with a special delivery. ETA, ten minutes."

Grimaldi was coming? Reaching a long straightaway, Lyons floored the accelerator and raced along, trying to glance down every side passage for the elusive Dodge.

"Is that EM spike still hot?" Lyons demanded, clipping a green shipping container lying in the middle of an intersection. Sparks flew, and their bumper came off with a grinding wrench.

"Bet your ass it is," Schwarz said, sounding puzzled. "Why the hell haven't they zapped us yet?"

Blancanales frowned and started to speak when there was a motion overhead. "Go left!" he bellowed. "Now!"

Lyons almost flipped the vehicle as he swung to the side. A shadow appeared on the pavement behind them and then a shipping box slammed into the ground. Asphalt flew out in chucks, and steel box groaned as if dying from the triphammer impact.

Looking upward, Lyons could dimly see the long arm of a crane moving across the sky, the dangling chains empty. But even as it swung aside, another crane moved into action carrying a second box. Damn! The

Indians had called in support from the crane operators. If one of those things hit the van, they'd be smashed flat. But why the hell were they trying that sort of desperate gambit when they had the cannon?

Leaning far out the rear window, Schwarz fired a long burst upward with his M-16 assault rifle. A shadow moved across the van and Lyons slammed on the brakes to spin around and lurch in a new direction.

Now his teammates both fired at the control booth of the crane, spent brass flying everywhere. Sparks flew as the bullets peppered the metal framework. The operator staggered and fell out the open doorway, plummeting straight into the river.

"Got him!" Schwarz cried, dropping a clip and slapping in a replacement. He worked the bolt with a snap. "Now if we can just find…"

The blue Dodge van shot out of nowhere, zigzagging down the passage.

Concentrating on his driving, Lyons kept two hands on the wheel. Blancanales and Schwarz leaned out of opposite windows and hammered the Dodge with armor-piercing rounds. The bullets bounced off harmlessly. Triggering the M-203, Blancanales sent a 40 mm shell at the Dodge van, but it missed and flashed by to strike a shipping box and thunderously blow open the side. DVD players poured across the pavement.

A square of darkness appeared overhead once more and Lyons reluctantly tried an evasion maneuver. A heartbeat later a steel box slammed into the ground directly alongside the van, a heaving wave of asphalt throwing the armored vehicle into a stack of boxes with a strident crash.

Battered and bruised, Lyons fought the shuddering wheel, trying to keep after the fleeting Dodge, but the van was shaking badly and a grinding sound coming from the transmission constantly grew louder.

A shadow appeared overhead.

"Out!" Lyons ordered, slamming on the brakes.

As the men poured from the rocking vehicle, another shipping box came down and smashed their van flat, glass erupting in a twinkling spray. A split second later the self-destruct charges ignited, and the crushed wreckage under the box began to glow as the thermite ignited, the military compound slowly growing hotter until reaching 2000 degrees Kelvin. The shipping box started to melt, rivulets of molten steel flowing down like ice cream in the sun.

Charging between the stacks on foot, Able Team maintained a steady fire upon the blue Dodge van even as the vehicle drove directly through the dying flames of the white phosphorous and vanished.

Rushing to the security fence, the Stony Man commandos poured gunfire onto the Dodge until it reached the civilian traffic. Merging with the honking madness, it took a corner and was gone.

CHAPTER SIXTEEN

Poltava, Ukraine

Calm and serene, the freight train rolled through the endless wheat fields, clattering along the old tracks. Poltava City was just disappearing behind the train, and there was a long haul ahead through nothing until curving past the radioactive ruins of Chernobyl.

In the engine room, the driver sipped hot soup from a plastic cup, trying to stay awake.

Dimitri Kleinov had been extremely happy to land the job of a railroad engineer twenty years ago. It was solid, reliable work, and he hadn't missed a week's pay in twenty years.

Just then, a red light flashed on the control board, and Kleinov picked up the radio receiver.

"Kleinov, engine room," he answered.

"Dimitri? This is the dispatcher," said a nervous voice. "I've gotten a priority message from the military, a general no less! You are to slow down the train on the next flat stretch of ground and pretend you have broken down."

"Is this a joke?" Kleinov snarled, placing aside the Thermos. He wiped the mustache of soup from his lips with a stained handkerchief. "We're behind schedule as it is!"

"Yes, I know, but—"

"Are the Russians pissing over our border again?"

The dispatcher gave a heavy sigh. "Dimitri, I have no idea what is happening. But you are damn well going to stop that train, or you're fired."

"Impossible! The union would strike! We would close down the entire nation!"

"No. The union has sent orders for you to obey," the dispatcher replied curtly. "Just do it, old friend. There is something in the wind, eh? I don't like this. But stop the train." He paused. "Then go hide."

"All right, all right," Kleinov muttered, looking out the window at the passing fields of green. It was October, and the cold had arrived in full force. But none of the fields was fallow, empty and bare, sleeping until the spring planting. Every inch of ground was thick with clover. Something about putting nitrogen back into the soil to make the spring harvest even bigger than before. He—

"Dimitri?" the voice interrupted.

"Fine, yes, I'm slowing down," the engineer huffed. "I'll call after I come to a halt. Out."

Hanging up the receiver, Kleinov chewed a lip, then went to the other side of the control panel and tapped a button on the intercom. Smuggling was more than a

way of life under the Soviets, it had been an act of re-
bellion. Now, it was a way of making his meager pay
from the railroad feed six children and his ungrateful
parents-in-law. Refugees, weapons, drugs, he never
asked what was in the specially marked cargo boxes. He
simply made sure they weren't entered on the manifest,
and dropped them off wherever he was told. If people
wanted to destroy their brains for a minute of pleasure,
or needed a gun to defend themselves, what did that
have to do with him? The law was for the rich, who
made the laws. The poor only had their hands and the
darkness of the night.

"Yes?" a voice hissed impatiently. "What is it?"

"Trouble, sir," Kleinov said to his real employer.
"The dispatcher has ordered me to stop the train, and
run away. I...I think the military is on the way."

"So soon?" There was a brief pause, followed by a
chuckle. "Very well. Thank you, Dimitri. Goodbye."

Goodbye? "Do you want me to stop the train, and let
you off, and then start up again, sir?" the engineer suggested. "I have done it before. The black box will show
nothing."

"A more than generous offer," the voice said. "But
that will not be necessary."

Suddenly, Kleinov felt a strange tingling cover his
body, as if his entire body had fallen asleep. But the
painful prickling only lasted a split second before it
was replaced by a soothing warmth and then blackness.

Less than a minute later, everybody on board Super-
Express Nine was dead, aside from the people inside
carriage fourteen.

FIVE MEN PUSHED OPEN the sliding gate of the carriage, and the night wind rushed in to buffet them hard. Swinging out an arm, one of them grabbed the access ladder and climbed onto the roof, to squat and scan the starry sky with field glasses.

Fifteen minutes later a NATO F-16 appeared on the horizon. The Ukraine and NATO had only recently signed a mutual agreement of cooperation. The Ukraine was happy of the extra firepower on their side and NATO was delighted to have a base smack in the middle of so many politically unstable governments.

"Incoming, five o'clock," the look-out muttered into a handheld radio. The Kenwood was state-of-the-art, with a ten-button scrambler whose coded signals were almost impossible to break.

"Five o'clock," a short man rumbled in acknowledgment, looking at the team leader.

"Now the fun starts." The bearded giant grinned, working the digital crosshairs on the small control panel for the neutron cannon. The Faraday Cage came alive once more with a pervasive hum. Thick power cables that snaked from the bottom of the machine fed into a powerful Sterling generator running in the corner.

Behind them, five street toughs were opening crates and pulling out heavy ordnance. Along with a few surprises. Mr. Malavade thought everything.

"Don't miss," a short man snapped, hoisting a U.S. Army Stinger missile launcher onto a shoulder. "Or Vinsara with have your balls on toast."

"Miss? I never have before, my friend." The giant

chuckled, using a joystick to swing the aiming mechanism around and fire.

A moment later the F-16 started to drift in the sky. Then the warplane moved off into the night, starting a slow barrelroll toward the misty Carpathian Mountains.

"Got him!" the rooftop sentry announced proudly. "Easy as shooting fish in a barrel!"

Unless there was also a rock in the barrel, the short man thought, easing his grip on the Stinger. The boxy radar array rested cool against his hairy cheek. Then the bullet would bounce back and kill you.

"Don't worry, my friend," the giant said, laughing easily, powering down the Sterling to save fuel. "Soon enough, we will be far away from here, and independently wealthy!"

The others cheered, but the small man checked the rocket launcher over again. He believed in karma and guns. Everything else was a song in the wind. At first, this crazy job had sounded exciting. But this was a lot different from breaking the legs of somebody who owed you money, or knifing a rival drug dealer in the back. This was more like warfare, cold, grim and unrelenting. Not very much fun at all.

A sign flashed past the open side of the carriage, announcing that there were fifty more kilometers before Chernobyl.

"How are you boys coming?" the leader called over a shoulder.

"Almost done!" a greasy man answered, waving a wrench.

One of the shipping crates in the carriage had contained a small hovercraft, just large enough to hold the eight-man team.

The leader grunted in reply. Excellent! The plan was that when the cement mound of the dead reactor was in sight, he would set the cannon on automatic, activate the self-destruct and they would flee into the night, flying their hovercraft across the fields and into the mountain caves where no nobody could follow.

As long as they hit Chernobyl, everything was fine. Russia would pay anything to prevent another nuclear incident, and the neutron cannon could make any reactor go critical. Once they understood, the money would flow like a monsoon. But Malavade was smart. The government would be told they had to pay the same amount every year, but it was a lie. Give them long enough, the Russian FSB would track down the criminals. This was a single payment plan, and then they would all disappear rich as rajahs.

Let the fools hunt for us, the big man thought. If they should ever find our boss, then may the heavens have pity on their miserable souls!

"Alert, bomber coming in from nine o'clock," the sentry reported in a hushed breath.

Stepping to the open side of the carriage, the short man squinted at the blinking lights in the sky. No military plane would announce its presence like that, unless it was pretending to be a civilian transport.

"I don't think that's a bomber," he said into the radio. "But no sense taking any chances, eh?"

Nodding agreement, the giant powered up the Sterling and used the joystick to realign the cannon, and sprayed that entire section of the horizon. There was no immediate change in the course of the high-altitude plane.

"Did you miss?" the short man snarled, readying the Stinger. His fingers were clumsy on the controls. "Malavade should have placed me in charge, by Shiva, at least that way—"

The blinking lights disappeared, then reappeared. The process repeated over and over, rapidly descending as the pilotless jumbo jet spiraled toward the ground.

"You were saying?" The giant chuckled, baring his teeth.

"Nothing." The short man sighed, feeling a trickle of sweat run down his back. "I was saying nothing at all."

"Good. Go help with the hovercraft."

"Yes. Of course."

A sign flashed by. Forty kilometers to Chernobyl.

Long minutes passed as the street toughs anxiously watched the sky for any suspicious movements. Sharing a bottle of wine, the men checked their weapons for the hundredth time.

Feeling a gnawing sensation in his guts, the short man turned on the radar. He knew it was foolish, but the blank screen would help him relax. Thirty kilometers to go. As the screen warmed, there immediately came a multiple set of images streaking low across the ground, coming at the train.

"Missiles!" he cried in horror. "Two from the east…and two—no, three from the south!"

"Use the decoy!" the giant ordered, revving the generator to full power. "And everybody into the hovercraft. We leave now!"

"But the reactor…"

"We'll turn the cannon on and let it sweep the countryside," the big man said, working the controls. "Eventually it'll hit the reactor." Along with several small towns along the way. But that really wasn't his concern. Everybody died.

Going to a small control box hanging by insulated wires from the wall, the short man pressed the first button. Instantly there came a muffled explosion behind them from the M-2 tetrytol charge wired to the coupling of the caboose. As the caboose fell behind, the train started moving faster from the lightened load. A moment later the second M-2 charge hidden under the caboose detonated and the car erupted into flames.

On the radar, the short man saw the missiles change course and lock on to the greatest heat source. A few seconds later the caboose thunderously exploded. Victory! Mr. Malavade really knew his weapons. There was a reason he was the biggest weapons dealer in Asia. There was no military system he couldn't outwit.

Then the radar beeped again.

"More missiles," he announced, swallowing hard.

"Then do it again," the team leader commanded gruffly.

Flipping the next set of switches, the short man disconnected the last carriage of the train and allowed it to fall far behind before the M-2 charge was ignited. Tetrytol was strong stuff, three times as powerful as C-4.

The missiles took the bait and struck the railroad car full of dead civilians with devastating results.

"And the cannon is live," the giant declared, stepping away from the device. Behind the shimmering Faraday Cage, the beamer was softly humming. Locked in position, everything in the east of the train was dying as it moved into the invisible beam sweeping along the Ukraine countryside.

Swinging in through the open door, the rooftop sentry paused to study the countryside rushing past. "How many people you think we're killing right now?" the man asked, his face shiny with excitement.

"Who cares? They're just peasants," the team leader declared cavalierly. "Smelly untouchables. We're doing them a favor taking away their miserable lives."

"Wish I could see," the street tough muttered, the sound becoming a lusty chuckle.

The short man looked upon the giggling fellow with open disdain. A death freak, just like Vinsara. Disgusting. "Just get in the damn hovercraft," he snarled, giving the fellow a hard shove.

As the team clambered into the craft, the short man went to the other side of the carriage and released the lock to pull aside the sliding door. They certainly weren't going to leave through the active beam of the cannon!

But as the wooden panel moved back, a hovering trio of helicopters was revealed moving alongside the train. Two of them were Apache gunships carrying the logo of NATO, and the third was a MI-25 HND emblazoned with the seal of the Ukrainian Air Defense Force. The rushing wind and the clattered of the rails under the metal wheels of the train muffling the sound of the throbbing engines to a low moan.

Still working, the radar screen showed clean, even as the beam moved across the three military gunships.

They jammed the radar! Snarling a curse, the short man dived to the side, scrambling for the neutron cannon. If he could just reach it in time...

In the hovercraft, the men pulled out their AK-101 assault rifles and started firing wildly. Grabbing a U.S. Army LAW rocket launcher, the giant team leader swung it toward the helicopters as he worked the unfamiliar controls.

With their targets in sight, and no hostages visible, the two NATO Apaches cut loose with the their rocket pods. The 35 mm minirockets tore the roof off the carriage, exposing the men and neutron cannon inside.

Slammed hard by the violent explosion, the short man was just able to grab the joystick of the neutron cannon when the cannon's locking mechanism released. He shrieked as the weapon swung around freely, killing the criminals in the hovercraft, taking out an Apache and then sending him into the Stygian blackness of forever.

The dead Apache drifted away as the Ukrainian Air Defense HND unleashed a salvo of 57 mm rockets at point-blank range. In a double explosion, the carriage was destroyed, reduced to wheels and burning floorboards. Tumbling off the train, the self-destruct of the neutron cannon went off, the thermal blast throwing out a hellstorm of shrapnel.

The two gunships were hammered by incoming debris. The windshield cracked on the HND, and the

Apache started trailing smoke from its engine. But the damaged helicopters retaliated with every weapon on board, determined to end this before another civilian died. In a seemingly endless series of explosions, the carriage was blown clear off the tracks, the attached carriages twisting along with the flaming wreckage as the train was pulled into the clover field, the tortured metal screaming like a dying beast as the charges on the couplings ignited.

Throwing out a tidal wave of dirt and plants, carriages rammed into carriages, the hideous crunch of wood rising into a deafening cacophony of destruction. Bodies crashed through the glass windows. Then as the engine tilted over, the fuel tank ripped open. With a roar, the thousands of gallons whoofed into flames, creating a hellish pyre visible for miles.

Circling the burning wreckage, the Apache and the HND landed in the field of churned earth, and armed soldiers came charging out to start searching among the fiery wreckage for any remaining pieces of the neutron cannon.

Bombay, India

DRIVING ACROSS TOWN, Phoenix Force slowly crept through the rush-hour traffic. Which never seemed to end.

Gazing at the buildings lining every road, McCarter saw old but clean stores filled with advanced electronics. Signs were everywhere, partially obscuring the buildings and in a few cases almost seeming to hold up the ancient structures. Pre-Victorian shops with twenty-first-century Plexiglas doors. What a wild country.

Along the way, James sent a coded radio message to the Farm. It took Kurtzman and his team only a few minutes to access the computer files of Thane High Security Prison, and grant McCarter limited access to the prisoner. That was about as far as they dared go. Anything more would have raised suspicions about the unannounced visit. Kantin Hu was a traitor, a spy for Pakistan, but granted life imprisonment because he released his hostages before surrendering. Many people in India were furious over the deal. But the government knew that peace with their hated enemy would only come from showing compassion, and establishing that their word was good. The spy would live, no matter how much they also wished to see him sitting in an electric chair.

Reaching a suburban area, the team was assailed by the music of drums and cymbals booming from CD players carried by pedestrians, and a score of live bands performing on the rooftops. Flowers were everywhere, festooning light poles or draped from balconies. The design of a blue lotus was prevalent. But just about every kind of flower imaginable was evident. The crowded streets smelled like an arboretum in springtime.

Slowly passing a bus stop, Hawkins could read a poster pasted on the side. It seemed to be there just for the tourists. Apparently, this was the October festival for Durga. Ten thousand years ago, a demon had been killing millions of humans, so Lord Shiva sent out some lighting from his third eye and it transformed into the goddess Durga. Equipped with a different weapon on each of her ten arms, Durga killed the demon and saved humanity. This was a celebration of life, and brotherhood.

Parking the car blocks away from the prison, McCarter got rid of his weapons and walked along the street to the monolithic building. Thane resembled a medieval fortress because it was; its massive stone walls designed to halt invading armies served well to contain the population of murderers, thieves and rapists. The walls were topped with concertina wire, and guard towers rose at every corner, festooned with search lights and heavy-caliber machine guns. The chance of breaking into the prison was as slim as anybody's chance of breaking out.

At the front gate McCarter showed his identification and waited for clearance. When it was finally granted, he was frisked by experts and taken to a holding area where he was frisked again and his ID checked once more. McCarter was impressed. Nothing illicit was being smuggled into Thane, which was probably why nobody had escaped in more than a century.

Eventually, a team of guards was sent to meet McCarter, and he was escorted down a long corridor, their footsteps echoing off the bare stone walls. The floor was painted concrete, the roof unpainted steel. The corridor felt like a morgue. Stopping at an iron gate, McCarter waited while his escorts used a hardline telephone to check on his credentials once more. When authorization came, the guard on the other side of the barrier undid the heavy locks, muttering under his breath in Hindi.

"Was that directed to me?" McCarter challenged.

Shocked at being addressed, the man recoiled slightly, then muttered an apology as he unlocked the gate to let them through.

"I thought you could not speak our language," a guard said in halting English.

"I can't," McCarter responded. "But I didn't like his tone."

The guard relayed this to the others, and the men shared a laugh.

"You are military, no?" the guard asked.

"Sorry, no," McCarter lied.

Frowning, the guard then shrugged. Everybody had their little secrets. Even the guards of Thane.

A bare corridor led to another set of gates, then another. McCarter had his credentials checked again and was finally shown into a small room. The place was bare, the only furniture being a steel table bolted to the concrete floor and a couple of folding chairs. The walls were solid, without windows.

A tall gangly man with scraggly hair sat in one of the chairs, his eyes watching McCarter intently.

Walking casually, McCarter took the opposite chair. There was no need to ask for any identification. The Stony Man commando recognized the spy from his dossier photo. Kantin Hu had been described as a cross between a snake and a rat. The depiction was apt. Hu radiated menace, and McCarter could feel the waves of hatred coming from the prisoner like heat from a furnace. This wasn't a man to be trifled with, and McCarter decided to play straight with the prisoner. Anything less, and Hu would probably close up like a bank vault on Sunday.

"They told me you speak English," McCarter said.

"I do," Hu replied sullenly.

"Good." Taking off his watch, McCarter placed it on the steel table and pressed the stud twice. The device began softly vibrating. "That's a Humbug. Every working microphone within fifty feet is now dead. We can talk freely."

Hu tilted his head. "And how do I know such a thing is true?"

Leaning forward, McCarter looked the prisoner straight in the face. "Because I give you my word."

After a moment, Hu grunted in acceptance. "Got a smoke?"

Expecting this request, McCarter set a fresh pack on the table and slid it across.

Eagerly, Hu unwrapped the plastic and breathed in the rich aroma of the fresh tobacco, savoring it like wine, before extracting one and placing it in his mouth. He waited.

McCarter tossed over a pack of matches. That had been a test. If the Stony Man commando had tried to light the cigarette for him, that would have been seen as pandering, and Hu would have ended this meeting on the spot.

Lighting the cigarette, Hu took the smoke deep into his lungs, then turned red and coughed for several minutes until getting it under control.

"Alas, it has been too many years," Hu said sadly, reluctantly placing aside the smoking cigarette. "I still want one, but my lungs…it was like trying them for the first time."

"And the longing never goes away," McCarter said

honestly, remembering his occasional attempt to stop the habit. "You just have to learn control."

The convict laughed bitterly. "Control? Yes, that I have learned many times over. When there is nothing else, there is always self-control." Taking the pack, he held it questioningly. "These would buy me many small pleasures." It was said as a statement, the question unasked.

Pretending he didn't care, McCarter gave a slight wave and the prisoner tucked the pack into his shirt pocket. Now, the two men understood each other.

"So why have you come here, British?" Hu asked. "What do you need from a dirty traitor, eh?"

"It's more a question of what you want," McCarter shot back.

"I want to be free!" Hu laughed bitterly. "I want my health. I wish for a woman, and a gun, and…"

"Malavade."

The prisoner scowled. "Him, I wish dead," he rasped. "Many, many times over. As painfully as possible."

"Perhaps that can be arranged," McCarter said softly.

Silently, the prisoner asked a question.

"My…associates wish to locate Mr. Malavade to tender our disappointment about a recent shipment," McCarter lied smoothly.

"That is a difficult thing to do," Hu replied, resting his arms on the metal table. The chains on his wrists clanked at the motion. "Mohad does his business through the wires, Internet, telephone, or through his staff. Nobody ever gets to see him directly."

"Unless they're being shot in the head."

Hu blushed at that reference and reached up to stroke the white scar between his eyes. He had tried to steal a shipment of weapons from Malavade, and received a bullet between the eyes for the effort. Hu survived, but spent six months in a New Delhi hospital learning to walk and talk again.

"Yes, that is one of the few times," Hu agreed with a lot of growl. "But why should I do this thing? Can you arrange for my parole?"

"No," McCarter lied. "But perhaps we can come to another type of arrangement." Actually, between Hal Brognola and Kurtzman, he could get Hu back on the street in a few hours. But that would only result in more civilian deaths. McCarter had to negotiate with the prisoner, while denying him the one thing Hu wanted most. Freedom. Hopefully, the second thing he wanted would suffice.

"Like what?" Hu scowled. "My family and friends are all dead. I have nobody, and nothing in the world. What can you offer me?"

"Revenge. Tell me how to find Malavade, and he will die."

Hu inhaled sharply. "You say such a thing out loud?"

"Yes."

Slowly the prisoner began to smile. "Accepted," he said. "All right, Mohad has a mansion in New Delhi. But he never goes there. The same with his famous mistress in Bombay. She's just a former whore, taken off the street and paid not to fuck. But she never gets any visits from Malavade. He is far too clever for that.

He has built a fake life, an artificial existence so that his enemies may search, and search, but never find him."

This was all new, but McCarter said, "Tell me something I don't know."

Slowly, Hu leaned back in the chair. "By Shiva, even if I cannot smoke, I still do miss cigarettes. And with nobody to send them to me…." He flipped a hand.

"I'll arrange for a carton a week to be delivered," McCarter offered.

"Five."

"Two."

"Three."

"Done."

"Done," Hu repeated with satisfaction. "There is a skyscraper in Calcutta…"

McCarter arched an eyebrow at that.

"Yes, Calcutta." Hu grinned. "The Victoria Towers. You know how many European buildings do not have a thirteenth floor, because it is bad luck?"

"Yes, but what…"

"Well, Indians do not have that superstition." Hu grimaced. "At least, the Hindus and Muslims, anyway. Now, this particular building does have a thirteenth floor." He paused. "As well as a pair of twenty floors."

"Two of them?" McCarter leaned closer. "And only one is listed."

"Exactly."

"Interesting. How do I find this hidden floor? Are there stairs?"

"No, the stairs have been altered somehow, they go

past that level. There is an elevator, yes, but it is heavily guarded, and explosives line the shaft. Along with video cameras, secret microphones, proximity sensors, pressure plates..." He waved at the technology, dismissing it. "Mohad is not a fool. He has access to advanced technology from around the world. All of it has been used to guarantee his safety."

"Then how do we get inside?"

Leaning back in his chair, Hu laughed. "If I knew that, I would not have this," he said, rubbing the scar.

"Fair enough." McCarter stood and donned his watch. "Thank you."

"Is...is there any chance of me seeing a photograph of the corpse afterward?" Hun asked plaintively, hope thick in his words. "I would enjoy that very much."

The request was ghoulish, but according to the medical reports, Hu should have died long ago from his injury. Hate was the only thing keeping the man alive.

"Look for a pack of Player's cigarettes in the cartons of Marlboros," McCarter whispered, going to turn off his watch.

"Wait!" Hu cried, raising a hand. "I thank you for the courtesy, and now offer a gift in return."

McCarter frowned. "What kind of a gift?"

"There are gunports in the front wall of Mohad's office, and mines in the ceiling. I never could get precise details. But if you walk directly to his office, you will not reach it alive."

McCarter grunted. "When we put him down, I'll mention your name," he promised.

"If you shoot him in the head, do it several times," Hu muttered, rubbing his scar once more. "One bullet does not always get the job done."

CHAPTER SEVENTEEN

Laputa Missile Complex

Six radios played softly along the control room of the underground base. Two of them were tuned to music stations, two to news reports. The last two were set for the audio broadcast of television stations in Moscow. The steel door behind him was locked tight. The seals were activated, and the lieutenant was breathing canned air from fifty years ago.

All around the control room, computers hummed and indicators blinked, while meters wavered with precise details on the five huge ICBMs fueled and ready to go only twenty feet away.

Listening to the radios, the lieutenant sat uncomfortably in the cushioned chair at his elaborate control panel, a 9 mm Gyrza pistol lying nearby. Even before the American President had informed the United Nations Security Council about the neutron cannon in orbit, the generals at the Kremlin had deduced what really happened to the MiG fighter over Moscow and placed the entire Rocket Brigade on full alert status. Ready for war. If any of the radios went suddenly off the air, or if some Russian official toppled over mysteriously, then the missiles would fly.

To be honest, the lieutenant didn't know what the ICBMs were aimed at, and he really didn't care. His trust in the Kremlin was absolute. If they said launch, then he would turn the key and unleash the thermonuclear might of Mother Russia at whatever enemy they deemed proper. The ancient Cossack blood in the officer flowed hot at the prospect, but the man forced down the savage feelings. He would wait patiently for the launch code, as was his duty.

Stony Man Farm, Virginia

THE DOOR TO THE COMPUTER ROOM swung aside and a blacksuit carried in a tray of sandwiches. The room was deathly quiet.

"Repeat, call off the bombing," Barbara Price said into a receiver. "Target location is unknown....roger. Out."

"Is Able Team okay?" Kurtzman asked from his workstation.

"They'll live," Price replied. "Just pissed as hell. It's strange the terrorists didn't use the cannon on them."

"Maybe it's broken," he suggested. "Or they have limited fuel to operate the device."

"More likely, they didn't want to start a city-wide panic and block the streets until their primary target had been hit." So far, all of their targets had been secret, no sporting events or shopping malls. It was as if Malavade only wanted the governments of the world to know of the weapon's existence, but not the public. What was the arms dealer planning?

"Okay, I have confirmation," Akira announced, turning away from his monitors. "There are six neutron cannons."

"Six?" Price demanded, frowning. "Are you sure?"

"Positive. I concentrated my search on only the more esoteric items needed to build the weapon. Based upon his theoretical work ten years ago."

"And you came up with six?"

"Either that, or Mohad has a million of them."

"All right, there was Braintree, the North Atlantic, the Ukraine and Sri Lanka," Kurtzman said, counting on his fingers. "Are you including the damaged one recovered from the wrecked van?"

"Of course."

"Then that's five, which leaves one more, whereabouts unknown," Price finished. "Hunt, how is the dummy coming along?"

"Already finished and ready to go," Wethers replied, rubbing his eyes. "Give the word and I'll flood the Internet with a hundred different copies of fake blueprints that will only radiate a location signal as to their whereabouts, but wouldn't harm a fly. NATO can then gather in the fools at gunpoint."

"Excellent."

"Carmen, any word on those t-bursts?" Kurtzman demanded.

"I finally tracked them. Mohad is having an auction for the weapon," she replied, sitting motionless. "I've traced the t-bursts to a VR room in Sweden, but there's no mention what is for sale. And all requests for information have been denied."

"If you don't know," Price growled humorlessly, "then you're not important enough, or rich enough, to partake."

"Exactly."

"Have any of the Dirty Dozen gotten an offer?"

"Checking," Delahunt replied.

Long ago, Mack Bolan had suggested the creation of some artificial buyers of weapon. In virtual reality that was relatively easy. But Kurtzman had decided to take the matter one step further. He and his team had created a dozen artificial personalities in all of the major areas of crime: smuggling, drugs, assassinations, money laundering, fencing stolen goods, along with a team of black op mercs called Blue Lightning.

When the Stony Man hackers patrolled the Internet, they would post coded messages of total gibberish to and from the Dirty Dozen. On the open Internet, one of them would rent a penthouse in Canberra, Australia, and another bought a Rolls-Royce in Paris, a third demanded a score of prostitutes in Tokyo for a party. The Yakuza were invited, caterers hired, a band was rented. Hundreds of people arrived, and afterward everybody chatted about the event, several of them boasting that they cut lucrative business deals with the nonexistent criminal.

During the Meternich incident a while ago, it had seemed strange to some terrorist organizations that none of the Dirty Dozen had tried to buy targets. Quickly changing their game plan, Kurtzman and his people planted rumors that Meternich had actually been the front man for the Dozen. With the well-known history of the group, the lie was easily accepted. After that, the Stony Man operatives were much more careful about maintaining the cover of their incorporeal agents.

"Absolutely. Sheikh Abdul "Benny" Hassan in Jordan was sent an invitation," Tokaido replied without looking up from his console. "And I still hate that name. The word 'ben' means 'son of,' it's not the short version of Benjamin."

"Just a bit of color to make the sheikh more memorable," Kurtzman replied, sipping from a fresh cup of coffee. "We've made it known that he hates his father and has renounced his family. That way, there are no ties to any folks who actually have the last name of Hassan. Besides, it makes him more sympathetic."

"To murderers and thieves?"

"Absolutely. Even terrorists have families."

"The secret history of a nonexistent criminal lord," Wethers muttered, sliding disks into his console slots. "We could have used you, my friend, during the cold war."

Walking closer to the NASA map on the wall screen, Price placed hands on her hips and made grinding sounds with her teeth. She still could not figure out where the blue Dodge van was going. Madison Square had the Ice Capades, and there were a dozen shows running on Broadway, but those were all very public. What was there in New York that involved the greatest amount of government officials, preferably with multinational ties…

"Oh shit," the woman gasped, turning around fast. "Bear, sound the alarm! I know where they're going to strike next. The United Nations!"

"Too late!" Kurtzman swore, slamming his fists on the console. "Malavade just released a t-burst telling everybody to watch the television for news from Manhattan. The crazy bastard is going to kill the delegates just to prove the weapon's power!"

He was no longer hiding the deaths. Price had been afraid of that. The kid gloves were coming off. Now it was going to be bare-knuckle fighting. But Stony Man could do that, too.

"Okay, send this message fast," she said, worrying a lip. "Tell Malavade that…tell him that…" Price smiled. "Tell Mohad Malavade that Sheikh Abdul Benny Hassan is at the UN, and offers one million dollars not to do the demonstration."

Kurtzman grunted in admiration of the brilliant ploy and got to work, his hands playing across the keyboards.

"Now to make it sound real," Price continued. "Counteroffer with two million dollars from…Richard Tucholka in Detroit to kill the sheikh anyway."

"And the sheikh responds with five million not to do it," Kurtzman continued.

A tense minute passed, then two.

"Malavade bought the deal." Kurtzman sighed, leaning back in his wheelchair. "He's shutting down the cannon."

Five million dollars to save several hundred ambassadors of peace. Price gave a hard grin. That was the best bargain she had ever purchased.

"Unfortunately, since three of the Dirty Dozen are so hot for the weapon," Delahunt said, fondling the air with her cybernetic gloves. "It's hit the fan. Like it or not, the auction has begun in earnest."

"Everybody hop on board fast!" Kurtzman commanded, slaving their readouts to his submonitors.

The team lurched into action, activating their artificial personalities across the world.

"What's the current price?" the mission controller asked, studying the wall monitor. It was scrolling with encoded data bytes, incomprehensible to a mere mortal.

"The Hamas has bid a million Euros for one of the units," Delahunt announced in a deceptively calm voice. "I've had Etta Caramico of Bolivia match that."

"Tucholka upped that to one million point three," Tokaido said, increasing the volume on his stereo. The thumping rock music pounded audibly from his headphones.

And so the bidding went, progressively climbing.

"The Koreans are offering seventeen," Tokaido announced. "And somebody named Unity has gone to twenty…"

"Thirty," Kurtzman said. "Time to flex some monetary muscle."

As he placed the bid, a terror group from France appeared and counteroffered with fifty million for the satellite. Then Libya bid fifty-one. Pakistan went to sixty. Unity came back with sixty-five.

This was becoming a feeding frenzy, Price realized. The governments of the world bidding against the criminal underworld. This was what Malavade had been planning along, to turn the prospective buyers against one another and drive the price through the roof. The woman had to admire the technique, even as she arranged for his violent demise. "Okay, offer seventy."

"Al Qaeda just upped that to seventy-five," Tokaido announced, leaning into the console as if physically involved in the auction.

"Eighty!" Kurtzman growled.

"Ninety from North Korea."

"A hundred million euros!"

"Hundred and ten for Syria."

"Offer a quarter billion," Price said impatiently, tired of the gamesmanship.

"No!" Kurtzman cried, swiveling around in his wheelchair. "That's too much, too fast!"

"And possibly too late," Tokaido frowned, popping his chewing gum. "Our hosts are suspicious of the sheikh and are trying to run a trace."

"On it," Wethers replied.

This was the tricky part, Price knew. If the trace succeeded, their bid would be ignored. If it failed, Malavade would probably cancel it anyway just to be safe. Either way spelled disaster. The only chance was to become Hassan.

Already established in sequence, a score of telecommunication satellites around the globe bounced the signals from the Farm through a maze of relays. But not so complex that Malavade couldn't follow. The arms dealer almost lost the trace at a Cray Supercomputer in Seattle, then Wethers let the probe break through to the final destination of a yacht off the coast of Chile. The registration was for A.B.H. Industries, Athens, Greece. A known alias for the fictitious sheikh.

"They've accepted that we are Sheikh Hassan." Wethers grinned in relief. "I must say that the person running his computers is very good. Very good, indeed. I beat him to the draw. But just barely."

"Syria offers seven hundred million."

"America counters with eight hundred." But was rejected. It was the target, after all.

Price saw the Mossad, the CIA and MI-6 had joined battering at the firewall. Soon enough, some government agency would break through and end the auction, killing Stony Man's only chance to retrieve the remaining weapons—if there was more than one—without the loss of civilian lives. Kurtzman probably could have slowed the other groups for a while, but he was too busy maintaining his artificial persona. There was nothing she could do to help at the moment, and she raged at the feeling of helplessness.

Red China raised to nine hundred million.

Suddenly alarms went off and Price saw the wall screen go blank. The firewall had been breached by the CIA! Instantly everything was gone, the links broken, the graphics fading into a haze of pixels. Soon, there was only the soft hiss of static from the dead connection.

"Well?" Price demanded anxiously.

"We…did it," Kurtzman said in amazement. "Sheikh Abdul Benny Hassan bought the damn thing for one billion euros. There will be no further attacks on anybody, until he gives Malavade a target."

"For the satellite that doesn't exist."

"Yep."

Kurtzman rubbed his face with both hands. "Of course, now Malavade has the funds to actually put the freaking thing into orbit for real."

"Bite your tongue," Price scolded with a frown. "But just in case, Akira, could you…"

"Already setting the Watchdog satellites to stay alert for any unannounced launches in the next twenty-four hours," he told her. "And if I find something?"

"Have the F-22 Raptors blow the rocket out of the sky before the payload reaches orbit."

"Done."

"Okay, people, we just bought the teams a day, maybe less, to find those remaining neutron cannons," Kurtzman declared, cracking his knuckles. "After that, we have to start supplying Malavade with target locations, or he'll get suspicious again."

"I'll begin lining up known terrorist training camps to take out," Delahunt said, accessing files. "And I have several deserted mesas in Nevada and Australia already listed with Interpol as possible drug factories."

Apparently the redhead was way ahead of them again. "Good. Add a couple of yachts far at sea, well away from the commercial lines," he directed.

"On it."

CHAPTER EIGHTEEN

Victoria Towers, Calcutta

"How soon can you transfer the money?" Malavade asked, almost dancing with happiness.

Still typing at the keyboard, Metudas shrugged. "Doing it right now, sir," he reported. "Just takes a while to wash that large an amount through sixteen banks. Are you sure that we need all of them?"

"Just do as you're told," Malavade snorted, then scowled. Through the cold window, he could see one of the lobby guards staggering along the hallway as if drunk.

Outrageous! Stepping outside the refrigerated room, Malavade started to curse the man when he notice blood all over the front of this shirt, dribbling down from the slash across his neck. What was going on here?

Reaching out for his employer, the guard fell to his knees, gurgling inarticulately, exposing the arrow sticking out his back.

"We have intruders!" Malavade shouted, pulling out his Desert Eagle and racking the slide.

Just then the dim sound of machine-gun fire made Malavade jerk his head toward the elevator. Backing toward his office, the arms dealer almost fired when a lavatory door was thrown open and another guard stumbled out, his chest riddled with arrows. For a split second Malavade saw a group of armed men in the tiled room. Big men wearing yellow masks striped with black.

Charging around the corner, Malavade was met by Vinsara and six more guards.

"Office!" the crime lord ordered. "It's Tiger Force."

Scowling darkly, Vinsara took the lead. Kicking open the door, he swept the room with his Chinese QBZ assault rifle, looking for live targets. But there was nobody in sight.

A guard started to close the door when a machine gun chattered and a rain of slugs threw the man backward to land dead at the feet of the furious crime lord.

"Shoot the doors!" Vinsara shouted, working the bolt on his assault rifle.

The remaining guards did as they were ordered, the pistol rounds smacking into the wooden veneer and slamming the doors shut.

Rushing to the wall, Malavade yanked off a picture and threw a switch, the doors locking tight.

"Arm up," Vinsara shouted, going to a closet, pulling aside the wall and a sliding panel to reveal an arsenal of weaponry.

"How did they find me?" Malavade raged, holstering

the Desert Eagle and taking down an American M-16.
He worked the bolt, chambering a round, then slipped
a belt of ammunition over a shoulder.

The door shuddered from incoming rounds, but the
steel plates inside the wood veneer prevented a breech.

Moving fast, the guards snatched INS assault rifles
and Neostad shotguns, plus bags of ammo.

"How should I know, sir?" Vinsara muttered, slinging the QBZ rifle across his back and grabbing an MM-1
grenade launcher. He cracked the breech to check the
load of 40 mm shells, then closed it with a clank and
flicked off the safety. "Maybe we have a traitor in the
organization!"

"If there is, I'll eat his living heart," the crime lord
snarled. "Try to save one of these attackers for questioning!"

Hefting the MM-1, Vinsara grinned. "I shall do my
best, sir. But no promises."

Malavade took heart at the bravado. He had been
startled at first, but now was safe in his office. His old
headquarters on University Street had been attacked
many times in the past by rival gangs, and once by the
Yakuza. The fools always seemed to think that he kept
huge amounts of supplies on the premises. His stock of
ordnance was kept in a series of warehouses outside the
city, and the cash was in a vault underneath the basement. How anybody could have gained access to this
floor was beyond his understanding. Besides, there was
nothing much here but the Cray supercomputers.

And him. For a brief second, Malavade felt a flicker
of fear.

Moving aside sections of the decorative paneling, the guards revealed firing slots in the concrete wall. The corridor was thick with swirling clouds of smoke. Malavade recognized the type. Those were an expensive German make, not something he kept in stock. That wasn't good.

Thrusting their weapons through, they opened fire, spraying the corridor with streams of high-velocity lead.

Fiery flowers appeared sporadically in the billowing fumes, the heavy-caliber bullets slamming into desks, throwing out a spray of splinters and annihilating a samovar.

A couple of guards caught outside the office stayed low behind the smashed furniture, then covered the area with a volley from handguns and machine pistols. One man lobbed a grenade into the cloud. A few seconds later there was a thundering explosion that rocked the entire floor. The cloud roiled with flames and the ceiling water sprinklers gushed into life.

There was no movement inside the computer room.

Insanely stepping into view, a guard carrying a street sweeper fired several rounds down the corridor, the spent aluminum shells arching high to the right and bouncing off the wall. The blasts were deafening.

A dull roar replied, a tongue of flame stretching out from the dark smoke. Caught reloading, the guard seemed to explode, his arms torn off his body as his chest burst in bloody gobbets. The shotgun went flying, still firing for a second into the ceiling. The acoustical foam tiles were shredded, exposing the metal strut holding them in place and a seamless slab of concrete.

"That was an elephant gun," Vinsara snarled, burping the MM-1 launcher through a narrow gun slot. "I wonder why they haven't tried to use it on the—"

With a strident bang, the door bulged, the veneer cracking off the burnished steel plating.

Quickly reloading, the guards started firing into the water and smoke outside the office, brass flying everywhere. The dull roar sounded again, and one of the hinges bent, the door collapsing at the top corner.

As the guards fired again, Malavade grabbed the phone and hit a red button. The line was still live, and there came an answering beep. He hung up the receiver with some satisfaction. Reinforcements would arrive from the warehouses in less than ten minutes.

The wall cracked and dented again, but again no penetration.

The crime lord began to smile. The fools in Tiger Force had made a very bad mistake in judgment tangling with him!

Going to a gunport, Malavade shoved the M-16 through and emptied a clip at the invaders. Incredibly, a fiery column extended up the corridor. Flamethrower! Malavade ducked, writhing tendrils of fire reaching through the gun ports. As the fire withdrew, he risked a glimpse.

Caught directly in the wash, the guards outside were covered with flames. Shrieking wildly, they dashed around waving their arms. Then their gunbelts started banging as the extra ammunition began to cook off from the heat.

"Poor bastards," Vinsara muttered, pumping a fast

couple of rounds from the MM-1 at the dying men. The fléchettes in the antipersonnel rounds mercifully tore the guards apart and annihilated everything in sight, gouging out chunks from the marble walls and floor. The water sprinklers ceased to gush, dribbling impotently from the bare ceiling.

"Hit 'em hard!" Malavade cried, switching to the 40 mm grenade launcher slung underneath the main barrel of the M-16.

The other guards sent out a hellstorm of lead and steel, and Vinsara adjusted the MM-1, then launched a couple of fat canisters. As they hit the ruined flooring, the canisters burst, gushing a hideous yellow smoke.

Almost immediately, the unseen attackers began to scream and curse.

"More! Give them more!" Malavade shouted in delight. The Punjabi terrorists might have been smart enough to bring along gas masks, but they wouldn't do them any good against mustard gas, which also worked on skin contact. The water would have neutralized that gas, but now that the sprinklers were off, there was no defense. He fired another long burst of perfectly imbalanced 5.56 mm tumblers into the yellow death cloud. Mercy was for the weak. He just wanted to hear the bastards start to scream in agony again.

Reloading, Malavade noticed a small light flashing near the built-in bar. The elevator doors had been forced open.

"They're trying to escape!" Vinsara shouted, dropping the empty MM-1 and swinging around his Chinese assault rifle. "Let's get 'em!"

Striding to the wall, Malavade pulled the release lever and the battered doors swung open with a groan of tortured metal. Shouting a rallying cry, the guards rushed from the office firing their weapons nonstop.

Letting the others mop up the would-be invaders, Malavade went behind his desk and dropped gratefully into the cushioned leather chair. What a day! He made a billion euros, and then some dirt-eaters from the south tried to take him down.

Tossing the assault rifle onto the desktop, Malavade hit the intercom to see if Metudas was still alive, when he heard a burbling from behind, like a samovar ready for tea. His blood ran cold and the crime lord swung around in the chair to see a team of window washers standing on a platform outside the building. The men were dressed in tan coveralls and cloth hats, but instead of carrying squeegees, they were carrying pressurized canisters on their backs and hosing some sort of foaming gray compound along the frame of the thick bullet-proof window.

It took a full second for Malavade to recognize it as as the new C-5 foaming gel explosive. A double attack! Grabbing the M-16, he ducked under the desk and prayed.

A heartbeat later the world was filled with a deafening blast, jagged shards of glass and big chunks of Plexiglas hurtling across the office. Hugging the assault rifle, Malavade was slammed by the concussion and hit his head against the armored front of the desk. The universe spun for a moment, but he didn't lose consciousness.

Crouching on the floor, the crime lord saw a dozen large men in janitor uniforms step through the jagged remains of the twisted frame, their gloved hands filled with Atchisson shotguns. Staying where he was, Malavade shot the men in the legs. In a spray of blood, three of them dropped, and the fourth staggered through the smashed window and fell from view. His scream seemed to last forever.

A gloved hand reached down from above and yanked the assault rifle from Malavade's grip. Snarling a curse, the crime lord fumbled for his Desert Eagle. But a man squatted in front of him, holding an Atchisson.

"Stand," the big man ordered, his voice oddly distorted.

The stranger grabbed the front of Malavade's shirt and physically hauled the crime lord out in the open. The arms dealer whipped out his .357 Magnum, but the stranger slapped the gun away, then beat his prisoner with a closed fist.

"Mercy!" Malavade begged. "Please, I'll give you anything you want!"

The stranger paused at that. "You say such a thing to me?" His voice rumbled. "Fat man, do you know who I am?"

Malavade shook his head, tears hot on his cheeks.

From down the corridor there came the sound of machine-gun fire and men dying. The voice sounded familiar.

"Fool, I am Ravid Komar, the commander of Tiger Force."

The crime lord went pale and seemed to have trouble breathing. He had thought the attackers were just impostors trying to frighten people by pretending to be the dreaded terrorists, or at worst some former members of the group, but not Komar himself. Killer Komar. Komar The Mad.

"Sir, I can understand your displeasure with me…" Malavade began in a rush of words.

With a snort, Komar flicked his left hand and a long, thin stiletto dropped into his palm. Bringing up the knife, the terrorist pressed the needle-sharp tip into the soft flesh just below Malavade's left eye.

The crime lord went absolutely still.

"You are going to die today," Komar said in an inhuman voice. "Have no doubt about that. The only question is how long it will take."

Malavade heard the words, but couldn't take his sight away from the shiny steel blade pressing into his face. A tiny trickle of red began to move along the stiletto, and he realized it was his own blood.

"But first…"

The blade flashed upward.

Screeching, Malavade dropped to his knees, cradling the gaping hole in his face. White-hot pain blossomed across his face, bloody fluids trickling through his trembling hands.

"That was just to get your attention," Komar snarled in his deep bass. "I want you to tell me everything about this new weapon you have stolen. This so-called neutron cannon. Where is it, how do I control it, and exactly how many people can it kill at a time?"

As a smiling Vinsara walked into the office flanked

by the masked members of Tiger Force, Malavade suddenly knew who the traitor was in his organization, and that his famous luck had finally run out.

CHAPTER NINETEEN

Manhattan

Sunlight slashed across the blue Dodge van from the nearby towering billboard advertising a new toothpaste. Two men and a woman hunched in their seats inside the vehicle, watching everything, their weapons at the ready.

However, there was no motion from the up ramp. Off in the far corner of the roof a group of teenagers sat drinking from paper bags and dangling their sneakers over the edge of the building. Occasionally, money would be exchanged for small plastic bags. Drugs were clearly being purchased. The Indian criminal knew Mr. Malavade had chosen this location well. It had to be an area infrequently patrolled by the N.Y.P.D.

The street traffic had been thin in New York, at least it was compared to Calcutta during rush hour. Many of the drivers were chatting on cell phones or drinking from plastic mugs. Some of the women were putting on their cosmetics behind the wheel. Incredible. But nobody had turned their car off to conserve fuel. The team had reached the parking garage with another brush with the American FBI, or whoever it was that had attacked them back at the holding facility.

The interior of the van was a bloody mess. The ballistic armor bolted to the sides had stopped the hardball rounds of the M-16 assault rifles from penetrating the chassis, but the hail of bullets that poured in through the broken rear window had rattled about inside the van like marbles in a can. Three of their brothers had been killed, the bodies almost minced from the fusillade. But their deaths had stopped the bullets from hitting the neutron cannon. Their families would receive a bonus from Mr. Malavade for that. Without ceremony, the riddled corpses had been dumped in a dirty alley near Central Park before the last three members of the team drove to the top of the parking garage to await the order to attack.

Straight ahead of them was the United Nations plaza. There was no direct access to the UN building itself; that was far too obvious a target. But the plaza had been deemed by the Security Council as nonvital.

"Its broken!" Salamalin Taralin snarled, inspecting the split ceramic ring in his hands. "May heaven damn the FBI!"

The ballistic blanket draped over the cannon had protected it from most of the ricochets, but not all. There were some dents in the control panel and a few loose wires sticking out from the massive electromagnet array. Nothing serious, but the aiming mechanism had been blown off. It was a small electromagnetic oval made of multiple layers of rare metals and ceramics fused into a homogenous whole under titanic pressure. It had arrived from the Fortress's deep storage facility packed in liquid Teflon. Now it was cracked in three places like cheap glass.

"Okay, fix it," Hadoch Ghaurdi ordered from behind the steering wheel.

"How?" Taralin demanded, proffering the oval for the other to inspect. "I don't even know what it is made of, so how can I make a repair?"

"Isn't there anything we can do?" Garunda Hai asked, an INS assault rifle lying in her lap under a sweater. One of the teenagers across the roof had been casting glances her way. Either the boy was interested in her looks, or, much more likely, he wanted to hijack the van.

"I'm no scientist," Taralin stated, tossing the twisted piece of junk on the floor. "Akim is dead. I just cut throats for a living."

The woman could only grunt in agreement. So did she.

"Hey, nice wheels," the teenager said, strolling up to the driver's window, a clenched hand in his bulging pocket.

Annoyed, Ghaurdi pulled the INS assault rifle into view and worked the bolt.

"Hey, hey, I was just talking." The teen smiled, pulling out an empty hand. "No harm, no foul."

Leaning across the driver, Hai leveled her silenced pistol and shot the boy in the temple. He staggered for a moment, then crumpled in a heap in the shadows. Nobody else on the roof seemed to notice or care.

"Why did you do that?" Ghaurdi demanded.

"Nervy bastard," she said, holstering the gun behind her back. A warm tingle filled her stomach, and her breath started coming fast. She often heard fools talk about cold murder. But murder was hot. Hot guns, hot screams, hot blood. Murder was hot, and infinitely better than sex, or even drugs.

"Fool," Ghaurdi muttered, but not too loudly.

If the woman heard, she didn't respond.

"All right, is the rest of it working?" Ghaurdi demanded, squinted at the milling diplomats in the plaza two blocks away. So close, and yet so far…

"Sure, the everything else seems fine. I mean, all of the indicators light up, and the meters go into the green," Taralin said hesitantly. "But if it will kill people, your guess is mine. And without the focusing lens, the beam could go anywhere."

Or everywhere, Ghaurdi agreed. Firing the cannon now could send out a halo of neutrons that would wipe out everything for a mile, including the people in the van. They could take out the United Nations, but only at the cost of their own lives.

"Okay, we have no choice," he growled. "Let's call Mr. Malavade, and get new instructions."

"He's not going to like this," Hai muttered.

"We're just lucky Vinsara is halfway around the world," Ghaurdi murmured, pulling out a cell phone and punching in a memorized number reserved strictly for emergencies.

Calcutta

TUCKING THE LAST FEW PIECES of Malavade's body into the garbage can, the men removed their stained gloves and secured the lid. Easing a handcart under the container, they hoisted it off the carpeting and left the ruined office to start down the long corridor for the elevators.

Coming out of the private lavatory, Ravid Komar finished drying his hands and tossed aside the towel. Walking to the cushioned leather chair, he sat and studied the top of the desk. Slowly, the terrorist pressed two different knotholes at the same time and the seamless wood broke apart, sections sliding away to reveal a miniature control console.

"Amazing," Komar whispered, watching the tiny blinking dot on a plasma screen that marked the location of the neutron cannons. His neutron cannons. At last, after all these years, the Punjabi terrorist finally had some real power to make people do as he commanded. Bombs and guns were nothing in comparison to the energy weapon. He could barely contain his eagerness to try the device. With this he could change the face of the world!

Whistling a happy tune, Metudas sauntered into the office, musically kicking the piles of spent brass out of his way.

"Everything under control?" the young hacker asked, plopping into a chair. There were frayed ropes lashed to the armrests, and he realized this was where Malavade had just died. That gave the man a vicarious thrill in the pit of his stomach that was almost as exciting as cocaine.

"Yes, and no. Do you have full control of these weapons?" Komar demanded, gesturing to the console.

"Of course, sir. I created the software that operates them! I can operate them from a distance, or make them explode." He gave a harsh chuckle. "Have I ever let you down before in destroying evidence, creating false identities or transferring funds?"

"No," Komar admitted, looking hard at the other man. "Paying your way through school was one of my better investments. Time and money well spent."

"You were the only one who believed that I wasn't insane," Metudas said softly, his eyes narrowing in hateful memory of his ancient tormentors.

In his mind there flashed a kaleidoscope of childhood images, slights, wrongs, insults. Ah, but his schoolmates were all dead now, every one of them. Either by his hand, or by their own, suicides taking the easy way out to avoid life in a maximum security jail from criminal charges created on his keyboard. Rapists didn't live for long inside an Indian jail, and the methods of their deaths from the other inmates was the raw stuff of nightmares.

"Sir?"

Kamar glanced up. "Yes, Hagar?"

Standing in the ruined doorway, a tall man removed his mask and breathed in the cool air blowing through the smashed window. A lean, whippet of a man, almost skeletal in appearance, his face was hard and unsmiling, with prison tattoos on his throat just visible above the collar of the overalls.

"I did a full sweep, sir," Hagar announced, resting the stock of his weapon on a hip. "The floor is clean. We found a few of Mohad's men hiding in a closet, and one actually made it through the hole in the lavatory before we captured him."

"And?" Komar demanded brusquely.

Hagar shrugged. "We added him to the pile."

"Good. Have the police arrived yet?"

"Come and gone. The rumors were true, Mohad owned them completely. They only came to see if he was okay, not to investigate all of the noise and falling glass."

"Even better," Komar sighed in satisfaction. "Have some of the men start cleaning this place, and replace the landmines. We're taking this building as our new headquarters."

"Are we going to start selling guns?" the man asked with a pinched scowl.

Leaning back in the chair, Komar laughed. "No, my friend. We are going to use the criminal's money and weapons to further our cause. If all goes well, Punjab will be a free and independent nation within a week. Maybe only a few days!"

The big man's face registered surprise at that, but he said nothing. If Komar said it was so, then it had to be true. One of the main reasons he ran Tiger Force was that he never lied to the freedom fighters.

"We also need to get the window fixed," Metudas suggested. "And with something stronger then Plexiglas. I would suggest Luxan. It's ten times stronger and just as clear, but also a hundred times more expensive. American C-4 plastique and dynamite will not penetrate Luxan plastic." Of course, an M-2 satchel charge or thermite grenade would, but the hacker kept that information to himself.

Hagar grunted. "Pinch rupees, lose lives, as the old saying goes. Malavade might still be alive if he hadn't been cheap."

Irritated, Komar waved that aside. "Cost doesn't matter now," he said. "The fat fool gave me the account numbers of his Swiss bank accounts. We have millions at our disposal now. Along with all of the advanced military weapons he has stored in those dozens of warehouses along the river. Those contain more guns and explosives than we can use in a lifetime."

"Plus, we have the cannons," Metudas added, his voice lowering to a mere whisper. "A Sheikh Hassan has purchased them for a billion euros. I was just arranging for the transfer of the funds when…" He didn't finish the sentence, and merely glanced around the decimated office.

"Too bad for him," Komar snarled, brushing back his ebony hair. "The cannons belong to Tiger Force, and aren't going anywhere." The weapons in the warehouses would keep them safe from COIN and NATO, but much more important things could be accomplished with the neutron cannon. Their homeland of Punjab had to be free, and the cost didn't matter.

A soft trilling sounded.

Reaching into his jacket, Metudas extracted a cell phone and flipped it open. The hacker started to frown as he read the text message being rerouted through the Cray Supercomputer.

"Trouble?" Komar demanded.

Turning off the cell phone, the young hacker sighed. "It seems that the FBI almost caught our Manhattan team, and the focusing mechanism for their cannon has become broken."

"Can they repair it?"

"No. They can barely fire it correctly."

"Useless," Hagar hissed, resting his assault rifle on a broad shoulder.

"Not entirely," Komar amended thoughtfully. "Have the Manhattan team go to its secondary target. Tell them to set the device on automatic, and then leave the region."

"What about the other three?"

"The same. The time for secrecy is over," Komar declared, slamming a fist on the console. "The whole world must know what level of mass destruction Tiger Force is capable of delivering."

"Punjab shall be free!" Hagar cried, shaking his weapon. Other men in the battle-scarred hallway took up the cry.

"Of course," Metudas muttered, rising from the chair to head for the computer room. The first thing to do was to tap into the lines of communications for the FBI, NATO and COIN to make sure armed troops weren't trying to track down any of the cannons. After that, it would be a simple matter to redirect Malavade's men to new locations. As long as the fools thought the crime lord was still in charge, they would do anything the hacker told them.

Within reason, he amended, entering his frigid computer room. After all, the men were merely criminals, street thugs only interested in money. But the hacker already had a plan to remove that weak link from their chain of command.

CHAPTER TWENTY

Manhattan

Flying between the skyscrapers and high-rise towers, the Black Hawk helicopter moved over Manhattan on a definitive seek and destroy. The sleek gunship was well-armed with 35 mm minirockets. Unfortunately, since they were going to be flying through civilian airspace, Jack Grimaldi couldn't arm the gunship with missiles. Those were too easily noticed. Hopefully, the minirockets should be enough.

Sitting at the side windows, Carl Lyons and Rosario Blancanales were watching the traffic below through binoculars, and Hermann Schwarz was operating a video camera mounted on the belly of the gunship, the view relayed to his U.S. Army laptop. Moving his finger along the mouse pad, Schwarz changed the focus on the telescopic lens of the camera and saw the faces of the people in the cars below. There were a lot of cargo vans in Manhattan, and half of them seemed to be blue, or a black so dark the man couldn't really tell if they were blue or not.

Strapped into a jumpseat along the wall, a replacement oscilloscope hummed steadily, spiking and cresting from the crisscrossing ocean of magnetic radiation emanating from the city.

Grimaldi had picked the team up only minutes after the escape of Malavade's men in the Dodge. The search had been fast, but fruitless. But Malavade's crew had successfully escaped into traffic as if they had done it a hundred times before. Now it wasn't a hunt, as much as a guessing game. Trying to deduce what the terrorists would do next, then jump ahead of them and lay an ambush. A direct frontal assault was virtual suicide, and would be used only as a last resort.

"Did you get the special equipment you asked for?" Blancanales asked, concentrating on the rooftops. Big machinery was everywhere in sight, but the man felt sure that he could recognize the cannon. It should look like nothing he had ever seen before.

"Sure did. Cowboy has never let me down," Grimaldi stated, flipping switches on the control board to thin their fuel mixture. "Although, I don't know if it will…." He frowned. "Just got a fly-by order. Guess we're too close to the UN."

"Ignore it," Lyons stated. "Barbara and Hal have our six."

Changing the yaw of the turbo blades, Grimaldi started moving over the neighboring buildings once more "Good call." He chuckled. "The N.Y.P.D. just granted us full access. Nice to have low friends in high places, eh?"

The usual banter of the pilot was falling on deaf ears, as Able Team was grimly determined to find the blue Dodge van again. And this time it wouldn't escape intact if they had to crash the gunship on top the damn thing.

"There's the UN," Grimaldi shouted over a shoulder. "Looks like most of the delegates have gathered in the plaza…correction, they're going back inside. I guess the danger is over."

"Nice to know," Lyons muttered, scanning the alleys. If Malavade had planned to take out the whole UN, then the Dodge had to be somewhere close by. But where? There were a lot of places where a van could hide in the city.

Passing a parking garage, Schwarz blinked in surprise, then zoomed the video camera in for a closer look. Yes, there was a blue Dodge cargo van with a broken rear window. And the UN Plaza was only two blocks away. A direct line of sight.

"Found it! Six o'clock, just below that billboard," Schwarz announced, checking the oscilloscope. But there was too much background hash. It was impossible to tell if the weapon was charged.

"I see it," Grimaldi said, swinging behind an apartment building. Rising high, he angled around, trying to arrange for an approach vector from the sun so that the Black Hawk would be invisible in the glare.

Everybody tried not to hold their breath as the gunship slid across the sky toward the van. Taking advantage of the billboard, the Stony Man pilot kept it between them until he was almost brushing the toothpaste ad. Then rising up fast, he swooped down. "Bombs away," he called, pressing a red button on the joystick of the gunship.

Attached to the belly of the Black Hawk, a fat canister trembled, then spread open wide, releasing a huge mass of pink-colored jelly. The glistening five-hundred-pound blob flattened as it fell through the air, but only slightly, then it slammed onto the van, the vehicle rocking as its roof buckled slightly and the bulletproof windshield cracked.

"Bull's-eye," Grimaldi said, starting a fast descent.

Releasing their seat belts, Able Team grabbed weapons. This was a calculated risk, but one they thought well worth it. Sea water had protected the British submarine, so hopefully the rest of the information about neutron weapons was also correct. There was something much denser in hydrogen than water in the Stony Man arsenal, although they had never used the stuff without igniting it first. Napalm. Designed to stick to enemy fortifications, the jellied gasoline was almost impossible to remove without the right solvents. Hopefully, it would be thick enough to coat the van and block the neutron beam. Methyl-ethyl ketone was the best solvent, but simple grain alcohol would also wash napalm off in just a few seconds. However, that wasn't common knowledge and few folks walked around with a couple of hundred gallons of alcohol just in case they got bombarded with unlit napalm.

The Black Hawk landed only yards away, six young

men stumbled from the dripping vehicle, coughing and gagging. Most of them had guns in their belts.

"What is this shit?" a teen demanded, touching the material with a finger. The thick goo stuck to his flesh and he couldn't shake it free. Wiping it off on his shirt, the fabric immediately stuck to his chest.

"Smells like gasoline!" another teen cried in horror.

The gang stopped talking as the Black Hawk dropped into view, the nose-mounted minigun spinning to full speed. None of the street toughs had any military experience, but they had all seen movies. They knew what a minigun could do.

"Freeze!" Grimaldi boomed over the PA. "Don't move, or we open fire!"

The side hatch opened and Able Team jumped to the rooftop, sweeping forward in an attack formation with their weapons at the ready.

"What the fuck is going on here?" a teenager demanded, trying to wipe the jelly from his face. Every attempt only made things worse. "We didn't do anything!"

Spreading out, the members of Able Team could plainly see that these were unfortunately not the owners of the Dodge, but just a bunch of teenagers. From the tattoos and colors, they were clearly part of a street gang.

Lyons and Blancanales kept the gang under cover as Schwarz went to the rear of the van. He cursed at the sight of the empty cargo area. The neutron cannon was gone. In spite of the napalm, he caught the smell of blood from inside. Some of the operators had to have died from the earlier gunfight.

"It's not here," Schwarz reported stoically.

"Okay, where is it?" Lyons demanded brusquely. "Tell us and you get to keep breathing."

"Where's what?" a gang member demanded. "We didn't do anything!"

That phrase seemed to be their mantra. "Okay, calm down," Blancanales said gently, resting his M-16 assault rifle on a shoulder to try to appear less threatening. "Just tell us what happened. All we want is the people who were driving the Dodge."

The gang was badly rattled. They were used to being in charge and feared. But now they had been slammed helpless in under a heartbeat. Panic was on their faces, and one wrong move could edge them over the line and the fools might start firing their guns. Making them all explode into flame.

"Which Dodge?" one of the gang members asked hesitantly, his entire body dripping a thick ooze.

"Shut up," Lyons said, playing the bad cop. "Or I'll flip a match at your sorry ass."

The gang paused. The teens didn't know what they were covered with, but from the reek, the thought of fire made them stop breathing for a moment.

"Look, man, we didn't steal the van," another youth said, trying to lift a sneaker from the concrete roof. It came free with a moist sucking noise. "The owners just left it here, the keys in the ignition."

"Bull," Lyons said in his best cop voice.

"Hey, it's the truth!" another teenager cried. "We just wanted to sell it to a chop shop! You know, all these spare parts are worth a lot."

Yeah, he knew. A fifty-thousand-dollar car was worth two hundred thousand if the parts were sold separately. Even in its present state with the chassis covered with dents, and the rear window gone, the armored van was worth a small fortune.

"Who's that?" Blancanales asked, pointing at a body lying in the shadows under the billboard.

"Just some nimrod from Queens." The leader sneered. "Got tough with the folks in the Dodge, and they iced him. No biggie."

"Bang, one shot in the head." Another member pantomimed with a finger.

Going over to check the body, Schwarz saw the youth had been killed by a small-caliber round in the temple. Somebody was a very good shot, and knew human anatomy. That smelled like a professional assassin to the Stony Man operative. Not a lot of those working with terrorists. Curious.

"Look, man, if you wanna bust us, then bust us," the leader of the gang said, pulling a plastic bag from his jacket full of a fibrous material. "But for Christ's sake, get this crap off us, whatever the hell it is."

Lyons decided to go for shock value. "Napalm."

"We're covered with fucking napalm?" the teen gasped. "Are you fucking assholes insane?"

"And what if we are?" Lyons asked in a cold whisper.

The gang went motionless, paralyzed by the startling question.

"And maybe we're not." Going to the Black Hawk, Schwarz returned with a bulging bag full of plastic bottles of alcohol.

"Okay, listen up, dill-holes. We're hunting terrorists," Blancanales declared bluntly, trying to be tough but amiable. "You guys remember what happened to the Twin Towers?" He used the New York term for the World Trade Center, trying to establish a closer rapport.

"You…you mean the shitheads who did that were driving this van?" the leader asked, jerking a thumb.

"Close enough," Blancanales said. "Friends of friends, shall we say."

"So you're not N.Y.P.D.?"

"Delta Force," he lied smoothly.

"Crap," a teen muttered softly, his shoulders slumping.

Laying the bag on the roof, Schwarz pulled out a bottle and tossed it over. "Use this to wash yourselves clean," he directed. "Just don't get it near your eyes."

"Smells like rubbing alcohol," one of them said, sniffing. There was no label on the military bottle, just a code number for the quartermaster corp.

"It is."

"And we're supposed to wash off napalm with alcohol?" The teen gave a nervous laugh. "Why don'cha just shove a charcoal briquette up my ass and finish the job?"

"Just shut up and use it," Lyons commanded, racking the slide on the monstrous Atchisson.

As expected, the noise of the shotgun got their attention. Hesitantly, the gang began using the alcohol and the thick napalm flowed off their skin like warm grease. Their clothes, however, were soaked all the way through.

"We going to jail?" a teen asked nervously, clearing his throat.

"Not if you tell us what we want to know," Lyons stated. "Now, start talking."

"If you want that thing in the back," a third teen added, washing off her pants, "they took it with 'em."

"In what?" Lyons demanded. "Describe the vehicle! How many of them are there?"

"Three, two old guys and a chick with big tits," the leader said, trying to rinse out his hair. "They jacked a dark blue Hummer and split, I dunno, ten…twenty minutes ago."

"What was the license-plate number? Did you hear their names? How were they armed?"

"How would we know any of that shit?" a teen said listlessly, tossing aside an empty bottle of alcohol.

"I heard their names," the leader said, opening a new bottle and pouring it along his arm. "Sounded foreign, Hatrack, Rumba, Salmon…" He put some alcohol into a cupped palm and smoothed down his glistening hair. Napalm flowed to the ground in gelatinous sheets. "And let me tell you, jack, they were hauling some serious iron. I know guns, but not the crap they were carrying. Weird, military stuff. Grenades, rockets, stuff like that."

"Sort of like what you got," another youth offered sheepishly, moving away from the puddle of napalm on the concrete. He left pink footprints behind.

"One of them looked like a Carl Gustav," a gang member suggested, doing the same. "Better stay clear of that."

The leader turned. "And who the fuck is Carl Gustav?"

"That's the name of the weapon, asswipe."

"Thanks, much appreciated," Lyons said, lowering the shotgun. That sounded like Malavade's people all right. He would expect the work crew of an arms dealer to be only packing the best guns available.

"Good enough," Blancanales said, deciding the gang had told everything they knew of any consequence. "We're taking off. You guys want an ambulance, or do you want to risk trying to reach a shower without blowing up?"

The woebegone expressions of the subdued street gang said that an ambulance was seriously desired, but they would rather detonate than ask for any assistance.

"Well, I'll send one along, just in case," Blancanales said diplomatically. "Thanks for the help."

"Sure, no problem," a youth muttered, pink jelly dripping off his beard. "But...no cops?"

"No cops."

"And we were never here," Lyons added in a stern voice. "Understand?"

"Hey, napalm falls outta the sky all the time around here." The leader smiled wearily. "Welcome to New York, and shit like that. Right?"

Shouldering the shotgun, Lyons nodded. "Right."

As Able Team started for the gunship one of the teenagers called out a hail.

"Yeah?" Lyons asked impatiently, turning.

"Watch out for the bitch with the tits," the gang leader said grimly. "I think she's crazy."

"Just blow their heads off," another teen suggested, flapping his arms in an effort to dislodge the quivering napalm.

"That is the plan," Lyons stated. "Keep washing until the ambulance arrives."

"That's the plan," the leader repeated, pouring more alcohol onto his shirt.

Climbing back into the gunship, Lyons moved to the copilot seat, while Blancanales closed the hatch. Schwarz was on the radio even before the Black Hawk was airborne.

"Stony Base, this is Able Two," Schwarz said, touching his throat mike. "I need you to monitor every low-jack signal on the east side of Manhattan. We're looking for a dark blue Hummer, maybe black, that was stolen within the past hour."

"Roger, Able Two," Kurtzman answered. "We'll track the GPS and block the police from receiving the signal. Give you a clear field."

"Thanks."

"Anything else?"

"Start ordering body bags," Schwarz stated grimly. "Able Two, over and out."

CHAPTER TWENTY-ONE

Calcutta, India

Arriving at the Netji Subhas Chandra Bose International Airport, Phoenix Force decided to act as any tourists would and took the subway across town to where they would pick up their weapons. Classical Indian music played over speakers, and the walls of the subway station were adorned with movie posters.

What a strange country, Manning thought to himself. But he found himself warming to the people. India was old and modern, chaos and order, all combined together in a wild Mulligan stew of life.

Just then, a group of Indian girls walked by wearing modern European dresses and stockings, but their trim wrists and ankles jingled with exotic jewelry. As they passed, dark eyes flashed in appreciation at the tall muscular Canadian.

He smiled in return. "A man could get used to this," Manning said amiably.

While the rest of the team chuckled, McCarter said nothing. Twice along the route, he felt sure the team was being followed. But just when he thought he had the person identified, he departed.

"Something?" Hawkins asked in forced casualness.

"Don't know," McCarter whispered. "But stay sharp."

Hawkins shrugged noncommittally, but there softly came the metallic click from under his jacket of a safety being disengaged.

They boarded the subway car and finally reached the town of Dum Dum. Phoenix Force went to a car-rental agency and found a truck waiting for them. Inside the rear of the vehicle were locked trunks filled with all of the equipment they had requested. How Barbara Price obtained some of the specialty items they needed from across the world was simply amazing. But the woman had never let them down. The combat soldiers considered the mission controller absolutely vital to the success of any mission.

Driving back through downtown Calcutta, McCarter avoided the Victoria Towers and circled past a museum dedicated to the British. There was no sarcasm there. The Indians were thankful the British dragged them into the twentieth century, but were equally glad they were gone now.

Beggars on the streets watched the foreigners in the rental truck, and McCarter wondered if that was all that he had noticed back on the subway. Possibly. Amid the sea of Asian faces, the Stony Man operatives were rather distinct.

Parking in a deserted alley, the team hauled out the equipment trunks and took a service elevator to the top level of an office building. The access door to the roof was locked, but Encizo opened it in less a minute with a keywire gun.

Throwing open the doors to the roof, Hawkins took point and moved fast across the open expanse, with Manning and Encizo close behind.

"Clear," Hawkins reported, holstering his 9 mm Beretta. "Just some hawks."

"Hawks?" James asked in surprise.

"The city buys them to deal with the pigeons."

"I thought Indians worshipped all life?"

"Hell, man, nobody likes pigeons."

Taking field glasses from a trunk, McCarter walked to the edge of the roof and scanned the sprawling city below. Through the hazy atmosphere, he could see the University of Calcutta to the south, the sluggish Hooghly River to the east, and far to the north he could just barely discern the whitish blur of the famous Taj Mahal. Suddenly he recalled that the Taj Mahal was surrounded by several fortresses all made of dark red stone. That had to be why the Indian military headquarters was called Red Fort. Their past was their future. To the west were only apartment complexes and factories, stretching on and on as far as the murky horizon.

"I see they finally got that second bridge built across the Hooghly River," McCarter drawled, tracking the waterway for any signs of a navy patrol. "About bloody time. The traffic here is terrible. Worse than Paris."

"So we noticed," Encizo replied, removing body armor from one of the trunks and placing it down on the hot concrete.

"And there she is," Hawkins muttered, adjusting the focus on his binoculars. Three blocks away, the blue stone edifice of Victoria Towers dominated the neighborhood.

"Pity we can't use that helipad," Manning muttered, packing items into an equipment bag. "Sure would make things easier."

"Their radar would spot us in a split second," Encizo noted dourly, slinging an MP-5 submachine behind his back. "And after that, we'd be flying corpses."

"How far is it?" Hawkins asked, studying the other skyscraper.

There were a lot of big machines on the roof. They appeared to be air-conditioning units. He sure hoped so. From that vantage point, a neutron cannon would wipe out most of the city and suburbs. One full rotation, and twenty million people would be dead. The concept was beyond ghastly, but the soldier didn't allow it to cloud his mind with unwanted emotions. Angry men died in battle. That was one of the first lessons a green recruit learned in combat. If they lived.

"Half a mile," McCarter stated. "And the wind is coming from the west."

"I like a challenge," Manning said, tightening the strap around his chest.

Suddenly, James went stiff and mouthed a curse.

"Trouble?" Hawkins asked pointedly.

"Yes. I can hear voices inside our Learjet," James said, turning up the volume on the transceiver. "Somebody is searching through our plane."

"I thought you left it locked," McCarter said as a question.

"I did," James said with a shrug. "On top of which, we're listed as U.S. couriers and have diplomatic immunity. Nobody is allowed to search our vehicles."

"Could they be thieves?" Hawkins asked, inserting a fresh clip of armor-piercing rounds into his MP-5. He worked the bolt, chambering a round for instant use.

"Don't know yet," James said hesitantly, fiddling with the gain. "They sure don't talk like—" He looked up. "Oh hell, they're Special Forces troops."

"COIN?"

"Yep."

James lowered the radio. "Damn it, they found the bug. These local boys are good."

"Is the plane clean?" Encizo demanded, donning combat boots.

"Yeah, no problem there," James said, lowering the volume. "Nothing on board could possibly be traced back to America, or the Farm."

"Okay, let's move," McCarter stated, tightening the last strap around his chest until it constricted his breathing. "Everybody ready?" There came a round of assent. "All right, people, let's go!"

Without hesitation, the team dived off the roof and into the sky. Rising thermals buffeted the team randomly. Encizo started to drift until James grabbed the man by a boot and physically dragged him back into the formation. Then the parasails took over, and the team angled its descent for the target building.

This was the only safe way to approach the Victoria Towers. On the ground there would be guards and video cameras. And there had to be radar on the roof. But the team should be invisible coming in sideways like this. NASA jetpacks would be perfect for this sort of maneuver, but even Barbara Price had her limitations.

Swooping around the rooftop like predatory birds, Phoenix Force checked for any visible obstructions or traps, then darted forward. Dropping heavily onto the concrete roof, the men quickly slapped the release button on their chest harnesses and gathered up the parasails. Their job was over. Now came the hard part.

Swinging around their MP-5 from behind their backs, the team worked the arming bolts and spread out to check for video cameras and guards. Weapons hung from the web harnesses strapped to their chests, and bulky backpacks gave them an almost hunchback appearance. Thankfully, the area was clear. However, the armed men had been extremely careful to not step outside the painted lines of the helipad landing circle on the roof.

Raising a hand, McCarter nodded at James.

Setting down a large case, James opened a panel on the side and extracted an electrical cord. Plugging it into the second case, he flipped a series of switches on top, and watched as the portable generator revved to full speed. When the miniature propane generator was operating at maximum capacity, he pressed a button on top of the second case and watched carefully as a gauge slowly climbed into the red zone. The moment the device was at full power, James pressed a button. The EMP bomb silently detonated, releasing an electromagnetic pulse equivalent to a five-kiloton nuclear explosion.

Instantly, all of the lights in Victoria Towers blinked out, the hidden proximity alarms and security cameras going dead.

All around them, the skyline of Calcutta was unchanged; only the upper fifteen levels of the skyscraper had been affected. Unlike in Hollywood movies, an EMP blast didn't somehow magically shut down electronics for a few minutes, then everything came back on exactly the same as before. In the real world, an EMP blast permanently burned out transistors and computer chips. They would never function again. Only shielded systems wouldn't be affected. And the systems here didn't seem to be shielded.

Leaving the painted circle of the helipad, the members of Phoenix Force raced past the dead sensors to the brick kiosk containing the access stairs. A wire gate blocked the entrance, but that was handled easily enough, the million-dollar EMP bomb clearing the way for a pair of twenty-dollar bolt cutters.

Kneeling before the steel door, Encizo tried to trick the lock and failed. Pulling on asbestos gloves, Manning extracted a long metal tube from his backpack. Scraping the end on the concrete, the magnesium top flared into life, then the thermite inside the tube ignited.

Applying the blue-white thermite lance to the door,

Manning melted a hole through the thick metal. Then he did it again in a different location, and twice more, searing the locking mechanism. With the power gone, the electronic door couldn't be opened with the keypad, so unless he found the restraining bolt holding it closed, their whole mission would fail before they even set a boot into the skyscraper.

On the plane ride from Bombay to Calcutta, Phoenix Force had studied every possible detail about Victoria Towers. Kurtzman and his team had ferreted out most of the modifications made to the skyscraper, but whoever ran electronic inference for Malavade had left a brilliant trail of false data and lost files. It was a pity the hacker worked for the other side. The Farm could use a man of his talents.

There came a clatter of falling steel from inside the kiosk and the perforated door swung aside.

Proceeding past the dead video cameras inside the kiosk, the team invaded the skyscraper. A plain steel door stood at the bottom of the stairs. C-4 plastique was packed around the edge of the door, timing pencils stabbed into the claylike material. The thermal lance was gone; now it was time for brute force.

"Ten seconds," McCarter commanded, working the arming bolt on his MP-5.

The men nodded, and snapped off the timing pencils at the lowest marking. The chemical sticks started to sizzle.

Retreating to the rooftop, the team waited. The entire building seemed to shake from the C-4 blast, and a hurricane of smoky wind buffeted the troops. But even before the concussion had faded away, McCarter flipped down his IR goggles and charged into the brick kiosk.

Whipping out a cell phone, McCarter hit speed dial, let it ring once, then terminated the call. Tossing the device away, he estimated it should take no more than thirty seconds for the signal to be relayed to the Farm, and then Kurtzman would—

The fire alarms went off, the din deafening as the small red squares on the walls started howling. The rest of the team flipped down their IR goggles, and Phoenix Force entered the building, tossing more grenades along the way.

People were already streaming out of their offices and charging down the stairs. Phoenix Force stayed out of their way, until the last person was gone. Then they quietly eased into the concrete stairwell and proceeded toward the hidden twentieth floor.

ACROSS THE STREET, five beggars lounged in the cool shade of an alleyway that just happened to look upon the front entrance of Victoria Towers. Several of them held EM scanners and palm computers.

"They're inside the building, and I'm getting a report of fire in the basement from the city," Private Jonkab reported, touching the tiny screen.

"In the basement? They must have very good computer support," Major Jagan Chandrasekhar noted. "Whoever they are."

The big man seemed barely able to fit into his uniform he was so heavily muscled, and there were ugly scars on his chest from months of torture at a Pakistani "education" facility. As a small child, Jagan had been kidnapped by narcoterrorists working for the Pakistanis. Starved and beaten, and given heroin, he had almost cracked to their brainwashing when he was rescued by the India army. He decided to become a soldier just then, and fifteen years later, joined the Special Forces. His hatred of their northern enemies was beyond intense; it was almost pathological.

"Better cancel the fire call," the major decided. "We have more than enough civilians running around the place without adding more."

"Yes, sir."

"Hey, what's going on here?" a policeman demanded from the mouth of the alley.

The major gave a sharp whistle, and two of his men shot the cop with stun guns. With a soft groan, the man fell and was stashed behind a garbage bin, safely out of sight for the duration.

Jagan grunted. His team had been after Mohad Malavade for almost a year, and they weren't going to lose him at the last moment because of some crooked cop. The major debated killing the man, then decided that was a matter for the public courts. Sad, but true.

"Alpha Team, disable that Learjet, and come back here pronto," Major Jagan said into a throat mike. "Enter the skyscraper through the lobby and make as much of a disturbance as possible. Give us some cover."

"Roger, sir. They'll think it's Independence Day."

"Good man." Jagan switched frequencies. "Beta

Team, pick us up in the helicopter. We're going in through the roof."

"Confirm, sir. ETA, ten minutes."

"Make it five."

"Roger, over and out."

"Who do you think they are, Commander?" a private asked, checking the clip on his assault rifle. Satisfied, he slapped it back into the receiver and worked the bolt.

"NATO Special Forces, probably," the major said, using a chemical rag to remove the last of his disguise. "Maybe CIA."

"Should we assist?"

"No, let them secure the weapon, then we take it from them. Our people invented it, and the neutron cannon belongs to us, not the United Nations."

There was a dark shape in the sky and the helicopter appeared.

The military gunship was modified to resemble a civilian news chopper, and had been flown past the skyscraper several times over the past month so that its appearance would seem natural to the arms dealer and his mercenaries.

Criminals my ass, Jagan thought savagely. Malavade was a terrorist and a traitor. Plain and simple.

"And if they refuse?"

"Let's just hope they'll listen to reason," Jagan muttered in a dangerous tone, checking the clip in his weapon.

CHAPTER TWENTY-TWO

Garden State Parkway, New Jersey

A dark blue Hummer rolled past the rest area on Route 95 at exactly the speed limit. Officer Daniel Carson cavalierly dismissed the vehicle until he caught a brief glimpse of somebody inside swinging an MM-1 multishot grenade launcher out of sight. The shape of the deadly weapon was unmistakable, and there was no civilian model available for hunters.

Buckling on his safety belt, the officer snorted. Hunters, that was a laugh. There was a word for people who used automatic weapons to hunt, and it wasn't considered very politically correct anymore.

"Mother of God, did you see that shit?" Officer Lucia Reed asked, starting the engine of the modified Chevrolet. The big V-12 engine roared into life, shaking the frame with barely controlled power.

"Bet your ass I did," Carson declared, reaching out

the open window and slapping a flashing light on the roof. "Those punks were getting ready to ace us if we dropped the hammer."

"Looks like we got a couple of hardcases from New York again," Reed snarled, shifting gears. "Goddamn drug dealers hauling their crap in a van trying to sneak their fucking goods past the chem sniffers on the turnpike."

Pulling a 9 mm Glock pistol from his gunbelt, Carson racked the slide and tucked the weapon into his belt holster. "So let's get the bastards."

"I hear you!"

The tires of the unmarked police car spun wildly on the gravel, lurched off the berm and onto smooth asphalt. Rapidly increasing in speed, the supercharged Chevy rocketed toward the Hummer.

Reaching over, Carson took the Glock from Reed's belt and worked the slide for his partner, then returned the weapon to her holster. With both hands on the wheel, Lucia couldn't prep her weapon without crashing.

"Whatever they're carrying must be hotter than the gates of hell to risk a run down the GSP," she added grimly. "Coke, maybe. Or Double-D."

"Could be designer drugs. But don't know, don't care," Carson snarled, snapping the lock on the gunrack and taking down the Remington 12-gauge to rack the slide. A shell popped out and rolled about onto the floor mat. The stun bag was a wise precaution for the first round, but this was no time for half measures. The people in the van were packing military ordnance. Time to get hard.

Pulling out an ammunition box from under the front seat, the officer started thumbing in shredders. Instead of buckshot, these carried stainless-steel slivers that tore car tires apart. The cartridges had originally been designed for blowing off the locks on doors, but they had quickly been adopted by every patrol car in America. And Carson knew that nothing stopped an escaping perp faster than having their tires violently disintegrate.

Rapidly building speed, the Chevy approached the Hummer. The van was still doing the speed limit, most likely hoping that the state troopers weren't after them.

Carson hit a switch, and the big siren behind the front grille cut loose. The noise rose like morning thunder and faintly shook the speeding unmarked police car. Long ago the patrolmen had abandoned the official state-issue siren as too damn wimpy to get the job done. This was a WWII air raid horn, slightly modified to match the wail of a police siren.

At the strident noise, the Hummer started to slow, then accelerated slightly as if the driver was thinking about making a run for it. Then the Hummer slowed once more, and started edging onto the soft shoulder.

The two patrolmen shared a quick glance, then checked their weapons and activated the built-in video camera. Bitter experience had taught the cops that folks who started to run, then decided to slow down, were always major trouble. Having a video record was just good legal sense.

"Stay loose," Carson said tensely. "That MM-1 can blow us into sushi."

"Only if it hits us," Reed said confidently. "But you better radio in for backup, just in case."

That was a good idea. "Car Nine to base," Carson said,

thumbing the switch on the hand mike of the radio. "Car Nine to base. We're just passing the Delanco exit—"

The radio began squealing as the transmission was jammed, and then the rear hatch of the Hummer lifted, exposing bulletproof vests lining the interior walls, several armed people, and a huge piece of electronic equipment.

"Freeze!" Carson said into the hand mike, his words booming from the PA speaker behind their grille.

In response, the busty woman in the Hummer opened fire with an odd-looking automatic weapon, and the man raised into view something that looked like a bazooka.

"Jesus H. Christ, that's a Carl Gustav!" Reed cursed, swerving the patrol car wildly.

"Bastards!" Carson snarled, triggering the shotgun. He missed, and tried again.

In response, there was a flash from the gaping maw of the Gustav, and the world seemed to explode as the antipersonnel round of stainless-steel fléchettes tore the Chevy and the patrolmen apart. Both died instantly.

Still in gear, the ruined Chevrolet burst into flames, but kept speeding along the road until it randomly veered onto the median. Smashing through the decorative bushes, the burning patrol car went straight into the northbound traffic. Honking steadily, a luxury sedan wildly arced around the rolling conflagration. A fancy BMW motorcycle dodged the car, but then crashed into the bushes. The driver went flying over the handlebars and hurtled into the decorative pine trees.

Blaring its air horn, a lumbering Mack truck hauling a double-load tried to get out of the way of the careening police car, but only succeeded in crashing into it headfirst. The wailing siren instantly stopped as the front of the Chevrolet erupted into a thousand pieces. Then the crumpling chassis flipped up and over in front of the unstoppable Detroit juggernaut.

Clutching the bloody ruin of his face, the truck driver screamed, a nest of steel slivers rammed deep into his skull. Blind and bleeding to death, the man let go of the steering wheel just as the truck jackknifed. He went through the windshield when the couplings broke, and the two trailers behind the truck went free. Flipping over sideways, the huge containers started tumbling along the road completely out of control. The rear doors jerked open, and hundreds of air conditioners went flying, raining down upon the oncoming traffic like meteors. Brakes squealed as a dozen cars smashed into one another trying to escape. Then the air conditioners hit and horrified screaming began. Moving too fast to stop in time, more cars plowed straight into the growing pile of mangled death. Fuel gushed out from a score of rupture gas tanks, and a fireball spread across the field of destruction, hellish flames and black smoke reaching high into the clear New Jersey sky.

Chuckling at the sight dwindling in their wake, Ghaurdi lowered the speed of the Hummer slightly. Hai and Taralin opened cans of soda and looked bored. At a steady five miles per hour under the speed limit, death rolled out of New Jersey and disappeared over a low hill into Delaware, heading straight for downtown Washington, D.C.

Victoria Towers, Calcutta

A LIGHT BOBBED in the darkness, and something large pushed open the door to the computer room.

"What the hell is going on?" Ravid Komar demanded from the hallway, brandishing a flashlight and a big-bore automatic pistol.

"We've been invaded," Metudas reported crisply, typing swiftly on his keyboard. The screen of the computer was sectioned into small windows. Most of them showed only blackness, but one displayed a greenish view of a stairwell. Several large men holding machine guns and wearing night-vision goggles were moving swiftly down the steps.

"So what happened to the lights?"

"My guess would be an EMP blast," Metudas said slowly, rubbing his scalp with stiff fingers. "But I've never seen one so powerful before!"

Slightly hunched over, Komar frowned. "Why is everything else down, but your computers and cameras are still functioning?"

"Shielded circuits and power supply," the hacker said proudly. "I can stay online for hours. I expected you to cut the power to the building before attacking, and took precautions. Now it seems…" He left the sentence hanging.

"Fair enough." The leader of Tiger Force leaned over the shoulder of the hacker for a closer look. "Any idea who they are?"

"None. But from all of that hardware I would guess they are not here to arrest us. Looks more like a CIA wet work unit."

Komar's eyebrows shot up at that, but he said nothing. He may be from the back hills of Punjabi, but he had heard about the secret teams of CIA assassins. They couldn't be bargained with, frightened, or paid off. They killed, and then disappeared. Lethal ghosts in the covert world of Intelligence.

There came the sound of running boots and Hagar appeared in the dark hallway, along with a dozen other men holding various weapons. Each man wore a black balaclava to hide their features from the police, and as they touched the triggers of the AK-101 assault rifles, red laser beams stabbed out from the small black boxes attached underneath the barrels of the weapons. Soon the gloom was a spiderweb of probing lasers.

"What's going on?" Hagar demanded gruffly. "Have some more scum come to rescue their boss?"

The massive .50 Desert Eagle pistol in his scarred hand didn't have a laser pointer attachment like the machine guns of the other men. The terrorist didn't need any aids to kill. Before he had been cashiered out of the army, he was considered the best pistol shot in India.

"Too late for that," Metudas snarled, accessing the city Web. He turned off the fire alarms. Blessed silence returned.

"I smell no smoke," a man in the hallway said, sniffing deeply.

"Of course not, this is a feint," Komar declared, cracking his knuckles. "They attacked from the roof, but set off the alarms for a fire in the lobby. That means they are frightened of us."

Metudas arched an eyebrow, but said nothing. In a room full of angry men with guns, it was a wise mouse that kept his mouth shut.

A moment later, the emergency lights came on, the nests of battery-powered bulbs extending brilliant beams of white light to bathe the exit doors and fire extinguishers.

"Who are they, sir?" Hagar asked hatefully.

Thankfully, the repairs to the defenses of the twentieth floor had been completed. The building was a hardsite once more, and the defenses were much better than what Malavade had in place.

"My guess would be COIN," Komar said thoughtfully, placing a hand on the shoulder of the hacker and squeezing hard. "The Indian army's counter intelligence operatives are well known for misdirection and surprise attacks. This seems to be their style."

"No guts for a real fight." Hagar laughed, relaxing slightly. COIN had been after Tiger Force for over a decade. He wasn't afraid of those silly men with their big talk.

"They're a Special Forces team?" one of the other men in the hallway whispered, clutching his new rifle tighter in both hands. "Perhaps we should use the neutron cannon!"

"The device is on the roof, fool." Komar sneered. "Aim it down at the invaders and we die, too."

"Is it still working?" Hagar asked, glancing at the ceiling as if he could see through five stories of concrete and steel. "Or did the EMP blast burn that out, also?"

"Of course it's working!" Metudas snapped. "I personally modified the subsystems to—"

With a sharp gesture, the terrorist leader cut off the technical explanation. All he wanted to know was that the weapon was still able to kill.

"Yes, it's working fine," Metudas amended, pointing at a submonitor. "See. All of the lights are green. We can threaten to beam down the city, if that is what you're thinking about trying." Thankfully, the invaders had to have gone right past the machine. Maybe they didn't know what it looked like. Interesting.

"Do it," Komar ordered. "Unless the device receives a command code from me in—" he checked his watch "—thirty minutes, then destroy the city. Let twenty million deaths be the reward for attacking Tiger Force!"

Feeling light-headed, Metudas did as he was ordered. Becoming one of those twenty million hadn't been part of his original plan. Something would have to be done about that.

"Well?" Komar demanded impatiently.

"Done. The cancel code is 'window washer.'"

"Excellent." Ravid chuckled, standing straighter. "Now have all of the other cannons attack instantly. Wherever they are. Beam down the nearest city until I tell them to stop. Make the death toll as high as possible!"

Hagar and the men cheered, rattling their guns overhead.

"Ah…more bad news," Metudas said awkwardly. "NATO has destroyed the cannon in the Ukraine, and the one in the Pacific."

Starting for the door, Komar snapped his head back. "What? Impossible!"

The hacker gestured at a monitor showing the symbol for NATO. "No, sir, there is no doubt. See for yourself."

The leader of Tiger Force had some trouble with the English words. The terrorist could speak the language well, but the spelling always drove him insane. In a darkening fury, he saw that the hacker spoke the truth. From six cannons they were down to three. Half of his forces depleted in a heartbeat.

Standing slowly, the man felt an insane rage build within, but kept it under control. NATO and the CIA were too much to handle. Suddenly, escape was their best option. Sadly, not everybody could go. Some had to stay here to be a distraction so that he could escape with the plans for the neutron cannon. He patted a pocket to make sure the disk was safe. He could sell this on the world market for billions, and hire an army to free Punjabi. As long as he lived, the war would continue forever.

"How many cannons does that leave us?" Hagar asked inquisitively.

"New York, the seaplane off the southern coast, the one on the roof," Metudas said. "And the one in America was in the middle of the swamplands of New Jersey. There might be cities nearby, but nothing major. Certainly nothing important enough to attract the attention of the world news."

"Bah. Useless."

"Until it reaches Washington."

Hagar grinned at that. Washington, D.C.? Now that was a real target! The Americans would force New Delhi to make Punjabi free to protect their beloved capital. The Yankees made wonderful movies, but aside from that were total fools. They talked to their women like equals, and all voted to decide who would be their leaders. What utter nonsense. None of that European filth would taint the shining freedom of New Punjabi!

"All right, prepare the American cannon to fire on my command," Komar said in a low voice, giving the hacker another warning squeeze until he heard the man whimper. "But don't tell the operators."

"Ah yes, well, there are always sacrifices in any revolution," Metudas replied softly, sweat forming on his brow in spite of the residual coolness of the room.

After a long moment, Komar released the hacker. "Exactly."

His hands moved across the keyboard, a chill running down his spine. The terrorists had to be planning to kill Malavade's people by turning on the cannon by remote control once it was in the D.C. area. Kill two birds with one stone. That would remove any possible link back to him, and horrify the entire world at the same time.

"Where is our seaplane on the coast?" Hagar demanded, checking the monitor.

Without speaking, the hacker hit a macro and a map of the world appeared with three blinking icons. He touched the Indian subcontinent with the cursor, and the map of the nation expanded to fill the screen. "They're taking on fuel at Nellor."

"Still?"

He shrugged, making his bruised shoulder ache. "It's a resort community. And they did not have a reservation."

Komar grunted in reply. "How close are they to Sriharikota Island?"

That caught Metudas by surprise. "The space launch facility? An hour by air, maybe less."

"Excellent. Arrange for the cannon to go on board the next available scheduled takeoff," Komar ordered. "Pay any price. Bump some other shipment. Use every rupee we have if necessary. But we need that weapon in space immediately. Only then will we be safe, and Punjab will be free from the iron yoke of New Delhi." The leader of Tiger Force paused. "And arrange for a random strike pattern if the weapon should not hear from us every hour."

Metudas swallowed hard. "Random?"

"If we no longer control the weapon, that means we are dead."

Pulling out a cigarette, Hagar applied the flame of a butane lighter to the end and sucked in the sweet smoke. "How long to convert the seaplane unit for space operation?"

"Already done," Metudas replied, feeling his stomach flutter. The terrorists were dangerously close to figuring out that this was exactly what he had planned to do from the start. The hacker had to speak carefully. His next words might be his last. "The units were…originally designed for space warfare. I kept all of the parts installed and the software loaded." He gave a feeble grin, trying to appear subservient. "Just in case you needed it, of course. I only have to activate the programs."

Komar said nothing for an uncomfortably long period of time, then laid his calloused hand on the shoulder of the small hacker once more.

"Excellent work! You will be the hero of the revolution," Komar said solemnly, this time giving a friendly pat. "Schools will be named after you!"

He'd rather have the satellite.

"Thank you, sir. I'll send the seaplane to Sriharikota Island immediately."

"How long until it is in orbit?"

"Just a few hours."

Hagar removed the cigarette and exhaled through his nostrils. "So soon?"

"I...found an opening on a commercial rocket launch this afternoon," the hacker lied quickly. "It cost a fortune, but our weather satellite is registered as cargo."

"Weather satellite." A man chuckled. "A death rain for our enemies, sunny freedom for us!"

The hacker joined in the general laughter. He had purchased the slot on this launch months earlier. Right after successfully suggesting that Interpol hold a convention in Sri Lanka. Everything was neatly falling into place, like data bytes in a stream of smooth code. If he could just live out the day, he would become the absolute ruler of India. The first maharajah of the entire continent! The nation would bow before him. The rest of the world could go to hell, but India would be his. And any other country that disagreed would soon no longer exist. People were plentiful. What did a few million deaths matter in the long view of history, eh? Nothing at all.

Suddenly, there came the soft rattle of distant gunfire. A man screamed and there was the dull thud of a muffled explosion.

"Our guests have arrived," Komar snarled. "Mongoose, continue your work. Hagar, cut them off at the landing. Lay an ambush. I'll prepare the internal defenses."

So this was to be a fight to the death. Hell, was there really any other kind? Hagar dropped his cigarette to the carpet and ground it under a boot heel. "They'll never get off the stairs," he promised, drawing his pistol and clicking off the safety with his thumb.

"Do not let them get past you at any cost!" Komar ordered. Then he repeated himself to drive the point home. "At any cost. Do you understand?"

"Yes, old friend," Hagar answered, and turning, the thin terrorist strode down the hallway with the dozen armed men close behind.

CHAPTER TWENTY-THREE

Garden State Parkway, New Jersey

The coming night was starting to darken the sky as Able Team raced the Black Hawk across the pine barrens and marshy swamplands. There had been a dozen low-jack signals coming from the correct time and place. Manhattan was paradise for car thieves, but only one stolen vehicle was a brand-new Hummer that was obeying the speed limit and had just passed by the crash of a police car. Not a definitive identification, but good enough for a hard recon.

A river of light marked the Garden State Parkway, and the gunship moved alongside the roadway, keeping a safe distance. The neutron cannon could kill anything it saw, so Jack Grimaldi kept the pine trees between him and the parkway. If they used radar, he'd know it in a second and could take evasive maneuvers. But otherwise, with the running lights turned off the black helicopter was all but invisible in the growing twilight.

"Did the FBI get the crane operator?" Schwarz asked, watching his laptop, a blinking star on the screen showing the location of the low-jack transponder. Strapping into a nearby jumpseat was a replacement oscilloscope. The screen was clean, but he had high hope for success.

"Yes, but he knew nothing," Grimaldi replied from the cockpit. "Just some fool paid to illegally move boxes. Homeland passed the buck, and the FBI is going to bring him up on smuggling charges."

"Not attempted murder?"

"And whom did he try to kill?" the pilot asked with a chuckle. "We don't exist, remember?"

"Oh yeah," Schwarz snorted. "I forget sometimes."

Miles passed in tense silence as the gunship came ever closer to the Hummer, the soft beeping of the low jack becoming faster and faster until Schwarz turned it off in annoyance.

"Anything in sight?" he asked, craning his neck toward a window.

"Rest stop up ahead," Lyons declared, shifting the Atchisson shotgun cradled in his lap.

"Let's see," Grimaldi said, angling in that direction. Then there came a series of fast clicks as the pilot armed the rocket pod and electric minigun.

Grimly, Lyons knew that there would be no trick napalm bombs this time, no sleep gas or other fancy maneuvers. Schwarz would track the Hummer and Grimaldi would blow it out of existence with the weapons on board the Black Hawk.

When the Farm had won the auction, everybody hoped that would be an end to the matter. They'd pay off Malavade, get the cannons and then kill the arms dealer. Nice and simple. But suddenly everything went straight to hell. The man had either changed his mind for some unknown reason, or else they were facing a new enemy who had seized control of the cannons.

The parking lot of the rest stop was filled with cars and motorcycles.

"And there she is," Blancanales announced, pointing downward.

A big dark blue Hummer sat all by itself in the parking lot, no other vehicle nearby.

Coming to a halt outside the nimbus of light radiating from the rest stop, the men looked the place over. The gas station was ablaze with fluorescent lights, the glow almost forming a haze around the refueling depot. A country-style restaurant was full of people, swarms of children were playing in a small park, and several families were playing miniature golf through a maze of comical figures, giant clowns, dancing windmills and pink alligators.

"Sweet Jesus, we got civvies up the ass," Blancanales growled as the Black Hawk eased closer over the treetops. "We miss, and it'll be a massacre."

"Not going to happen," Grimaldi declared, stroking the control panel of the military gunship to flip the safety off the joystick.

A tiny plastic square swung out from his helmet. On the clear square was a glowing crosshair, and now wherever he looked, the nose-mounted minigun would precisely track. The accuracy of the helmet was astounding. However, the minigun fired only AP rounds, nothing more. There also was a 35 mm rocket pod, but that wasn't a servo mechanism, and the minirockets didn't track. If the Black Hawk was carrying a complement of Sidewinders, or Red-Eye missiles, he could take out the Hummer from a mile away. But those were also hellishly destructive, and the vehicle was surrounded by noncombatants. This attack had to be a surgical strike, up close and personal.

"Infrared reads clean," Schwarz declared. "Engine is hot, but there are no passengers on board."

"No live passengers," Lyons corrected. "Lord knows where they dumped the owners. Take it."

Nodding, Grimaldi placed the crosshair on the Hummer and mashed down hard on the trigger. Instantly the minigun revved to a whine as the eight barrels started spinning, and then a stuttering stream of armor-piercing rounds and tracers extended across the trees and playground to savagely hammer the Hummer.

The front hood literally exploded off the vehicle at the arrival of the heavy-caliber rounds, and the engine burst into flames. The windshield disintegrated, the seats were torn apart into springs and foam padding, and then the roof caved in, displaying there was nothing inside. Tattered clothing flew from the annihilated luggage in the rear.

"Shit, it's empty!" the pilot cursed, releasing the trigger. Tilting away from the rest stop, he headed west, then south. "All right, I'll circle and land behind the restaurant. Try to give you some cover when you go EVA to hunt for the bastards on the ground."

"Forget it. The cannon's not here," Blancanales said softly, his face grim. "They didn't come here for food or fuel."

"Then what… Oh, crap. Hostages."

Behind them, people were rushing out of the restaurant, running, waving, shouting, pointing in shock. The punctured gas tanks of the Hummer erupted, throwing the vehicle sideways into a creek. Cameras flashed in the growing darkness as the Black Hawk dipped low and out of visual range.

"Heads up, people," Schwarz said, touching his earphone. "Akira is now reporting another low-jack signal from the parking lot we just hit. He checked as soon as we had a precise location. It came on…sixty minutes ago. Seems to be moving at exactly the speed limit on the southbound GSP—no, it just crossed over into Delaware…Route 95. That's sixty miles away!"

"Not for long," Grimaldi said resolutely, touching controls. The big turbo-engine increased in power. Moving off the parkway, the sleek Black Hawk cut straight across the rolling countryside, the ground streaking below them in a continuous blur.

"What are we hunting now?" Lyons demanded, placing aside the Atchisson and checking a satchel charge. Even if the big man died, he could drop the charge and take out the cannon.

"A Cadillac convertible." Lyons frowned. "But that can't hide the cannon worth a damn."

"But it's perfect for striking at other cars," Grimaldi added solemnly, his face covered with the twinkling rainbow of lights from the control panel. "And helicopters."

"Oh hell, they picked up a crew wagon," Blancanales cursed, smacking a fist on the jumpseat. "Which could mean they also got some fresh troops." For the first time, Able team was facing an enemy with computer support as good as the Farm. He hoped Kurtzman and the gang were on their toes, because this could get real ugly, real fast.

"But if they're in a Cadillac, then where is the cannon?" Jack asked, glancing at the reflection of the grim men in the tinted windshield of the gunship.

"Right alongside that fat daddy Caddy," Ironman said as a guess. "In some replacement vehicle, probably another armored van. Ready and waiting for us to arrive."

"Well, then, let's not keep them waiting," Grimaldi replied stoically, moving off into the deepening night.

Victoria Towers, Calcutta

THEIR MP-5s chattering nonstop, Phoenix Force hammered a path through the terrorists boiling up the stairwell.

A dozen civilians died in the first barrage before Phoenix Force could get a clear shot to return fire. After that, it was chaos, noise, smoke and death. So far, only the terrorists had fallen, but there wasn't a member of Phoenix Force who didn't have a couple of holes in their clothes from incoming rounds deflected away by body armor.

McCarter fired a long burst into the group of masked men, and they staggered but didn't fall.

"Looks like this new group also has armor," McCarter said into his throat mike, slapping in a fresh clip.

A hail of bullets rose up the stairs, zinging off the iron rail and cracking the concrete steps. Then a big-bore gun boomed and Manning was thrown back against the wall.

"No damage," the big man wheezed, gingerly touching his aching chest under the body armor. "But somebody down there can really shoot."

"Okay, let's see how well he can play catch," Hawkins snarled, priming a grenade and counting to five before throwing it down.

Three seconds later the AP charge detonated in midair. Wild shrieks sounded as the deafening halo of hot shrapnel tore the defenders apart.

Rushing down the stairs, McCarter stopped at the twenty-first floor and poured gunfire into the smoker, taking out another set of emergency lights. As darkness descended, James pulled a gray wad of C-4 plastique from his web harness, set the timer on the detonator and slapped the explosive to the wall. The team raced back up the stairs and the charge cut loose. Going back down, they found only a gaping hole in the wall revealing a deserted office, papers fluttering in the air like a quarterly report snowstorm.

"Think Hu lied to us?" Hawkins asked angrily, peering through the dust and smoke. The air was becoming oppressively hot in the stairwell from all the explosives.

"No, the secret twentieth floor is here," McCarter said confidently. "We just have to find the thing!"

There came a series of odd bloops from below, and Phoenix Force charged down the stairs, firing their weapons nonstop.

The two masked men armed with MM-1 grenade launchers looked up in shock at the unexpected tactic just as the 30 mm shells detonated high above in hellish flame.

Even as he gunned down one of the terrorists, Mc-

Carter recognized the light of the blaze as Willie Peter, white phosphorous. These men were either fanatics, or else they didn't care if the skyscraper burned down. Which could only mean…

"This is a holding action!" Encizo bellowed, firing his MP-5 into more onrushing enemies. "The leader is trying to escape!"

Suddenly there came a hail of bullets from above, and Encizo stumbled back as a slug ricocheted off the iron railing to hit him in the belly. The slug flattened on the bottom of his body armor and fell off to tumble down the concrete stairs. Pulling in a ragged breath, the Cuban swung his MP-5 upward and poured hot lead into the foggy darkness. A man screamed and a body fell past them wearing night-vision goggles.

As Hawkins and James threw grenades down the stairs, McCarter, Encizo and Manning shot their weapon upward. The team knew they were in big trouble, caught in a classic pincher trap. How the masked men had gotten behind them, McCarter had no idea. Another secret set of stairs? Maybe. The EMP should have fried the elevator controls, and the fire alarm would have shut them down tight. Secret floors, trick walls, Malavade was either a genius or flat-out insane.

"This isn't a skyscraper," McCarter muttered over the radio, slapping more C-4 to an undamaged section of the wall. "It's a freaking funhouse!"

"Why, are ya having fun?" Hawkins taunted over the chatter of his weapon.

Slapping in a fresh clip, McCarter started to reply

when he heard a metallic thumping sound. Two grenades came bouncing down the steps.

Slapping the remote detonator on his belt, McCarter ignited the C-4. The blast opened the wall like a birthday piñata, the concussion throwing the grenades over the railing and into the blackness. A double explosion sounded from far below, but this time there were no screams of pain. The enemy was learning, and fast.

Pulling a canister from his belt pouch, McCarter detached the steel ring on top and dropped the bomb over the railing. Encizo and Manning did the same, while James and Hawkins threw their canisters upward. Seconds later, there were muffled explosions, and dense smoke poured over the railing from both directions.

"The tower is on fire!" a man shouted. "Run for your lives!"

"Shut up fool," another man snarled, followed by the sound of an open-palm slap. "Those are just gas grenades!" An M-60 machine gun chugged from above, the massive slugs chewing chunks off the concrete steps.

Racing down another flight, McCarter pulled a second canister from his pouch, this one marked with military color codes. His went up, and the rest of the team's dropped down. Immediately, the team members slipped breathing filters into their mouths, pressure clips closing their nostrils tight.

As these grenades gushed forth yellow smoke, the sounds of ragged coughing began, closely followed by the stomach-turning noise of men being violently ill.

Moving through the billowing clouds of smoke and

retch gas, Phoenix Force started to place yet another C-4 charge on the wall when Encizo whistled softly. Turning in his direction, the team saw the last charge had blown a hole in the wall as expected, but this time it showed two offices separated by a concrete floor.

"Which one is it?" Manning demanded, adjusting his filter. A whiff of the retch gas had slipped past the mask and he was fighting heroically to keep his lunch.

Looking around, Hawkins found the dead body of a masked man. Taking the man's AK-101 assault rifle, he flipped it into the top level. Nothing happened. Getting the idea, McCarter yanked off the dead man's ammo belt and tossed that into the lower level. Instantly, there came a flurry of gunfire peppering the ragged sides of the opening.

"Block the stairs," McCarter ordered, pouring lead into the crack.

Hawkins and Manning pulled out their own Willie Peter grenades and tossed the incendiary charges up to the next landing, while Encizo and James did the lower. Soon the stairs were filled with writhing flames, blocking any possible progress in either direction.

Going to the hole in the wall, the Stony Man commandos checked inside and saw nothing moving. They knew it was a trap, but there was nowhere else to go.

Flipping through a couple of stun grenades, the team waited for the flash-bangs to cut loose, then they scrambled into the marble foyer and immediately took cover.

A split second later, a long chatter of sustained gunfire and a hail of small-caliber rounds kicked up loose papers and tore a fern apart, the stream moving back and forth nonstop as if the gunners had an endless supply of ammo.

McCarter tossed through the last Willie Peter, and Hawkins added a thermite grenade. He tried for a bounce, and succeeded, the canister sailing over the railing and dropping out of sight.

The charges filled the stairwell with flames and screams, a wave of fear rushing out of the crack as if it was a doorway to Hell.

"Son of a bitch, it's another AutoSentry," Encizo growled, recognizing the boxy shape in the swirling smoke.

"No, there are two of them," James corrected, staying low as the desk shuddered from the impact of the tiny .22 rounds. The sentries on Wake Island were armed to kill. These were for maiming an enemy, holding them in place until… "They're going to use the cannon!"

"Then shoot better!" Swinging his MP-5 in that direction, McCarter tried to take out the sensor array on the right AutoSentry when a big man appeared briefly behind the robotic weapon on the left. The muscular fellow looked nothing like Malavade, yet he carried a definite air of authority and his clothing was spattered with dried blood. Had there been a hostile takeover? Maybe Malavade was no longer in charge.

Shooting from the hip, the stranger boomed death at Phoenix with a Glock .45 pistol. Locking the man's face into his memory, McCarter emptied a clip of 9 mm hardball ammo into the man. The rounds hit him in the chest and the big man dropped the handgun but didn't fall. More body armor!

"Ravid, here!" somebody shouted from around the corner and tossed over an assault rifle.

Making the catch, Komar worked the bolt and returned a full clip of armor-piercing 5.56 mm rounds from the INS assault rifle. McCarter flinched as something smacked painfully into his shoulder like a red-hot poker. Rolling sideways, he got behind a smashed desk and inspected the wound while the other members of Phoenix Force maintained the deadly hail of gunfire. The wound was bleeding steadily, but seemed shallow. At least, it wasn't squirting, or pumping, sure signs that a vital artery had been nicked. The round had to have just missed his body armor by the thickness of a sinner's prayer.

Slapping on a field dressing, McCarter flexed the shoulder gingerly, then kneeled into position and started firing once more. One of the AutoSentries was down, but the other was still holding court.

"Ravid," Hawkins muttered, working the bolt on his submachine gun to clear a jam. "Think that might be Ravid Komar of Tiger Force?"

"Let's see," James muttered into his throat mike, then took in a long breath and pulled the filter off his face. "Hey, Komar!"

The terrorist leader jerked at the sound of his name and sprinted around the corner.

Suddenly the elevator doors exploded off their tracks and tumbled into the darkness. Even before the smoke cleared, a group of armed man wearing combat armor rappelled into view and swung into the lobby. Landing in a crouch, the big man in front fired a 30 mm grenade launcher bolted underneath his assault rifle, the hellstorm of double-aught buckshot blasting the AutoSentry into sparking trash.

McCarter and Phoenix Force stopped firing for a moment at the unexpected arrival. The newcomers were dressed in black raid suits, and draped with military ordnance. Grenades festooned their web harness, and belt pouches bulged with ammunition clips for their sleek INS assault rifles, most of the weapons equipped with a 30 mm grenade launcher.

For a long moment the two groups looked at each other, the tension in the smoky air thick enough to chew. That's when McCarter noticed the crest of a charging lion on their shoulders. They were Indian air force? No, these were COIN troops, Indian army Special Forces commandos, the equivalent of American Green Berets.

"Identify yourselves, or die," Major Jagan Chandrasekhar of the COIN unit demanded, leveling his weapon at the Stony Man commandos.

But then the Indian troopers started violently gagging on the vomit gas billowing into the room, one of them almost tumbling down the elevator shaft before a comrade made a desperate grab for his arm.

Without replying, Phoenix Force started past the choking COIN troopers as the men struggled to shove breathing filters into their drooling mouths.

Just then, terrorists appeared around the corner, carrying a sheet of glass in front of them as protection, and firing their stubby machine guns around the edges.

In unison, COIN and Phoenix Force cut loose a thunderous barrage, the soft lead and hardball ammo smacking into the windowpane of Luxan and just staying there like flies in amber. In a fast move, Manning dropped his MP-5 and brought up the .50-caliber Barrett rifle. Working the bolt, he triggered a round. The startled crowd of men behind the thick Luxan shook from the triphammer impact, but incredibly, even the 660-grain round failed to penetrate.

As the Tiger Force terrorists started shooting again, James and a COIN trooper both grunted as they were hit in the chest, their body armor deflecting the 7.62 mm caliber rounds.

Now both covert teams dived to the dirty floor and opened fire at the grinning members of Tiger Force, approaching behind their adamantine shield. But instead of aiming at the exposed weapons of the terrorists, the assault rifles and submachine guns hammered the feet of the men into bloody gobbets.

Shrieking in hideous agony, the terrorists dropped the sheet of Luxan and were mowed down by the combination fusillade of 5.56 mm and 9 mm bullets.

Slapping in fresh clips, McCarter and the major looked at each other once more, then nodded, and the two teams proceeded side by side into the fortified headquarters of the former international arms dealer, now a military hardsite for Tiger Force.

But the moment they left the foyer, the glass window of an office halfway down the next corridor stridently shattered, spraying the ten men with twinkling shards. Grinning triumphantly as if they had already won the battle, a pair of terrorists stroked the triggers of their M-60 machine guns, throwing out a maelstrom of heavy lead.

Returning fire, Phoenix Force sprayed the pair of gunners inside the office, their rounds throwing out coronas of splinters from the huge mahogany desk. Dropping into firing positions, the COIN troopers started carefully sniping at the enemy as if trying to capture them alive.

Then the Barrett roared once more, a foot-long lance of flame extending from the long barrel. The monstrous round slammed into an M-60 and smashed it sideways into the other heavy machine gun. For single heartbeat, the two terrorists just stood there, stunned and vulnerable. Then the teams filled the office with gunfire and the shuddering corpses were riddled before they smacked into the wall cracking the wood paneling. Slowly, the twitching corpses slid to the floor leaving a contrail of life fluids smeared on the polished wood.

Racing along the corridor, Ravid Komar directed the last of his men to erect a barricade of wooden desks in the hallway, then he bodily charged into the computer room.

"NATO is here! Fire the rooftop cannon in two minutes!" he cried angrily. "Wipe out the entire city!"

But the room was empty, and Metudas was gone.

"Coward!" Ravid screamed, smacking the deserted chair with the barrel of his INS assault rifle.

As the chair wheeled away from the console, the leader of Tiger Force could now see there was a package of plastic bottles resting on the cushions. Bound with a nylon strap, each was a different color, and connected with a maze of plastic tubing. On top was a complex mechanism and a digital timer silently clicking down from twenty…nineteen…eighteen…

Dropping his weapon, Komar dived for the corner and barely made it into the former office of the arms dealer when the entire floor shook with a titanic blast and a wave of roiling flame filled the hallway.

CHAPTER TWENTY-FOUR

Nellor, India

Finished refueling the seaplane, Atman Basat shut off the pumps and closed the gas tank.

"Done," he announced, wiping his hands on a dry rag. "Let's get going for Sriharikota."

"We're being watched," Neeja said from the cockpit of the aircraft.

"Could just be a horny sailor watching the pretty girls on the beach."

"And it might be a sniper zeroing his scope before blowing off our heads." The man licked dry lips and forced himself not to look in that direction. "What should we do?" There was nobody near them on the dock. But that didn't mean missiles weren't getting ready to arch over the horizon and blow them into pieces.

"To hell with them," Basat snarled, climbing into

the plane. "Get ready to take off, while I get the cannon working."

"Here?"

"Better them than us," the man growled, flipping a row of switches. "Mr. Malavade said we could use it in self-defense." There was a low hum of electrical power as the Faraday Cage came alive, then the cannon boosted to full power.

"Goodbye," Abdeleb whispered, starting to swing the aiming mechanism along the coast in a long smooth gesture.

WALKING THE FOREDECK of the India navy corvette *Akshay,* Lieutenant Na Runta abandoned his sunglasses and smiled at the clear sky. The sun was just rising behind the radar hemisphere atop the bridge. It was going to be a really hat day, as his grandmom used to say. Hat, not hot, that was her thermometer. It was ninety degrees, maybe more, and by noon they'd all be longing for that tiny patch of shade.

Belowdecks, the *Akshay* was fully air-conditioned, the environmental system capable of keeping the thirty-six members of the crew safe and alive for a month from any known radioactive, chemical or bacteriological agent. The air smelled a little artificial, like the inside of a new car, but an open porthole fixed that. He dragged in a deep breath. Ah, wonderful! Many sections of India were rank and smelly, other parts were paradise, lush gardens of delight. But the sea was always a delight, even during a massive storm, the beauty becoming terrible to behold. Yet it was still magnificent. Merely a beauty to avoid until the sea calmed down and welcomed the sailors back once more like a temperamental lover.

Crewmen were moving around the ship checking ropes and chains, oiling a hatching or using one of the new palm computers to run a maintenance check on the quad rail for the SAM launcher. The four deadly Stellaclass missiles gleamed in the morning light like polished sin on Sunday. Belowdecks, he knew the torpedo tubes were spotlessly clean, the deadly arsenal lying in their armored battery.

Turning aft, the lieutenant checked the progress of the crewmen greasing the master gymbol for the portside mortar. The five fat tubes formed an angular arch around the sweating sailors. Normally, the mortars weren't loaded, but because of the mysterious disasters that had been happening lately at sea, the Navy High Command at Red Fort had decided to keep the ships ready for instant battle. The five tubes were loaded with two depth charges, two mines and a chaff-flare bundle that would fill that sky with protective confusion for hundreds of meters. It could also sink a Chinese fishing boat. Runta had seen a tube misfire once, and the bundle shot straight through the canvas sails of a Chinese junk and exploded inside an ore freighter. Ever since then, the arms book has been slightly modified to list the defense bundle as a potential aid for troops on the ground.

Grabbing his hip flask, Runta unscrewed the top and carefully took a sip of the steaming coffee inside. A lot of his brother officers insisted on sticking to the old British rule of serving tea, but he hated the wretched stuff. He wanted something hot and black, not weak and pale.

Just then, the lieutenant frowned. A couple of sailors on the aft deck were ogling the tourists on the beach with field glasses. That was strictly prohibited. They were navy men, damn it! The pride of the nation, and they should all damn well act like officers and gentlemen. Especially if they weren't.

Then his blood ran cold, and he dropped the flask. People were toppling over on the sand and falling out of their chairs. At a beachfront café, waiters were crashing out of sight and numerous diners were limply collapsing into their meals.

Rushing to the aft deck, Runta grabbed a heavy pair of field glasses from a horrified sailor and adjusted the focus. The whole city seemed to be affected. As he watched, dozens of cars veered wildly on the roads to crash into other cars, the side of a building, or just plow through the hundreds of bodies lying on the sidewalks. People toppled off balconies and hit the sidewalks like bags of red sauce. In a few moments it was over, and Runta couldn't seem to find anybody moving in the entire city.

Terrorists! the man rationalized. This had to be some sort of nerve gas attack! What other possible explanation could there be?

Then he caught a small motion near the civilian refueling station. A fixed-wing seaplane was motoring away from the pumps, the airfoils moving, their course change showing that the pilot was still very much alive. Unlike everybody else on the dock.

Shoving the field glasses into the hands of the stone-faced sailor, Runta sprinted to the nearest ship's phone and dialed up the bridge. Nobody answered. Glancing upward, Runta saw the captain hanging over the railing of the observation deck, a pair of field glasses dangling from the cord around his neck.

Adrenaline pumped into his body, as the lieutenant canceled the call and tapped in the code for the PA system.

"Attention all hands, get ready for action!" the lieutenant barked into the hand microphone. "Get ready for action stations!"

Klaxons and sirens and bells started all along the ship, a different sound for each primary task. The main 76 mm cannon rose for battle, the missile quad-launcher spun around as its radar searched for a target, and dull thumps sounded from the mortars as the safeties disengaged. Crewmen rushed to the forward and aft to the 30 mm gun emplacements. A few of them were shoeless, and one chap was dressed only in his underwear. But the sailor grimly worked the arming bolts on the big weapon ready for battle.

Suddenly a dozen crewmen raced out of a hatchway carrying INS assault rifles, several of them tipped with grenades. He almost smiled at that. If anything came within the range of the rifle-grenades, the 76 mm cannon would blow it apart. But he applauded the preventive action.

As the tiny plane lifted off the shimmering waves, it buzzed past people swimming in the ocean. They went still and sank from sight, while others in sailboats fell overboard.

A speedboat skipped past the seaplane and rammed directly into the fuel station, the resulting fireball spreading across the boardwalk and dock in a tidal wave of flame. But nobody moved within the writhing flames, and the lieutenant somehow knew there weren't any screams of pain. Dead. Everybody was dead. Wherever the plane went, death followed. In spite of his military training, the lieutenant felt as if he were watching some ancient prophecy come true, as if the Hindu god Shiva had was striding across the land. *I am death, the destroyer, the shatterer of worlds.*

"Not on my watch," Runta snarled, then spoke clearly into the receiver. "Fire all guns! Repeat, fire all guns! Destroy that seaplane!" But nothing happened. The main cannons didn't boom and not a missile went airborne.

Stepping out from behind the housing for the main water pump, Runta instantly felt oddly warm, sort of itchy all over, and then fell into an infinite pool of Stygian blackness.

Behind the thick steel hull, men died in their tracks, falling into the working gears of the generators, tumbling off catwalks, collapsing in the corridors. A helicopter gunship lifted from the deck and the crew perished. Without the autopilot engaged, the aircraft followed the dead hand of the pilot and slipped sideways across the deck to crash into the sea and quickly sink from sight.

A few moments later, the little seaplane flew over the heavily armed corvette, then turned away the fifty thousand dead civilians of Nellar, and assumed a leisurely course for the nearby commercial space port of Sriharikota Island.

Newark, Delaware

A SIGN FLASHED BY the Cadillac with the name of the next town. Salamalin Taralin frowned in consternation. "Are we back in New Jersey?"

"No, this is Delaware," Jimmy "The Ice pick" DeMarco said.

"Crazy Americans," Taralin muttered, "with their cities of the same name."

Unconcerned, DeMarco shrugged. Across his lap lay a brand-new Barrett XM-109, the 25 mm rifle his payment for riding shotgun with the Indian. The Sicilian mobster really didn't care what the fellow was guarding in the dark blue Dodge van—a ton of drugs, illicit weapons, an experimental prototype for corporate espionage—who gave a fuck? This new 4-shot monster Barrett would give the local boss a killing edge against those goddamn Jamaicans trying to take over his Atlantic City casino. Personally, he was just itching to give it a try.

"Hey, you're from India, right?" DeMarco said, the wind ruffling his dark hair.

Both hands on the steering wheel, Taralin kept a close watch on the two Dodge vans ahead of him. The FBI had to have some way of tracking the stolen vehicles, perhaps even that low-jack thing that Mongoose Metudas had warned them about. But the hacker had easily arranged for replacement vehicles for the van they had abandoned in Manhattan. Newer models, bigger, with more armor.

Something dark appeared in the starry sky behind the

Cadillac, briefly eclipsing the twinkling lights as it moved across the interstate.

"We have company, seven o'clock high," Taralin announced.

Turning in the seat, DeMarco stared skyward, his hands moving slowly across the big Barrett. "Alive or dead?" he asked, raising the barrel and closing an eye to take aim.

"Dead, and don't miss."

Flame belched from the huge maw of the titanic weapon, the acoustical suppressor reducing the muzzle-blast to something no louder than a .38 Police Special.

At the same moment, a stuttering lance of 35 mm rockets lanced out from the weapon pod of the Black Hawk gunship, stitching both Dodge vans. The vehicles erupted into twisted metal and flame as something in the sky loudly exploded and started to fall to the ground, trailing smoke and flames.

Wildly careening, the smashed vans rocked back and forth colliding with each other like mobile bank vaults. Every other car on the road started to race out of the way, .The dome light came on inside a BMW and a man in a business suit started punching numbers into his cell phone.

"Stop him," Taralin ordered.

Laying down the Barrett, DeMarco pulled a .357 Magnum S&W handgun and fired twice. The side window of the Beamer shattered and the driver bucked as his head burst open like ripe fruit, brains and fluids spraying across the inside of the windshield.

Veering sharply to the right, the car went straight off the road and crashed into an outcrop alongside the road.

Trailing smoke and flames, one of the damaged vans swayed dangerously close to the gravel berm. A bump shook open the rear doors and loose items tumbled out—ammunition clips, plastic drinking cups, fast-food hamburgers, and a couple of round metal spheres. In the bright halogen headlights, the men could see the handles fly away free.

"Look out!" DeMarco cried, throwing an arm across his face.

Heading straight for the grenades, Taralin drove directly over the charges and a split second later they thunderously exploded behind the Cadillac. Shrapnel peppered the big car, smashing the sideview mirror and ricocheting off the windshield, leaving a star-shaped impact crack.

"Sweet Jesus, that was close," DeMarco swore, trying to catch his breath. Turning sideways, he gave the driver an impressed look. "You got balls, Sammy-boy, I'll give ya that."

Grinding his teeth, Taralin started to correct the man when a dark shape appeared above the trees ahead of the burning vans. Once more, a staccato barrage of minirockets reached down to sweep across the vans, and then roadway far ahead of them thunderously exploded.

Bracing his legs against the seat, DeMarco pressed himself against the windshield for support, and fired the remaining four rounds in the Barrett as fast as possible. The minirockets spoke again, along with the high-pitched whine of an electric minigun. The hood of the Cadillac was stitched with gaping holes, and oil squirted into view like thin blood from a wound. With a ragged sputter, the engine died as two fiery blossoms appeared in the sky. This time, Taralin could dimly see the outline of a fire-covered Black Hawk falling sideways into the rocky Maryland hills. It disappeared behind some pine trees, followed by a satisfying explosion.

Unexpectedly, one of the burning Dodge vans dived into a gaping crater in the road and thundered into a roiling fireball, the driver and the five gunmen in the back silhouetted for a single moment before vanishing within the blast.

The concussion hit the second Dodge and the Caddy like an invisible fist. Multiple tires blew as the van slammed into the car, shoving them both onto the safety railing. DeMarco cried out and the big Barrett went flying to land safely in the rear seat.

Throwing off a contrail of sparks, the Dodge and Cadillac scraped along the railing. The corrugated steel beams bent alarmingly, then gave way in a grinding crunch. Both vehicles plowed deep into the thick woods, careening through bushes and saplings, slowing in speed until coming to a rest in the middle of a grassy field dotted with wildflowers.

A mile down the roadway, a reddish light began to intensify in the dense woodlands as a blaze started to spread through the dry October weeds.

CHAPTER TWENTY-FIVE

Victoria Towers, Calcutta, India

Even before the staggering explosion dissipated, spreading along the hallways and offices, gunfire came from the crack in the wall. McCarter and Hawkins were on the move, Major Chandrasekhar and one of his men close behind. A sergeant stayed behind with two more troopers.

Stopping at the source of the blast, McCarter could see the charred ruins of computers. The blast had smashed down a plastic room divider, revealing a Cray VSG Supercomputer. It was the exact same model as the one at the Farm. He even saw pressurized nitrogen tanks in the rear to keep the supercomputer as cold as possible. The tanks were ruptured, and many of the units and servers were glistening, frozen into fragile crystals from the spray of ultracold·liquid nitrogen. So this was the home of the mysterious enemy hacker, Mc-

Carter thought. A smashed picture of a mongoose lay on the smoking floor, and a cracked nameplate on the splintery desk also bore the same moniker.

"Mongoose." Hawkins snorted. "At least he has a name now."

Removing the filter from his face, the major looked over the ruins with marked disdain. "I always knew I would never capture the Mongoose alive," he said, the words low and guttural. "Pity. There are many old debts his imprisonment would pay."

"Mongoose works for Ravid Komar?" McCarter asked bluntly.

The major paused for only a moment. "No, and yes. He worked for Malavade, past tense, but apparently…"

"He also was working for Tiger Force," Hawkins finished grimly. "Or switched sides. It doesn't really make a difference. He's working with the terrorists now."

"Or is he working for himself?" McCarter asked, lifting a piece of the chemical bomb from the floor. He recognized the liquid feeder device and knew what it was used for. "T.J., get the team and spread out. Find that hacker, or Ravid Komar. One or the other of them—" He broke off.

"Has a remote control for the neutron cannon," Chandrasekhar said, resting his ISN assault rifle on a shoulder. "I know what we both seek, NATO."

"Never heard of them," McCarter said, glad the rip on his sleeve didn't expose the SAS tattoo on his arm.

The major gave a hard grin. "And I never heard of COIN."

"Just as long as we understand each other."

"Agreed. However, the weapon will not leave this country. Our scientists invented the machine, and so only we should have control."

An armed private stepped closer to the major and worked the arming bolt on his assault rifle.

"At ease, Kinnah," the major said softly.

"How about we find it first, then argue pissing rights later," Hawkins drawled.

The men looked at each other and finally nodded. They would work together, and argue possession afterward.

Machine-gun fire erupted in the foyer, and a man screamed.

Abruptly starting that way, McCarter noted the sagging door of the office at the end of the hallway, and changed directions. The COIN soldiers were close behind.

Charging into the office, McCarter and Hawkins found the place was empty. If Komar had been here, he was gone. But where? There didn't seem to be another exit. A broken sheet of plywood covered a window, and to the side was a weapons cabinet, most of the racks empty, drawers askew, and loose bullets rolling on the ground.

Rolling? Going to the cabinet, McCarter studied it carefully for traps, then pressed several times along the inside jamb. His questing fingers found a soft spot and he pressed hard. With a sigh, the wall slid aside to reveal a dark staircase spiraling downward.

"Mongoose, or Komar, somebody went this way, I want them both," the major stated forcibly.

McCarter checked the clip in his MP-5 and tossed

away the half clip to load in a full magazine. "You realize this is almost certainly a deathtrap," he said, coolly working the slide.

"Of course," the major snapped. "And every moment lets them get farther away."

"Gary, you're going after Komar and a hacker named Mongoose," McCarter said, touching his throat mike. "Find that cannon. If I know Malavade, the damn thing is somewhere on this floor in another fake room."

"Not the roof, or the basement?" the Canadian replied over the earplug.

"Check everywhere! Find it, and fast. If we ever have to abandon the…headquarters, self-destruct charges would remove it from the face of the earth shortly afterward."

"More likely, they'd use the cannon."

"Yeah," McCarter said woodenly. "I know."

The major was touching his own throat and muttering, obviously relaying instructions to his own troops.

"Will do," Manning replied. "Good luck."

Without further comment, McCarter and the others started down the stairs.

IN THE FOYER, Encizo and a COIN trooper tossed AP grenades through the opening in the wall. The explosives detonated, but there were no screams from the stairwell.

"Rafe, stay here and guard our six," Manning directed. "Cal, with me. Let's find that cannon if we have to tear down the whole building!"

"Wait," Sergeant Akbar Raman said, holding up a restraining hand. "Private Goshkal, stay here and help… Rafe. Private Banjerea, check the computer room."

"It's smashed," Manning started in annoyance, then gave a smile. "But Mongoose must have planned for the use of an EMP. It's too obvious a ploy. Hell, the neutron cannon is similar, effecting an aspect of a nuclear explosion."

The barrel-chested sergeant grinned. "Which means fiber optic cables to operate the weapon. Wherever they go, we'll find the cannon."

The four men rushed down the corridor and easily found the destroyed computer room. Small fires were burning all over the place, and some of the metal pieces of the Cray seemed to actually be melting.

Returning into the hallway, Manning grabbed a fire ax and came back swinging randomly at the walls. The other men started using their belt knives, hacking apart the softened wood paneling and the drywall underneath.

"Here!" Banjerea cried, tugging the clear plastic cables into view.

Using the ax, Manning attacked the carpeting and traced the fiber optic to the smoking pile of electronics mixed in with the pieces of the burned desk.

"They stop here," Manning announced, displaying the ragged ends.

"And go up," Raman answered, looking inside the wall.

The neutron cannon was on the roof, hidden somewhere inside the air-conditioning units and water pumps. Both teams had to have gone right past the disguised weapon without knowing it. But then, Malavade's profession was hiding things and smuggling weapons.

Returning to the foyer, the teams split, the remainder of Phoenix Force going through the crack for the stairs. The three COIN troopers attached the dangling cables inside the elevator shaft to small mechanical devices on their belts and started moving upward.

Charging up the stairs, Manning and the others found only dead bodies wearing masks. Those last grenades seemed to have done the job and taken out the last of Tiger Force.

With a cry, Encizo sprayed his MP-5 at a corpse, the rounds ricocheting off the body armor.

From the bloody floor, Hagar fired three times, hitting each member of Phoenix Force dead in the middle of the chest, his own rounds deflecting. Both sides fired again, changing their targets, the noise nearly deafening in the enclosed space.

As the submachine guns ceased firing, the ejected brass danced musically down the cracked stairs. Hagar clicked his empty weapon twice more, crimson squirting from a large hole in his neck. Drawing his .357 Magnum Desert Eagle, Manning fired once more, and left the faceless terrorist sprawled in a warm pool of his own blood.

Exiting the kiosk, Manning, Encizo and James found the three COIN troopers already there scanning the assortment of complex machinery with handheld EM scanners.

Breaking out their own scanners, the Stony Man commandos took the other side of the roof, probing everything.

"Power surge over here," James reported, touching a large vented metal housing. Then he saw the digital meter start to rapidly climb. "Damn, the cannon is charging to fire!"

"Cut the wires. We want it intact…" Raman started, then clearly changed his mind at the sight of the city spread out below. Helpless and vulnerable, Calcutta waited for his decision.

"To hell with that," the sergeant roared, leveling his assault rifle. "Take it out, boys!"

The Phoenix Force members moved back quickly as the three COIN troopers swung up their assault rifles and triggered the grenade launchers. The 30 mm shells punched through the thin metal cowling and blew it off, exposing a large ceramic oval covered with complex wiring in a hundred colors, and covered with a fine silvery mesh. Manning inhaled sharply at the sight of the ripped Faraday Cage, the wide rent crackling with electric sparks.

The sound from the accumulator got noticeably louder.

"Everybody!" Manning commanded, triggering his MP-5 and the Desert Eagle at the same time.

Side by side, the six men unleashed their weapons, soft lead and armor-piercing steel hammering the delicate controls and ceramic rings. Pieces flew off the neutron cannon under the pummeling barrage, wires snapped. A small oval shattered and fell away. The noise got louder, and blue short circuits crawled along the weapon like demented insects. Dropping clips, the men reloaded and kept firing.

A pressurized pipe was punctured and liquid nitrogen hissed free, forming a dense white cloud that extended across the rooftop. A wave of bitter cold seized the soldiers, chilling them to the bone. Breathing became difficult. Ricochets went everywhere, but not a man retreated. The 30 mm grenade launchers spoke again, fléchettes chewing chunks out of the humming machine. It tilted sideways, pulling a fiber-optic cable from the mounting.

The Faraday Cage fell away completely as the grim soldiers advanced upon the still revving neutron cannon, probing desperately for a weak spot on a weapon far beyond their comprehension…

CHAPTER TWENTY-SIX

Maryland

Siren wailing, a police car rocked to a halt on the berm alongside the smoking crater in the highway. Clambering out, the two policemen stared in horror at the crashed Dodge van sticking out of the depression, then one man rushed to the trunk for a medical kit, while the other leaned into the car and grabbed the microphone clipped to the dashboard.

"Car Nineteen to base," the man said quickly. "Car Nineteen to base. We have a—"

A pistol roared in the dark woods and the patrolman twisted inside the car, blood and brains blowing out through the open window as the .357 magnum round took him in the ear.

"Freeze!" the other patrolman shouted, drawing his 9 mm Glock.

A fiery flower spoke from the darkness, the 5.56 mm

rounds from the M-16 stitching the officer from crotch to crown. He staggered, discharging his handgun at the pavement, then toppled over, sighing into death.

"Tough bastard," Garunda Hai said, stepping out of the darkness. A large section of her hair was burned off, and she walked with a pronounced limp. "Get those bodies off the road, and take his gun."

"Right," Taralin said, rushing to the job.

"Well, now we have wheels," DeMarco said, leveling the Barrett in his big hands. "But stealing a cop car isn't smart."

"We are taking these vehicles," Hai declared, sniffing hard. A rivulet of thick blood began to trickle from her nose. "Get some flares from the trunk and circle off the crater."

"Then what?"

"Then we wait for a ride to arrive," she said with a cold smile.

Waiting in the bushes, the terrorists watched several motorcycles, an expensive coupe, a battered pickup truck and numerous sedans roll past the illuminated blast crater and police car. Everybody slowed slightly, but then sped up again once they were past.

"This isn't going to work," DeMarco stated. "I say we use my cell phone, call a cab and get the fuck out of here. If the FBI sends another copter..."

"Chopper," Taralin corrected him.

"Who gives shit what it's called?" the man exploded. "I was hired to ride gun on a shipment. Okay, here I am. But gunning down FBI agents wasn't part of the deal. Those boys have got a long memory."

"So do we," Hai murmured, working the bolt on the M-16 assault rifle.

Then a delivery van came into sight.

Instantly moving into the police car, Taralin turned on the flashing lights, then flipped on the siren for just a moment.

Slowing reluctantly, the van eased over to the berm and stopped. Nervously, the driver stayed behind the steering wheel, trying to see past the rotating light.

A shape walked out of the lights holding up a hand and wearing a police hat.

"Something wrong, Officer?" the young driver asked.

"Not anymore," DeMarco said, slashing the teenager across the throat.

Red blood gushed from the hideous wound, and DeMarco grabbed the dying teen by the hair to haul him bodily through the window. The teenager hit the pavement making horrible gurgling noises. Walking to the fellow, Hai fired the M-16 once and the body went flat.

Shouldering the Barrett, DeMarco drew a pistol and got behind the steering wheel. Checking the rear to make sure there were no passengers, the hitman next turned the headlights off and on. At the signal, Taralin turned off the flashing lights on top of the police car.

Climbing into the passenger side, Hai briefly checked over the vehicle. "It'll do," she said grudgingly. "Let's move."

Easing the delivery van into gear, DeMarco crept forward and paused near the police car to let Taralin get into the rear. Turning off the road, the man followed the path of destruction left by the speeding Cadillac, branches and broken tree limbs scratching the body of the delivery van. Trundling carefully through a shallow creek, he finally reached the grassy field and parked alongside the sagging ruin of the Dodge van. Fluids were dripping from the engine, and the rear doors were agape, the neutron cannon visible inside. The ballistic cloth was still draped over the machine.

Openly holding shotguns and machine pistols, four big mercenaries hired by Metudas over the Internet were standing around the tilting Dodge, one of them with his left arm in a sling made from a torn shirt.

"Hot damn, you did it," the largest men rumbled, lowering his Ingram. "Okay, lady, I'm impressed."

"Shut up and get the machine into the van," Hai commanded, watching the sky. If the FBI had sent one Black Hawk, they could easily send another. The only thing holding the federal agents back was the impression that the cannon was working and that she could shoot down anything coming her way. Or turn it on the countryside, wiping out hundreds of civilians. The closer they got to Washington, D.C., the greater their leverage.

Opening the rear doors of the delivery van, Taralin started throwing out the cardboard boxes and packages. Using a tire iron, the mercenaries forced open the Dodge and removed the heavy sheet of cloth. Grunting and groaning, they awkwardly maneuvered the heavy machine and waddled toward the delivery van.

Checking the load in the clip, DeMarco reloaded his weapon and stayed behind the wheel, keeping alert for any suspicious movement on the leafy path through the forest. Dimly, he could see the reflected light from the flares on the quivering leaves.

The delivery van rocked as the mercenaries deposited the cannon onto the corrugated steel floor, and fumbled to shove it deeper into the interior. When it was balanced roughly in the middle of the vehicle, the mercenaries draped the ballistic cloth over the machine again. Then added several of the bulletproof vests that formerly lined the Dodge.

"That'll do?" the head merc asked.

"For the moment," Hai said from the passenger seat. She dropped a nylon bag full of weapons and cash on the floor. When the van was parked near D.C., they would steal a car and drive to another state. Once there, Metudas would give them new identities, and they'd fly home in comfort.

Collecting their weapons and supplies from the crumpled Dodge, the mercenaries clambered inside the delivery van and pulled the rear doors' shut.

"Want one?" Taralin asked, offering the woman a spare bulletproof vest.

Using a handkerchief to tie back her wild hair, Hai started to reply when Able Team and Jack Grimaldi walked out of the trees. The men were battered and bruised, their clothing burned, and Grimaldi had bloody bandages wrapped around his neck. But their weapons gleamed with oil, and the Stony Man commandos opened fire with their assault rifles, dealing death in every direction.

"Kill them!" Hai screamed, triggering her own M-16 assault rifle.

Diving for cover, the Stony Man operatives rolled into the shadows, firing constantly.

The rear doors of the delivery van were thrown open, and the mercs charged out, brandishing weapons.

DeMarco killed the headlights and reached for his Barrett, but Hai held it.

"Drive," she commanded, flicking off the safety.

Looking down the huge barrel was like peering into a subway tunnel. Inhaling sharply, DeMarco glumly nodded and shifted into gear.

As the van started rolling, it exposed the mercenaries, and they dropped to the grass, sending out a maelstrom of 9 mm rounds from their MAC 10 machine pistols. The leaves in the forest shook wildly and bark flew off the bare trees. Rosario Blancanales grunted from a hit, and Hermann Schwarz sprayed the mercenaries with a wreath of 5.56 mm tumblers. One of the men cried out, and stood clutching at the horrible wound in his face.

Tracking to the right, Carl Lyons fired a half dozen rounds from the Atchisson at the delivery van, trying for the tire, but there were too many rocks and broken branches on the ground. Debris filled the air, leaves flying, and the van disappeared into the trees.

Breaking into a run, he gave pursuit, firing occasionally just to see in the velvety darkness. The bastards were driving with their lights off to make sure their taillights didn't offer him a target. That was smart. And unnecessary. Until he knew what happened to the original driver of the delivery van, Lyons would only shoot at the rear if he thought the cannon was getting ready to fire.

Bursting onto the highway, he saw the van speeding away even as he spied the dead man in a delivery uniform on the side of the road, and the two dead cops. A former Los Angeles policeman himself, Lyons felt a visceral surge of rage at the sight, but controlled his temper for the moment and headed for the patrol car. The dead didn't matter at the moment; getting the terrorists was his only goal.

Getting into police car, Lyons reached under the dashboard and fumbled with the trick switch hidden there for officers to use in case of trouble. The big engine roared into life.

Maintaining a standard three-man formation, Blancanales, Schwarz and Grimaldi rushed from the bushes, their weapons at the ready.

"In!" Lyons yelled out the blood-smeared window.

Schwarz scrambled into the passenger seat, ignoring the grisly stains, and the others climbed into the back seat. Tromping on the gas pedal, Lyons took off in a spray of loose gravel.

"Windows," Grimaldi said, tapping the glass with his Glock.

Steadily accelerating, Lyons hit the controls and lowered the rear windows so the men could shoot outside. Cop cars were primarily designed for passengers wearing handcuffs, but ferrying other cops in an emergency had thankfully been taken into consideration in most of the newer models.

"To the best of my knowledge, there aren't any hostages," Lyons said quickly. "We can take them down."

"If we can catch them," Grimaldi countered.

"Just give me one shot," Blancanales said, leaning out a window. His hair was a riot in the wind of the speed. "That's all I ask, once clear shot."

"Aw shit, they smashed the on-board computer and radio," Schwarz snarled, casting down a tangle of wires. "And our radios are deader than disco!"

"Then we're on our own," Lyons said in a voice carved from ice.

"How long before the police track the lowjack and come to investigate?" Grimaldi asked, thumbing loose rounds into the partial clip to fill it completely. There was a spare box of ammo in his jacket pocket, but only the one clip. Thirty rounds was all he could fire at a time, then he had to reload.

"Too long," Lyons replied, trying to will the engine to go faster. Steadily, the needle crept to ninety and then quivered at the hundred mark.

Suddenly, taillights winked out up ahead.

"That must be them," Lyons declared, turning on the siren.

Every other vehicle on the road started to move aside, just as somebody leaned out of the passenger window of the van and opened fire with an M-16 assault rifle.

Swerving out of the way, Lyons held a steady course as the others peppered the van. The rounds easily penetrated the side panels, but only dented the heavy rear door.

The M-16 was withdrawn, and now a much larger weapon came into view. It looked halfway between a 40 mm and a .50-caliber.

As the gun went steady, Lyons twisted the wheel hard. An instant later the roadway alongside them exploded in a shower of dust and rock.

"That's a Barrett 25 mm rifle," Grimaldi said. "Cowboy just bought one for the Farm!"

"Any suggestions?" Schwarz asked loudly, firing the M-16 assault rifle. A stream of spent brass shells flew into the night.

More shots were exchanged.

"Yeah, don't get hit!"

By now, all of the other cars in sight were pulling off the road, several of them bouncing across the median in their haste to escape the running gunbattle.

Suddenly the van swerved, almost clipping a Fiat, and took the exit for Baltimore with squealing tires.

"They're going downtown!" Blancanales cursed, slapping in his last clip. "They must have realized D.C. was impossible and now Baltimore is the target!"

"That's not going to happen," Lyons growled, streaking down the exit ramp at full speed.

A headlight shattered and sparks flew as the police car scraped along the concrete divider. But the grim man maintained their speed and flashed through the intersection nearly getting hit by the crisscrossing traffic.

"Nine o'clock!" Blancanales shouted, pointing a finger.

There was the van, sliding into an alley barely large enough to pass its bulk.

Slamming on the brakes, Lyons fought the police car into a sharp turn and then pushed the pedal to the floor.

The big engine surged, and the two vehicles collided louder than foundry triphammers. Glass shattered and metal crumbled, and everybody in the police car lurched forward, straining against the seat belts. Instantly the air bags deployed, shoving the Stony Man commandos hard against their seats, pinning them helpless.

Even before the car stopped rocking, Lyons used his pocketknife to slash at the air bag holding him prisoner. It violently deflated, the exhaust smelling oddly like gunpowder.

Squeezing out the door, Lyons blasted the rear tires off the van with his Atchisson, the rubber disintegrating in the fusillade of steel fléchettes.

There came a crash of glass, and then somebody scrambled onto the roof of the van. Grinning fiendishly, a busty woman aimed the Barrett at the stunned men trapped in the police car, and Lyons cut loose with the autoshotgun.

Her face vanished as the fléchettes chewed through her body, the Barrett tumbling away from hands no longer connected to a living mind.

As the corpse dropped from sight, soft bangs came from the police car and the other men struggled from their impromptu prison.

Clambering onto the hood of the car, the Stony Man commandos climbed onto the roof of the van, and jumped onto the hood, their weapons seeking targets. A large man lay slumped behind the wheel, his head half caved in from violently striking the steering wheel. An opening lead to the rear compartment, and light unexpectedly arrived as a short man threw open the rear doors and aimed a Carl Gustav at the police car.

He gaped for a moment in confusion, then spun and fired. The RPG streaked through the van and past the men on the hood to strike a brick wall and thunderously detonated.

Coolly, Lyons reloaded and fired the Atchisson once, removing the terrorist from this plane of existence.

Mindful of the little glass squares everywhere, the Stony Man commandos crawled into the van and moved to the lump under a pile of bulletproof vests and a heavy ballistic blanket.

Clearing the obstructions, Lyons scowled at the un-damaged neutron cannon, the indicators glowing softly, meters steadily rising as the accumulators began to charge.

"If we shoot, will it go off?" Blancanales asked.

"Can't take the chance!" Lyons snarled, tearing at the Faraday Cage with his bare hands. They couldn't use the guns. In this small a space the ricochets would kill them with the first volley.

Yanking wires loose, the four men cast them away to grab more. But the hum only got louder and some-thing loudly clicked. Nobody had to tell them that the weapon was about to discharge.

Risking everything, Lyons reached deep into the guts of the weapon and ripped loose a thick coaxial cable. Instantly, he began to writhe as high-voltage electricity crackled through his body. Every muscle locked. His heart seemed to stop beating. The pain was unimaginable. The stench of roasting flesh filled his nose.

Even as Blancanales and Schwarz reached for the

next coaxial cable, there was a loud snap. The discharge abruptly ceased, and Lyons limply fell to the floor, wisps of steam rising off his still body.

CHAPTER TWENTY-SEVEN

Below the Victoria Towers, Calcutta, India

Moving swiftly down the winding steps, McCarter exited into a room full of thumping water pumps and heavy machinery. He could only guess this was a pumping station for the city, part of the massive network of substations that directed the river to the purification plants.

By now, the pounding could be felt in the floor, like the beating of a gigantic heart. Pipes were everywhere in a complex maze that was filled with the deepest blackness. Light sockets lined the low ceiling, but the bulbs had been smashed, the shards twinkling on the damp floor.

Sliding on their night-vision goggles, the darkness vanished and the men saw a body crumbled near a heavy wrench, blood and hair matted on the rusty tool.

Turning the body over, the major snorted. "That's

Metudas," he declared. "It seems that justice finally caught up with him down here in the bowels of the earth."

"One down, one to go," McCarter retorted. "Any computer disks on him? Or a personal digital assistant?" He had never known any hacker to be without a PDA of some sort.

"We call it a pocket computer," the major said, checking the body. "No, nothing here."

"Which means Komar has them."

"Yes. Operational commands, blueprints...everything."

"Blueprints," Hawkins said as if it were the filthiest word in existence. "I thought this was the end of the matter. If Komar gets away, we could soon be facing hundreds of cannons operated by every terrorist group in the world."

Snapping his fingers for their attention, McCarter pointed at the damp floor. Amid the small vibrating puddles was a set of bloody footprints leading into the darkness and out of sight.

Readying their weapons, the six men moved fast and low, checking both sides and expecting an attack at any moment. The dwindling tracks went around a housing moist with condensation, and then under a yard-wide pipe faintly humming from the rushing river water being sent to the filtration plant.

The beating of the big pumps was a tangible thing, pounding against their exposed skin. McCarter knew that the pressure inside the pipe had to be tremendous, probably more than a ton per square inch. If released,

the stream of water would cut through the men like
laser beam.

Past the huge feeder pipe, McCarter and Chandrasekhar found a small area for the maintenance workers,
the floor a raised metal lattice inches off the ground.
There were several chairs, a folding cot, a crate of ammunition, and a card table covered with detailed maps
of the skyscraper. Food wrappers were everywhere, and
a bucket was filled with cigarette butts.

Easing his finger off the trigger, the major snorted at
the mess. "This must be where Ravid Komar planned
his attack on Malavade. Right under his nose."

"No sign of a PC or the disks," Private Kinnah said,
glancing around. "I wonder if—"

Appearing in the shadows, Komar leveled the Chinese QBX and fired. The 20 mm AP shell in the grenade launcher blasted a thundering hellstorm of
fléchettes. The antipersonnel charge annihilated the private in a nightmarish explosion of flesh and blood. The
tattered remains of the trooper fell over without even
giving out a sigh.

With hundreds of ricochets zinging wildly about the
workroom, the other men dropped and returned fire
with their assault rifles. Bullets zinged among the pipes.

Spraying rounds from the QBZ wildly, Komar
slipped into the dark labyrinth and started running.

McCarter started to touch his throat mike, then realized that the major wouldn't be able to hear the commands. "Flanking sweep," the Briton whispered
hoarsely. "T.J., go wide and try to get ahead of the man.
Major, go left, I'll go right."

Chandrasekhar nodded and started to leave, then paused and laid down his assault rifle to pick up the bloody weapon of the dead man. With an almost feral expression, he moved off to the left.

"After the son of a bitch!" McCarter shouted. "Don't let him get out of sight!"

Adjusting his night-vision goggles, Hawkins went back the way they came.

Pulling the pin from a stun grenade, McCarter dropped it on the metal floor and charged off an angle, completely ignoring the direction that Kamar had taken. They had to find the man fast or else the world would never be free from the threat of the superweapon.

Sidestepping a ladder going up, McCarter briefly thought about the other members of Phoenix Force, hoping they were still alive. Then he shut down those distracting thoughts and grimly concentrated on tracking the prey.

BENDING UNDER A TRIP WIRE attached to the grenade tucked among the thumping pipes, Ravid Komar went to his knees and crawled away below an array of hot pipes, cold pipes and an insulted gas line. When the explosive charge tripped, this whole section would become a raging inferno.

Going to an access ladder, Komar descended a level, ran along a catwalk, then went down again. The escape route from the pumping station was through the sewage tunnel, but without air tanks, the journey would be lethal. Komar was in unknown territory now, running blind and hoping for the best.

A dull explosion sounded in the distance. Almost smiling, he fervently hoped that the trap had taken out his pursuers. But he couldn't risk capture and kept moving, proceeding faster and deeper into the heart of the colossal maze.

Reaching another maintenance area, the panting terrorist checked the pocket computer he had taken from Metudas. The files containing the construction details for the neutron cannon were in the drive, along with a tracking icon for the cannon heading to Sriharikota Island. But at the moment, the screen was blank.

Raising and lowering the minicomputer, Komar gnashed his teeth in frustration. The metal pipes lining the walls and ceiling had blocked the signals from reaching this far down. He might be able to fire the cannon, but had no idea where the thing was! Once he got outside, he would be fine, invincible. Master of the world! But until then…

SPOTTING A LONE FIGURE not wearing night-vision goggles, McCarter fired from the hip, hammering a fast salvo at the pipes above the crouching man. The ricochets bounced down and Komar cried out, his arm streaming blood.

Almost dropping the pocket computer, he stuffed it into his jacket and fired a long burst from the QBZ assault rifle. The heavy rounds thudded among the pipes, ricocheting everywhere, but there was no answering shout of pain.

Then gunfire sounded from far ahead of the man, and from above. They had him in a box!

Abandoning all thoughts of reaching the surface, Komar scrambled through the pipes and vertical columns. Condensation trickled along the exterior of some of them, and the air became rank with the tang of chlorine and lime soda. His eyes began to sting as he squeezed along the concrete wall behind an icy cold pipe. A ricochet zinged by, leaving a shiny mark on a pipe where it had scraped off the protective layer of paint.

Metal stairs lead to the next level, and Komar gratefully used them to reach another catwalk, confident that the pounding water pumps would mask the brief sound of his boots.

More gunfire sounded. Another explosion. Then somebody gave a muffled yell and a brilliant light flicker off to the side. Flares? Those spelled trouble. But in the dim illumination, Komar saw a ladder leading up, straight past an inspection port for the gas line. Easing off his boots, the terrorist started to silently climb, and incredibly saw a dim glow of sunlight from far above. A sewer grating! Freedom was only moments away.

"Freeze!" Major Chandrasekhar snarled from the darkness of the catwalk below. "You are under arrest!" A flare came to life showing the leader of COIN holding an assault rifle. "Now drop that gun, or die!"

Without pause, Komar brought his assault rifle crashing down on the inspection port. The brass nozzle bent and started loudly hissing, a white cloud engulfing the major and igniting.

Covered with flames, the major dropped the flare and staggered inside the hellish cloud, firing his assault rifle blindly. Streams of bullets went everywhere. Then the ammunition in his belt pouches began to detonate, blowing off bloody pieces of flesh.

Komar was already twenty feet away, climbing for his life. From the growing daylight and the fire down below, he was able to see his surroundings better. Risking a pause, he checked the pocket computer. Faintly, a single bar appeared. Not good enough. Quickly, the terrorist climbed another fifty feet and checked again. Three solid bars appeared, the fourth wavering in and out of existence.

"Excellent!" Komar sighed, tapping the screen with a finger to access the remote-control function. Victory was only moments away.

Highlighted by the whooshing fire, a figure stepped out of the shadows. "My very thought, asshole," Hawkins snarled, crouching on another catwalk. He triggered his assault rifle.

The high-velocity stream of AP rounds from the M-16 hammered across the terrorist, slamming him flat against the rusty ladder. Blood erupted from his arms and legs.

In horror, Komar saw that his NATO body armor had only stopped some of the AP bullets, and he was bleeding profusely. Weakening by the second, he stubbornly raised the PC high and fumbled for the fire-control button when a second stream of hot lead tore him apart. With a strangled cry, Komar was thrown off the ladder, and as he fell through the air the terrorist very briefly saw McCarter holding a badly charred INS assault rifle, right along the roaring inferno of the escaping gas leak.

Snarling with bloody lips, Ravid Komar, supreme leader of the dreaded Tiger Force, fell directly into the writhing flames, but never had the time to feel the flesh cook off his bones before he violently impacted on the hard metal lattice and died.

Catching the pocket computer on the first bounce, McCarter back away from the reeking conflagration and checked the display, but the screen was blank.

Dropping the borrowed weapon, the leader of Phoenix Force hit the ladder and started climbing like it was the end of the world.

WHISTLING A TUNELESS SONG, Atman Basat checked his compass heading to make sure the seaplane was heading in the correct direction for Sriharikota Island. Then the pilot saw the four islands of the space complex on the horizon. On the eastern island was a black landing strip surrounded by glistening white sand. On the other three islands the flat expanse of rock was crisscrossed with concrete roads and railroad tracks. Squat brick buildings stood everywhere, and slim gantries rose impossibly high at four different launch pads. But the grinning pilot saw that only one held a colossal white rocket, the top misty from the steam of the LOX/LOH fuel being loaded. *That's our baby.* In just a couple of minutes, it would be all over, and they would be billionaires.

"Hey!" Neeja Abdeleb cried from the aft section of the plane. "The cannon just made a weird sound."

"Is it broken?" the pilot asked, frightened. "Or worse, getting ready to fire?"

Frowning, Abdeleb checked the readouts and displays. Then his face went pale. "Vishnu save us! It's going to—"

In a clap of thunder, the seaplane was vaporized as the self-destruct charge of M-2 plastique ignited into a monumental fireball. Writhing tendrils of flame extended across the clear blue sky. A few seconds later, a handful of melted debris sprinkled onto the Bay of Bengal and disappeared from sight forever.

EPILOGUE

Washington, D.C.

"Hey," Carol Lyons whispered from the hospital bed.

Talking to a nurse, Barbara Price spun around at the word as if it was a pistol shot. Anxiously, the woman looked hard at the reposing giant, and slowly gave a weary smile.

"Hey, yourself," Price replied, going to the man. "How are you feeling?"

"Been better," he said, trying to smile. The man hurt all over, and for some reason his kidneys were killing him. Had he been shot? No, he'd been in the van, yanking wires, then came a flash of light…

"Electrocuted," Lyons rumbled, relaxing slightly. No wonder his kidneys hurt. He dimly remembered from his police academy days reading that kidneys were the organ most susceptible to electricity. Not the brain, or the heart, but the kidneys. Heart attack victims saved by an EMT using electro-shock paddles, often found themselves with terrible backaches the next day from their sore kidneys.

"Backache?" Price asked, nodding to someone.

Even as Lyons reluctantly agreed, the nurse brought over a tray and gave him two pills and some water. A few minutes later a soothing warmth began to spread throughout his body and the pain started to lessen considerably.

Checking his pulse, then looking professionally into his eyes, the nurse nodded in satisfaction. "You'll be fine after some sleep. Just try to go easy when you relieve your bladder. There could be some strong discomfort." Then the nurse left, closing the hallway door tightly behind.

"Now we can talk freely," Price said, pulling a Humbug from her pocket. She flicked on the device and set it on the bedside table.

"Okay, what's up with the cannon?"

"Gadgets and Rosario are fine. Apparently you caught most of the discharge. They escaped with the cannon before the Baltimore police arrived. They hauled it to the farm, where the cannon was personally disassembled by Cowboy and reduced to fine ash."

"Even better." He grunted. "And Phoenix Force?"

"They're alive, just battered to pieces when the self-destruct of that other cannon on the roof went off. Malavade, Komar, Mongoose Metudas… Everybody involved is dead." Price sighed and shook her head. "Including a couple of COIN troopers who fell trying to stop Komar. They paid in blood for the weapon, so

Hal insisted that the White House cut a deal with New Delhi."

"We're going to share the plans?" Lyons asked, then corrected himself. "The files have been destroyed."

"All of them. Every one. A neutron cannon is just too dangerous to have in the world. My God, when you think about how many people died in just Nellor…" She stopped, her face a hard mask.

"That bad?" Lyons said.

"The estimates are over fifty thousand civilians."

Stunned, Lyons gave a low whistle.

"New Delhi is claiming Nellor was a natural disaster, carbon dioxide gas vented by an underwater volcano. The whole region of the world is very geologically active, so folks will believe the lie."

"Called the Ring of Fire, isn't it?"

"And deservedly so," Price said, leaning back in the hospital chair. "As for Sri Lanka, we're denying the whole incident at the hotel ever happened."

Yeah, Lyons thought Interpol would do something like that. No one wanted it known that key law enforcement personnel the world over were dead.

"When you come to think of it," Price said with a deep sigh, "we actually got off pretty lightly. If Malavade or Komar had gotten one of those cannons into orbit, the death toll would have been astronomical."

"Make World War II look like a fistfight."

"Pretty damn close."

"Fifty thousand?"

"Yeah."

Lyons and Price contemplated the staggering numbers, incredibly thankful that it wasn't a thousand times that amount.

"Okay, that's the ten-minute mark," Price said, rising from the chair. She turned off the Humbug and stuffed it into her purse. "Get some sleep, Carl. You're on sick leave until further notice."

The blond man tried to reply, but only an unintelligible mumble could be heard as he drifted off into sleep.

Don Pendleton's Mack Bolan®

War Drums

Iran's hardliners are pushing an extremist
agenda, defying U.N. rulings and amassing
an arsenal with bio and nuclear capabilities.
They've got stolen U.S. technology and
unlimited financial backing by China.
With Russian black market weapons dealers
eager to profit from international terror,
the Stony Man warrior's multifront mission
becomes one of infiltrate and confront,
uniting him with Bedouin brothers-in-arms
and other unlikely allies across enemy
territory in a race to shut down an explosive
situation before the deadly fuse is lit....

**Available July
wherever you buy books.**

JAMES AXLER

DEATH LANDS®

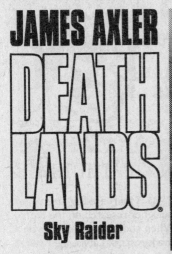

Sky Raider

Raw determination in a land of horror…and hope

In the tortured but not destroyed lands of apocalyptic madness of Deathlands, few among the most tyrannical barons can rival the ruthlessness of Sandra Tregart. With her restored biplane, she delivers death from the skies to all who defy her supremacy — a virulent ambition that challenges Ryan Cawdor and his band in unfathomable new ways.

Available June 2007 wherever books are sold.